Burning and Dodging

A Novel
by Julie Wittes Schlack

Black Rose Writing | Texas

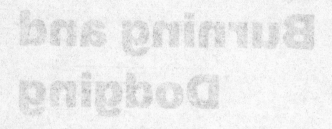

First printing

This is a work of fiction. Names, characters, businesses, places, events, and
incidents are either the products of the author's imagination or used in a
fictitious manner. Any resemblance to actual persons, living or dead, or
actual events is purely coincidental.

ISBN: 978-1-68433-842-9
PUBLISHED BY BLACK ROSE WRITING
www.blackrosewriting.com

Printed in the United States of America
Suggested Retail Price (SRP) $19.95

Burning and Dodging is printed in Book Antiqua

*As a planet-friendly publisher, Black Rose Writing does its best to eliminate
unnecessary waste to reduce paper usage and energy costs, while never
compromising the reading experience. As a result, the final word count vs. page count
may not meet common expectations.

Cover art by Liz Chalfin

For Katie, Layla, Chloe, and Melanie

Burn (verb)

: to give off light

: to be hot

: to produce or undergo discomfort or pain

: to become emotionally excited or agitated: such as: to yearn ardently

: to increase the light exposure to areas of a photographic print that should be darker

Dodge (verb)

: to move to and fro or from place to place usually in an irregular course

: to evade by a sudden or repeated shift of position

: to decrease the light exposure to certain areas of a photographic print that should be paler

Burning and Dodging

"Unlike the other children in Lucile's photos from that day in Eden Park, Ally Harris knows he is a Subject. Not so different from those leafy vistas. Head cocked to the side, one foot placed carefully behind him, he looks not just uncomfortable but unwilling. ... That guarded expression, shy, maybe recalcitrant. Ally Harris is a boy, not a view. His overalls are his overalls, not a costume. His feet are bare because he has no shoes. How hard it is to remember that people exist outside of our ideas of them."

— **Suzanne Berne,** *Missing Lucile*

"But the camera is not a mirror with a memory, and it never was — or if it was, or if it is, it's a fun-house mirror, because from the beginning, it's been used to trick people. People have taken this thing defined by the fact that it cannot be faked — and they've faked it. With this machine that promises to tell the truth, they've lied."

— **Sarah Sentilles,** *Draw Your Weapons*

"While there is perhaps a province in which the photograph can tell us nothing more than what we see with our own eyes, there is another in which it proves to us how little our eyes permit us to see."

— **Dorothea Lange**

June 2011

The house was one of those enormous, faux English manors that dotted too many Thousand Islands shorelines. But when Tina pressed the big oval button on the door frame, she heard not the deep tolling bell she expected, but the hilarious amplified screeches of a laughing baby. Startled, she pressed it again. This time a hidden speaker emitted a donkey's nasal baying.

"You've discovered one of Dad's audio games," said the tall, middle-aged woman who opened the front door. "I hope you're not put off."

"Surprised, maybe, but not put off," Tina answered. "Actually, sort of amused."

"Well, great. That's a good start. I'm Melissa Bright, Peter's daughter." She stuck out her hand and gave Tina's a bony shake. "Come on in."

Tina stepped from the shaded landing into an enormous pool of sunlight. The living room she'd entered jutted out from the rest of the house and felt as if it were suspended over the St. Lawrence River. The wall in front of her was made almost entirely of windows. To her left, rows of diagonal weathered pine boards soared over a fieldstone fireplace, tall and pointed as a bishop's hat. A grouping of abstract landscape paintings adorned the third wall, meadows and rivers and beaches, all of them suggesting light burning through fog.

"What a stunning space!"

"Yeah, well, this house is my father's pride and joy, his baby and his mistress. He used up two architects and three contractors getting it built just how he wanted it."

"He's got quite an eye." And quite an income to afford some of these paintings, Tina thought.

"He's got quite a strong will. 'This is the last place I'm ever going to live,' he kept saying, 'so I'm going to make it the house I want to die in.' " Melissa gestured toward the kitchen entrance. "Can I offer you coffee? Tea? Beer?"

"Coffee would be great, if it's no problem."

"Is drip okay?" Melissa asked. "I'm a surgeon. I can operate robotic instruments, but I'll be damned if I know how to use that thing." She pointed to an industrial-sized gleaming espresso machine occupying half of the granite kitchen counter.

"Well, I've never done surgery. I've never even had surgery. But I used to be a barista, so if you feel like a cappuccino, I'm happy to make you one."

"I like you already," said Peter Bright, humming into the room in an electric wheelchair.

"Use your arms, Dad." Melissa knotted her forehead and pursed her dry lips. "You've just come from your study twenty feet away. Save the motor for hills, or avoiding oncoming trucks."

Peter winked at Tina. "She's so strict, my daughter."

Tina forced herself to smile back. She hated the jocularity and false intimacy of the wink. But she loved Peter's plummy baritone voice. Its resonant lilt had made him CBC's prime time newscaster when radio was still king, and his lean, patrician face had paved his transition to anchor of the televised national evening news. Though shrunken, the man who had presided over millions of Canadian dinners and drinks in the 1960s and '70s was still recognizable beneath a shock of luminous white hair.

"I'll take your word for it."

"Oh, a diplomat," Peter cooed. "Another point in your favor. If your cappuccino is any good, you've got the job."

"Whoa, not so fast, Dad. Let's give Tina a chance to tell us a bit more about herself."

"Just point me to the coffee beans and then I'm all yours," Tina answered, walking toward the counter. How had she become so adept at ingratiating herself? she wondered. Or, more to the point, why?

Peter wheeled himself to the cherry-wood pastor's table in the center of the kitchen, and Melissa sat down next to him. "Have you been a caregiver before?" she asked Tina.

"Not a hands-on personal caregiver, no. But my impression was that you already have someone to help Mr. Bright with bathing and dressing and that sort of thing. Was I mistaken?"

"Call me Peter, please." He flashed a dazzling smile.

"You're right. We do," Melissa answered over him. "Jean-Pierre is a certified nursing assistant and a big, strong guy. Since my husband and I are here for the weekend, we gave him a few days off, but he's usually here 24/7. I guess I meant to ask if you've ever been a chef and personal assistant before."

"Absolutely," Tina answered, turning away to steam the milk. The din of the machine gave her an excuse to stay silent for a few moments and decide who she was auditioning for—Melissa or Peter. Peter, she decided. "I was a den mother of sorts for a communal household of Haight-Ashbury old-school hippies at the age of 17, and I've been cooking and corralling and coordinating ever since." She placed a steaming cup of cappuccino in front of Peter and another next to Melissa's tapping fingers. Then she sat down opposite them both.

"You alliterate with alacrity," Peter said.

Tina smiled and nodded in acknowledgement. "I've spent the past twenty years or so in Toronto as an event planner, specializing in art-related affairs—openings, fundraising galas for the Art Gallery of Ontario, that sort of thing. So I know how to both cook and hire good caterers, and more importantly, how to manage logistics and personalities."

"You mean big personalities," Peter observed.

"Well, yes." He was old, but still sharp, she thought. "Artists, philanthropists—people who invest a lot and expect a lot."

"Artfully said." He turned to his daughter. "I like this woman!"

"Forgive me, but where's Haight-Ashbury?" Melissa asked.

Tina and Peter exchanged a look. "It's a neighborhood in San Francisco," Tina answered. "Back in the day, it was the unofficial capital of the counterculture."

"I was born in 1968," Melissa said almost angrily. "You don't look older than me."

"You're very kind," Tina said, "but I am. I'm 59."

"Years young," Peter finished.

"Shouldn't you be starting to wind down?" Melissa asked.

"I'm not the retiring type," she answered easily, but seething inside at the cluelessness of this woman who had clearly never had to worry about how to pay the rent. "But I'm hoping that living in this beautiful home assisting your illustrious father will be a nice change of pace."

Melissa glanced quickly at Tina's left hand.

"No," Tina said. "I'm not married. Free as a bird."

"Children?" Peter asked.

"Only some of the men I've dated."

Peter chortled. Melissa frowned, but pressed on. "So, are you originally from San Francisco?"

"No, I'm originally from New York City." She shifted slightly in her chair. "Like you, Peter, my father worked in television, but behind the camera, as an engineer and producer. So I grew up in Manhattan, then ran away to California like many young women my age were doing back then."

"How did you end up in Toronto?" Melissa's interrogation continued.

Peter covered his daughter's restless fingers with his own elegant hand, milky and marbled with almost sapphire veins. A true blue blood, Tina thought.

"Let me guess," Peter said. "You were living with a guy who didn't want to go to Vietnam."

Tina nodded. "There were a lot of us moving to Toronto and Vancouver and Montreal in those years. I imagine you interviewed draft-dodging expats like my boyfriend at the time."

"You imagine right."

"So you've been an event planner for the past twenty years." Melissa doggedly steered them back on track. "It sounds like an exciting life. Why would you want to stop doing that and move to sleepy old Brockville, Ontario?"

"Where is he now?" Peter asked, as if his daughter hadn't said anything.

"Living on Facebook," Tina said to Peter, then turned to Melissa. "I'm ready for a bit of serenity. Toronto is frenetic and polluted, and the rental prices are astronomical. It's not that I'm slowing down—I'm as energetic and fit as ever—but I'd like … I don't know, I'd like a bit more beauty in my surroundings and a bit less din."

By which she meant: I need to make money, spend less on rent, and chip away at my complacency before I run out of time.

Peter leaned closer to Tina, as if preparing to divulge a secret. He smelled of Old Spice and Polident. "Technically, we're not in Brockville, you know. We use the same postal code, but when you crossed the bridge to get here, you entered Refugee Island."

"That's fitting," Tina said, then wished she hadn't. But Peter just laughed.

"What's your citizenship?" Melissa asked. "If we hire you, I want to do this on the up-and-up. No under-the-table payments."

"As far as the U.S. is concerned, I'm American. As far as Canada is concerned, I've got dual citizenship, and I travel under a Canadian passport."

"See that big rock sticking up out there?" Peter pointed out the kitchen's bay window. "Breaststroke your way out to it and you'll be back in the States. No passport required."

"Ah, but you can't swim home again."

Peter raised his cup in tribute. "Bravo."

"Did you go to college?" Melissa persevered.

"Off and on. I studied drawing at the Montreal Museum of Fine Arts when I first moved there, and spent a year at the University of Toronto about a decade later doing museum studies." She was suddenly and acutely aware of how flaky she sounded. Why not just announce *I'm a dilettante?* "When it was clear that I couldn't create great art, I thought that perhaps I could curate it."

Melissa brightened. "Really?! My husband Michael teaches in the museum studies program."

"What a coincidence! I'm sure a lot has changed since I was there. Everything's gone digital."

"He's a Renaissance tapestries scholar, Michael."

"He must be a very bright man."

"A genius," Peter said briskly. "We can all just stipulate that. So, do you know anything about archiving?"

"A bit. I worked in a gallery when I was still in Montreal and created catalogues for a couple of exhibits. Despite my somewhat chaotic life, I'm actually extremely organized." She studied Peter's lit-up face. "Why do you ask?"

"I collect photographs. Collect them and write about them. I could use some help, though, in researching and cataloguing them."

"I would love to help." Tina felt a flutter in her chest, a stirring of excitement that she realized she hadn't experienced in a long time.

"So you've got curiosity, a smattering of expertise, but no degree?" Melissa was determined to wrest back control of this interview.

"No degree. I needed to make a living, and I was always very motivated to learn on my own, so, much as I enjoyed some of my classes, college felt mostly like an expensive constraint."

"Let there be no book but the world, eh?" Peter said. Then, looking at his daughter, "I'm quoting Rousseau. Trust me, it's very impressive."

Tina laughed. Here, in this honey-colored kitchen, with this undeniably charming old man and his cross, tightly wound daughter, she was letting herself imagine an intriguing future, at least for the next year. No more hustling for the next gig. No more people-watching on the subway, either, of course. She'd have to say goodbye to spontaneous dinner dates at the newest Burmese or Slovenian restaurant, to invigorating afternoon walks with her friends through the churning streets of Queen West or Greektown. But after years and years of soaking up energy from the sensory carnival surrounding her, maybe it was time to be still. Maybe without distractions or excuses, in this house that felt like a retreat, she'd finally produce some good art that was exclusively a product of her own vision and labor—not "work by committee," as her father liked to characterize her efforts, but a solo achievement.

A bright red-and-yellow tour boat—one of the many that wended their way through the channels between the islands—glided into sight. Tina fought the impulse to leap to her feet, run out onto the deck, and wave madly at the passengers on board. "Can you swim in the river?" she asked, her gaze still focused on the water.

"I can't," Peter answered briskly.

Tina felt herself blushing. "I'm sorry. I meant 'Can one swim in the river.' "

"One can if one doesn't mind frigid water and the occasional oil slick from the Jet Skis or whatever the hell they are whizzing around out there."

"It's not too polluted, if that's what you're asking," Melissa said.

"So, when were you planning to ask about the wheelchair?" Peter casually asked Tina.

"When you were out of the room."

Peter's eyebrows shot up in surprise. "You don't pull your punches, do you? Well, no need to be discreet. I know I'm in a wheelchair. It's a recent development. Post-polio syndrome. The virus was dormant for 75 years, and then just when I was starting to congratulate myself for being such an active octogenarian, bam. Muscle wasting, sleep apnea, and I'm cold all the goddamn time."

"But at least you don't have Alzheimer's," Melissa droned. Tina had the sense that Melissa reminded him of that at least once a week.

"If I did, I wouldn't know about the goddamn polio."

"Can you walk at all?" Tina asked.

"Not at the moment. I can get myself from the bed to the wheelchair, from the wheelchair to the toilet or the shower, but that's about it. But I'm doing strengthening exercises every day with Jean-Pierre, so who knows. I might regain some mobility."

"I'm sorry."

"Thanks. But the good news is that my eyes and arms and brain still work pretty well."

"That's obvious." Tina smiled, and she meant it.

"And this iPad, it's changed my life." Peter pulled a sleek tablet out of a mesh pocket below the seat of his wheelchair. "World at my fingertips and all that. But it's true. I can read the news, watch the news, see myself when I was young and debonair delivering the news. I can find new photos and research the ones I've got, dig deep into what's going on all over the globe ..."

"Let's be honest, Dad. Not all of your pursuits are that lofty. I know you binge on old episodes of *I Love Lucy* and that reality show — what is it? *Who Wants to Marry a Bachelor*? *Dancing with the Over-the-Hill Television Star*?"

Peter laughed scornfully. "What's the difference? It's just like McLuhan said. 'Anyone who tries to make a distinction between education and entertainment doesn't know the first thing about either.'"

"We're not all quite so cynical, Dad."

"That's because we haven't all been in the entertainment business."

Melissa sighed. "Sorry I brought it up." She pivoted, halfway turning her back on her father. "If we want to pursue this, Tina, could you provide us with any references?"

"Of course. I brought some letters with me, but I'm happy to supply more."

"Tell you what. Let me chat with my father—"

"It's okay, Melissa." Peter looked skyward. "We don't need a private confab. Tina, we're interested in you. Are you interested in us?"

She paused for only a beat. Get the offer first, she thought, then decide later. "Absolutely."

Melissa tapped the tabletop. "So, yes, can I see your recommendations?"

Tina pulled an envelope out of her purse and handed it over, then stood to go.

"You're not leaving, are you?" Peter asked.

"I thought I was."

"Don't be silly. Stay for dinner."

"Dad, I wasn't planning on cooking anything fancy ..."

He shushed her. "Don't worry about it," he said magnanimously. "Tina will cook. What better form of trial run, right?"

And there it was, Tina realized with a soul-wracking thud. Once a service worker, always a service worker. She was a refined one, of course—smart, pleasingly sassy, a woman that wealthy women and men could pretend was a peer, a colleague, almost a friend rather than a mere employee. *Don't you get it?! You're either the exploiter or the exploited,* her father, Bob, had fumed almost forty years ago when she told him she was coming back from the West Coast and moving into a commune in Vermont. His words and the exasperation behind them had shocked her. She'd thought he agreed with her, believed that a society of equals, bound by shared work and shared values, was possible. *It's an aspiration,* he'd said more gently over the crackly long-distance call, *not a reality.*

It had been decades since she thought of those years with anything but wry nostalgia for an age when she didn't know better. Tina, her close friend Marnie, and others in their circle would still hum snatches of old melodies and recite song lyrics with ironic gravity. They distilled the era to a time of fashion appropriated from Third World cultures, and culinary despair courtesy of earnest vegetarians who knew how to cook nothing but rice and beans. But much as they mocked themselves, they rarely demeaned what they'd aspired to.

Now, though, standing alone at the granite counter, watching her own newly age-spotted hands chop shallots and ginger to stir fry with two kinds of bitter greens and some Kobe beef, she felt unsteady, as if standing on the deck of a shuddering ship. How had she gotten here? Yes, she could and just had recited the succession of choices and events that had brought her from a hippie commune in San Francisco to a farm in Vermont to an impeccable multi-million-dollar estate in Ontario almost forty years later. Idealism. Sectarianism. Richard the Red. Poverty. The diaspora of friends (and its corollaries: Law School. Fixer-Uppers. The conservatizing influence of kids. Whole Foods.) Art as a political force. A steady paycheck. Routines, mostly beloved. Millennials. Dissolution. Craig's List. Carl, who waited for her at home. The urgency to finally discover whether her art—whether any work she could do by herself—was worth doing.

She could still find the woof of continuity in her own history. But in this July dusk, staring out at the green-tufted river, that logical progression felt like a fairy tale, like a story invented only for its moral. *Follow your passion.* Or *It is better to have loved and lost.* She hadn't experienced her life as a well-plotted narrative, not even a coherent one. The threads that led from there to here were pasted on it like a sequined spangle. No, her life felt more like a sequence of trips through a wormhole, as Carl had described it to her one night — their only night of winter camping. Space and time were woven into the same mesh that here and there folded in on itself, burrowing shortcuts from one place and instance to another. One moment she'd been a five-year-old child sitting on a sled with legs straight out in front of her, mummified in her cherry-red snowsuit with white stars, as her parents pulled her through a hushed Central Park. The next, she'd been marooned in the arms of this most unlikely lover, in a tent in a forest on a lake in Northern Ontario, as happy as she had ever been. Now she was here, charming her way into a castle that its owner meant to die in.

When dinner was over, when Peter and Melissa declared their satisfaction and formally offered her the job, it was with relief that she said yes. She would have one day off per week and a reasonable salary ("Paid monthly," Melissa had specified. "We can't have helpers in and out of here through a revolving door.") Best of all, she'd have blocks of down time — between meals and while Peter napped — to "pursue your own interests."

Before Tina left, Melissa escorted her to the second floor to see her future bedroom, just down the hall from Jean-Pierre's. Equipped with a queen sleigh bed, a good-sized teak desk, some sort of Danish Modern chair and a tall, sleek dresser with many drawers, the room was large and airy, with an Eastern exposure and a view of the river. The morning light would be great for drawing. Would she take advantage of it? Would she finally accept the risk of taking her own art seriously?

Through an opened window, Tina heard the smoky, dark cry of a loon. Here in the handsome house of strangers, under the sardonic eye of a man old enough to have witnessed and reported on her life's full trajectory, her distant youth throbbed like a phantom limb.

• • •

Carl was asleep when Tina got home. Just as well, as she wasn't ready to talk about it. But over breakfast the next morning, she got straight to the point.

"So, I've got some news," she said, studiously buttering her bagel.

"You're pregnant," he deadpanned.

"Just pregnant with possibilities. I got the job and I think I should take it."

Carl's head jolted back. "Whoa, wait. Just like that?"

"Oh sweetie, it's hardly just like that. This isn't really a surprise, is it?"

Two weeks earlier, still vacillating about whether to join Carl on his year-long residency at an astronomical observatory in the Canary Islands, she'd passed her downstairs neighbor, Alan, walking his ancient dog. Darius the spaniel had waddled slowly down the block, and when he'd teetered onto a section of pavement where the sun broke through the trees, he had stopped and slowly circled, bathed in warmth.

"Come on, Darius," Alan had said, lightly tugging at the leash. "Come onto the grass and do your business."

But the dog didn't comply. *Warmth!* Tina imagined him thinking, however dogs thought. *Yellow light!* No moment had existed before this one, and this one was lovely.

"Darius," Alan had repeated, "come on. Do what we came out here to do." He'd cast Tina a needlessly apologetic look.

Blissed out by the feel of the sun's rays, the dog had circled again, then carefully lowered itself to the pavement.

"Darius! Get up. Come on. You're a dog, for God's sake, not a cat. Do your business. Do *something*."

Alan's tone, annoyed and entreating, had startled her. He'd sounded just like the voice in her own head that had gotten louder and more insistent since Carl had told her of his residency in Tenerife and asked her—no, expected her—to go with him. Do something beyond what feels right in the moment. Make something that's your own, she'd told herself, knowing as she did that she was parroting her father's words, the exhortations that had stalked her since her adolescence. ("Test your mettle! Don't hide in the crowd!") And for reasons she could only sense, if she was finally going to hold her own feet to the fire, she had to do it alone, independent of the man whose unqualified love made it too easy to keep drifting.

"The house is huge and modern and airy, and the mystery man, my new employer, is Peter Bright."

"The nightly news guy?"

"Yup."

"So you're going to pass up a year with me in the Canary Islands to live with an old man—I assume he's an old man—and do what?"

This was the even harder part. "Cook. But not just that. Do my own work—"

"Which you could do in Tenerife—"

"—but also be his research assistant. I'll be able to use my skills, Carl, and maybe—I know this sounds stupid, or childish—but maybe actually help to produce something with my name on it."

He threw up his palm, as if to stop her from saying more. "I get it. What I don't get is why you have to do it in Brockville instead of with me."

"I'm not—this isn't a rejection of you. It's just a temporary separation, a—what do they call it? A distance relationship. You'll be sleeping all day and up all night, and I just can't see myself sharing a tiny dorm room with you on a mountaintop, sketching for a year. It's not like I can be your astronomer's helper." That came out more sharply than she'd intended. She took a breath. "I'm sorry. I know that's not what you're asking from me." She looked down at her buttery hands. "I need to do real work too, and I don't know how to do it alone. I need to be accountable to someone besides myself."

Carl gazed at her in silence. Was that sorrow on his face, or pity?

"What's Peter Bright like?" he finally asked.

"Old. Charming. Erudite. He's working on a book about documentary photography and how it's been perverted, about the manipulation of imagery in this evil century. I'll help him archive pictures and organize the book. Maybe even help with the research."

"That's right in your wheelhouse," he said. This was one of Carl's anachronistic phrases. But what should she expect from a guy who was raised with wolves and learned about the world from Boy Scout manuals?

"I'm not sure what a wheelhouse is, but I do think it'll be interesting."

"You'll be so far from everything—your friends, the museums, the Joy Luck Café—are you okay with that?"

As usual, he'd unknowingly tapped into her biggest fear. She was so accustomed to the hassle and joy of collective endeavors. Putting up a show, managing an event—these projects required her to work with carpenters, caterers, publicists, and the artists themselves; to be focused, gracious, and always outward-looking. That was the thrum that nourished her, and the prospect of solitude and silence was both exhilarating and terrifying.

"I guess we'll find out," she said, appalled by the forced lightness she heard in her own voice. "Marnie's sister wants to sublet our apartment, so that's taken care of."

"You're making sure you can't change your mind."

Tina was silent for a moment. "You do know me well, love," she said.

"Should I bother trying to change your mind?"

"Thank you for asking," she said, and meant it. "And the answer is no. I said I needed to shake things up for myself. Well, holing up in the boonies with an old man, some deadline-driven work, and lots of photos to inspire my own art should do the trick."

"Did you tell them you might only stay until my research residency is up?"

"They didn't ask how long I would stay, and I didn't volunteer it. But I'm sure the time will fly by." She was not at all sure.

"I wish I shared your confidence," he said.

"Don't be sad," she implored. "If you're sad, that'll make me sad, and that's the last thing I want right now." She paused. "It's bad enough that I'll be leaving our brand-new foam mattress behind."

"And the stovetop meat smoker," he offered, trying to play along.

She wasn't about to tell him that Peter's kitchen and deck were larger than their whole apartment and certainly better equipped. "Right. Saying goodbye to you will be tough, but the smoker ..."

"I'm not sad," Carl said abruptly. "I'm getting paid to do work that I love. I just hope that when you go there, you do work that means something to you. Or that you don't, but stop regretting that fact."

Was it possible to live without regret? Or just self-deception?

July 2011

While it was a joy to work in such a well-equipped kitchen, neither the cooking nor the sketching Tina did in her downtime brought much passion to her days. She'd brought two photo albums and a shoebox of pictures that she'd randomly assembled when leaving Toronto, with plans to draw some of them for a series about ... childhood? Families? Aging? She wasn't sure yet. But so far, she'd largely avoided them, and instead stepped up her efforts to help Peter not just research but actually write portions of his book.

After a fiery Introduction denouncing the ways in which even "legitimate" journalists staged, enhanced, or otherwise manipulated photographic images to tell a more compelling story, *Framing the Shot, Shaping the Story* was organized around a series of iconic photos. For each, Peter meticulously documented not just when and how the images were shot, but what he believed to be the beliefs and biases of the photographers who took them. Their artistry, he argued, laid the foundation, however unintentionally, for the more egregiously doctored images that now defined "reality" for an increasingly lazy and credulous public that demanded stories, not truth.

So many of the photos in Peter's collection were posed or, as he was determined to establish, staged. That was, he'd told Tina, his mission in his waning years – to excavate and tease out mundane facts from burnish in a medium that claimed to document reality. And if that meant proving that the iconic candid image was posed, that Cartier-Bresson's "decisive moment" was actually the product of hours of fussing, well, so be it.

"Facts, my dear—not spin, not interpretation, not narrative, and God knows, not Photoshop—just undeniable who's, what's, where's, and when's." They'd been sitting in his archive a few days after she moved to Brockville—a thick-walled, precisely humidified, dimly lit room. Shelves were vertically stacked with flat cardboard boxes containing photographic prints and, in some cases, negatives. The boxes were labeled in Peter's slanted script and ordered chronologically from top shelf to bottom: *Vishniac 1933, Lange 1933, Rothstein 1934, Shahn 1934.* "The east wall is the Great Depression and the War," he'd explained, waving vaguely behind him. "The north wall is the 1950s. The west wall, the 1960s, up until 1974."

"And nothing after that?" she'd asked.

"Oh," he'd answered with faux gravity, "you can't believe *anything* you see after that."

Tina's tasks were varied—from the tedious process of indexing and documenting the provenance of the pictures, to researching the context and veracity of the images themselves. At what time would the sun have hit that hillside in Espejo, Spain, in Capa's viewfinder during the first week of September 1936? Had that arid, crumbling plain outside Norman, Oklahoma, ever been a pasture, and if not, why would Rothstein have "found" the bleached skull of a cow there? And was it really the remains of a cow, or, based on its dimensions, really that of a bull or even an elk? How about that tawny-haired girl clinging to Robert Zimmerman's arm on the cover of *The Freewheelin' Bob Dylan?* Was she already his girlfriend at the time, or a hired model who later became his girlfriend? Did that montage in Santiago consist entirely of portraits of those who had disappeared under the Pinochet regime, or was it just a random collection of Chilean students?

"You've got quite the eye for detail," Peter said late one afternoon after Tina had walked him through the spreadsheet she'd created, showing him how to filter and sort based on the photographer, the subject, the locale, and the date of every image. "Good organizational skills are hard to come by."

"I can't take any credit for mine," Tina answered. "I inherited them. One of my father's great joys in life was organizing stuff— condiments in the fridge, spices in the cabinet, records on the shelf.

Alphabetically by artist? Or alphabetically first by genre, then by artist?"

"What did he do for a living?" Peter asked. "Was he perchance a librarian?"

Tina laughed. "That would have been way too quiet for him. No, he was a television engineer."

"That's right. You mentioned that, didn't you? What's your last name again?" Peter asked.

"It's Gabler."

"Gabler," Peter said pensively. *When people ponder your last name, it's because they're trying to figure out if you're Jewish, or Italian, or Irish,* Tina's father had told her when she entered high school. "I'm just wondering if I might have known your father, you know, as one television guy to another. What was his full name?"

"Bob Gabler."

"And where did he work?"

"He started at NBC, then went to National Educational Television, then to ABC. He kind of specialized in live broadcasts, though. Do you remember a short-lived documentary series called *Now and There?*"

"That rings a bell..."

"They did these one-hour shows about mostly human-interest stuff—quirky people, off-beat events, the hot-dog-eating competition on Coney Island, some sport like polo that guys in Afghanistan played on horseback using a goat's head instead of a ball, that kind of thing. Anyhow, each show was broadcast live from countries all over the world. Unfortunately, the hope that they would also be broadcast live *to* every country in the world never panned out beyond the debut episode."

"I remember that! I think I may have even been on one of those episodes, though for the life of me ..." Peter shook his head ruefully.

"Small world!" Tina said. "Anyhow, that experience made my dad perfect for sports and the Olympics. So eventually he migrated to ABC, to shows like *Wide World of Sports.*"

"'The thrill of victory, the agony of defeat," Peter intoned, perfectly imitating the voice-over that started every episode.

"I see you remember that program."

"Oh, that opening reel is impossible to forget. You see a ski jumper hurtling down an almost vertical slide, knowing that at the end of that frightening descent isn't rest or safety. No, he's going to launch himself off it into naked space. Of course you're terrified that he's going to fall, and then he does. Over and over, at 30 frames per second and again in slow motion, he fulfills your worst prophecies."

"I know an astronomer who loves to ski," Tina said. "Fast, not on the bunny slope like me. When I admired the leg strength he used to navigate the black diamond hills, Carl said that gravity was responsible, not strength; that skiing was falling, not charging." They fell into silence, then she added, "I've always kind of liked that."

"I know that viewers have seen many falls since then, accidents far worse than that. But that's the one we remember, isn't it? I wonder whatever became of that guy. Did he live?"

Tina shrugged.

Peter pulled his iPad toward him and after a few moments triumphantly announced, "Vinko Bogataj. The guy who fell was Vinko Bogataj. He's alive and well and living in Slovenia. He looks like a beaten down slob, like Walter Mitty, and he spends his time painting landscapes." He swiped and squinted. "Very pedestrian landscapes." He handed the computer to Tina.

"I agree. Dull. Lifeless."

"Another insignificant question instantly answered," Peter announced, "encouraging more such questions, and discouraging the ones that can't be answered by simple facts or video clips."

Tina suddenly wished that her father had lived long enough to have a smart phone or a tablet. He loved gadgets and was delighted by trivia, or as he preferred to call it, "serendipitous knowledge."

"Did you know that the Band-Aid was invented for someone much klutzier than you?" she remembered him asking her one Sunday morning as he cleaned a gash on her thumb, which she'd earned by trying to open a can of sardines at age five, unassisted, to make her parents a surprise breakfast. Tina remembered how he'd sat her on the closed toilet and squatted down in front of her. "Yup," he said, gently cleaning the cut with a facecloth, "Mrs. Josephine Dickson lived with Mr. Dickson in New Jersey, and she was very accident-prone. Every night when her husband came home from work at Johnson & Johnson"—he paused and pointed to the container of baby powder perched on the sink—"Mrs. Dickson would have cuts and burns on her fingers from her adventures making dinner. Mr. Dickson would cut little pieces of gauze to cover her injuries, then seal them with adhesive tape. But he wanted her to be able to bandage herself, so he took one big strip of tape, put squares of gauze at regular intervals along the length of it, and covered them with crinoline."

"What's crinoline?"

"The light, scratchy fabric under the party dress that you hate to wear. Anyhow, he covered each square with crinoline and left the whole strip hanging from the window frame like fly paper."

"What's fly paper?"

"It's the subject of a different story. Then"—Bob daubed her wound with iodine, speaking more rapidly, as if that would somehow ease her pain—"the next time Mrs. Dickson injured herself, she could just cut off a length of the tape, peel back the crinoline, and voila! The Birth of the Band-Aid!"

Even then, Tina had sensed that this and the other "Did you know…" stories he told her tickled him as much as they were intended to delight her. And when later that morning she'd colored a picture of Mrs. Dickson—her enormous left hand a pulpy claw dripping blood onto the counter, her tiny right one holding up a scissors the size of gardening shears to snip off a bandage—Tina's father was happier still.

"This belongs in MoMA, right next to the Picassos!" he'd declared, ruffling her hair and holding the picture up for her mother, Joan, to see. Then, looking at Tina's apparently puzzled face, "It's brilliant, Tina. You'll be a great artist someday. You've got your mother's sensibilities and talent."

But "talent" seemed to mean different things depending on who it was applied to. On the handful of times Bob had taken her into the control room at work, he'd guided her hands across an array of levers and switches and knobs. "This is how we make the talent sound better," he'd say of one set of controls. "And this is how we make them look good," he'd continue, pointing to another. While he clearly admired the devices, he had less use for the people on the other side of the glass that they were designed to serve. "Talking heads," he'd say of the broadcasters dismissively. "Not like Billie Holiday or Jackie Robinson or Isaac Asimov or you—people with real talent!"

By the time she was thirteen, she'd grown to hate the term and, thanks to her father's constant nagging, which he called "encouragement," to doubt that she had it.

Now, decades later, here she was sitting with The Talent, feeling bemused, with just a hint of guilt.

"Live broadcasts," Peter mused. "No room for error. It's just you, the teleprompter, and the little voice in your ear."

Hardly "just you," Tina thought, remembering the artful bedlam of the production crews she'd seen in action when visiting the studio. The producer would be instructing the cameramen and the engineers in the booth, the director murmuring to the people on camera as the make-up artists fussed with their cheeks and noses and hair while simultaneously bickering with the lighting crew—and all of them magically receding into invisibility and silence as the producer counted down to zero. She had loved the choreography behind the chaos. Everyone had a role to play; they all depended on each other to make their efforts succeed.

Her work at the studio was tedious, but it had a rhythm to it. Tina thought of a Western she'd seen as a kid in which a hay-filled barn, ignited by a bolt of lightning, started to burn. Someone madly clanged a bell and neighbors came running, many in nightshirts and bare feet. They formed a line snaking from the well outside the farmhouse to the blazing building, passing buckets of water towards the person closest to the flames, then passing the empty buckets back for refilling. She couldn't remember if they'd succeeded in dousing the fire. But what she recalled, what she loved, was how the night-shocked crew, unkempt and urgent, had glowed in the light of the flames.

This was her first and formative impression of work, she suddenly realized—a process in which "me" was subsumed by "we." No wonder she'd been so drawn to this job. No wonder she'd moved so quickly and effectively to find a role for herself not just as Peter's chef and archivist, but as his collaborator.

Safe again.

August 2011

Peter was staying with his daughter Melissa in Toronto for the weekend, lured by the National Press Association awards banquet and the promise of center orchestra seats at a revival of *Camelot*. ("It's a grossly underestimated show," he'd told Tina the night before he left. "And I'm not just saying that because Robert Goulet was Canadian and Richard Burton couldn't sing. No, it's got some memorable tunes, and God knows, we could use a little courtliness right about now.") Jean-Pierre took advantage of the time off to go visit his son in Montreal. And Tina, much to her own surprise, had passed on the chance to go to Toronto herself to see friends and let someone else do the cooking for once, choosing instead to lounge around the house on her own and do a little work.

She'd risen early each of the last two days and spent a few hours each morning studying the Roman Vishniac archives. He seemed to have travelled throughout Eastern Europe almost constantly from 1932 to 1944, and before she could examine his work with the skeptical eye that Peter demanded rather than the reverent one she'd grown up with, she felt she needed a firmer grasp on the facts—where he was taking photos, and on whose behest.

But on Sunday, lured by the dazzle of a sunny if unusually cool day, she instead took a long walk down the road hugging the river. Most of the homes had the soaring roof, sharp angles, and huge picture windows of Peter's, and almost every one had a swimming pool or tennis court between the house and the rocky shore. But every so often she spied a compact little ranch house made of sensible brick and vinyl siding, planted resolutely on its own quarter-acre, resisting upscaling or any other manifestation of concern for property values.

Stolid, these little houses were, but still a far cry from rustic. Nothing like the slanted, wind-and-snow-bleached cottage overlooking Borden's Pond that her family spent vacations and many weekends in when she was a child. There she'd learned to find adventure, not anxiety, in isolation. She'd gather kindling for the fireplace in the winter, probably not venturing more than twenty yards from the cottage but feeling herself a brave pioneer in the deep woods of Chatham, New York. And at night, she'd bundle up and pad silently out the door, down the shoveled, moonlit path to their rented car. In the cold, cocooning silence, she'd brush the snow off the Pontiac's roof, windows, and headlights, even as new snow fell to replace it. Sometimes she pretended she was on a pit crew, that she was the first and best girl to frantically service the world's fastest winter racing car. While the rest of her imaginary team thrust the car up on jacks, popped off and replaced its tires, refilled it with gas, and did mysterious things under the hood, she removed every last flake of snow from its windows. What could matter more than good visibility for the winter race car driver who was also her boyfriend—Rick, his name usually was—as he sped around the icy track?

But her more frequent fantasy—the quieter, more solitary one—was of being the polar explorer, alone in the Arctic, recording the weather and studying the bears. In that story, the Pontiac was not a car but her winter home, an ingenious construction that was half wooden hut, half igloo. She'd clear its windows the way a Zen Buddhist monk raked his garden—slowly, precisely, with immense satisfaction in each measured swipe. She knew her efforts were fruitless; no sooner had she cleared a strip of windshield than the snow flurry would once again quietly coat it. But the pleasure in making something clear, even if just for a moment, was self-reinforcing. She was calm in those moments, alert only to what lay outside her—the muffled thump of accumulated snow falling off a tree branch, the groan of wood shifting under the weight of it.

Maybe I was wiser as a child than I am now, Tina thought as she sat in the living room, looking out at the dusk, the Sunday jazz show on the radio, *The Grapes of Wrath* untouched in her lap, the grapes of Ontario in a wine glass next to her. Futility didn't trouble me. I knew how to be still. Would any of that have been evident in a photo? Or would a portrait in that moment, even one taken by a skilled photographer, merely have revealed the red nose and glittering eyes of a young girl's face enveloped by a sealskin hat and the high collar of her woolen winter jacket? We're unknowable, Tina thought. The meaning of a picture is imbued, not inherent. It's what we bring to the act of looking.

The temperature had dropped dramatically along with the sun. Outside the window, the wind had picked up, and desiccated pine needles swirled over the deck.

"Would you like some company?"

Tina startled as Jean-Pierre walked up behind her. For a large man, he moved with exceptional quietness and grace, like the grizzly bears she and her friend Marnie had watched in Alaska as they padded silently down the rocky lakeshore.

"Sure," Tina answered. "I didn't even realize you were here. When did you get back?"

"About an hour ago. My daughter-in-law's family was having a big Sunday dinner this afternoon. I was invited, but—she's a good girl, Francette, a good wife and a good mother, but not too bright, if you know what I mean, and her family makes up in noise what they don't have in brains—so I said I needed to head back."

Tina smiled sympathetically. "I know. Too much family can be too much of a good thing."

Jean-Pierre chuckled, a deep, mellifluous wave of sound.

In the two months that she'd been living there, this was the first time she'd conversed with Jean-Pierre one-to-one. Most days after helping Peter bathe, shave, and dress, he'd escort him to breakfast, then disappear until lunch time, and again until dinner. Tina had no idea what he did in those off-hours. She imagined him returning to Peter's room to straighten up, to make his bed, drape his Scottish wool cable-knit cardigan from the night before on a wooden hanger, briefly buff the alternating pair of brown or black loafers that Peter wore every day. She'd never actually been in Peter's bedroom, just glimpsed it through an open door en route to the sun porch at the end of the hall. But even just in passing, she caught the scent of aftershave and leather and, though she hoped she was wrong, urine.

That wasn't unlikely, after all. Peter was in his late eighties and effectively paralyzed. But the thought of him being swaddled in a diaper and lifted into Jean-Pierre's arms like a life-sized rag doll broke her heart. Did Jean-Pierre enfold him in silence, showing respect in the face of Peter's humiliation? Or did he chat with him about sports or the weather, about the gutters or the grounds, about anything that would make this process of pulling off his padded underwear not even worthy of notice?

And how did Jean-Pierre feel, mothering a grown man (as, despite her own father's tenderness towards her, Tina couldn't think of bathing and grooming and dressing as fathering)? Was he proud? Demeaned? Indifferent? He was so self-contained behind that broad, pleasantly bland face. At meals he ate quickly and neatly, periodically dabbing at the corners of his mouth. He'd compliment Tina on the food in his lovely Haitian patois and gently tease Peter about the performance of the Blue Jays or the Raptors, critique the performance of their new electric van, or seek approval for some small household repair. Their conversation—at least their public conversation—was unfailingly guy talk. When the conversation turned to politics or books or even the irritating way that Peter's son-in-law plugged "frankly" into every sentence he spoke, Jean-Pierre fell diplomatically silent. Tina didn't know, didn't even sense, what he really thought or felt about much of anything.

But her ignorance wasn't unnerving; their side-by-side silence in this moment was companionable. Louis Armstrong's chuckling voice, emerging from the background, now seemed to fill the living room. Jean-Pierre started humming along.

"Do you sing?" Tina asked abruptly.

"Only in the shower. And in church, when I go to church, which I don't do around here. In Montreal there are Haitian churches, with singing and tambourines and drums, but here, just pinched-face Protestants. No offense."

"None taken. I'm Jewish."

24

Jean-Pierre smiled broadly. "I knew I liked you. Your people, they're like my people."

"How so?"

"You love music, you love to eat. You laugh loud and cry louder. You have five senses, and you use them all."

"And that's how you'd describe Haitians?"

"I shouldn't make such big statements about your people or my people or any people. Let's just say these are the kind of people I like. And there aren't a lot of them, especially now, with all of us burying our noses in these things." He waved his smart phone, which was dwarfed by his large palm.

Just then it vibrated and a loud ding rang out. He peered at it. "Ah, *Live From*," he told her. "Now this I like. This is a good use of a smart phone."

"Live From?"

"You've never seen it?" Jean-Pierre looked astonished. "I thought everyone played it." Tina shrugged. "Here, I'll show you."

Jean-Pierre held up his phone, turning it sideways. Squinting against the setting sun, Tina could see two boot-clad feet walking down a narrow path through sparse woods, and hear the crackle of breaking twigs. Slowly the image panned upwards, and in the distance, gray against a brilliant blue sky, was a conical mountain, strewn with fallen trees and boulders. For just a moment she heard the sound of breathing as the cinematographer lowered the camera, once again focusing just on the trail.

As she watched, little heart-shaped bubbles floated up over the video, followed by a series of comments. "Mount St. Helen's, right?" said one. "I love that view of Mount Kilimanjaro!" said another. "Swoon," wrote a third observer, and so it went, the guesses as to location and commentary on the video.

"So, is this some kind of game?" Tina asked.

"Yeah. Somebody live-streams these videos, and people guess where it is. The first person to guess right gets a text message from The Traveler telling them how many miles they've won."

"You mean like airline miles?"

"No, like miles on a journey. The goal is to earn as many miles as The Traveler is actually logging."

"How many is that?"

"Nobody knows."

Tina smiled uncertainly, finally looking away from the screen and into Jean-Pierre's face. "Is this some kind of scam?"

"No," he answered gravely. "Nobody knows, because nobody knows where The Traveler is going. Is she visiting every country? Every continent? Some people say she's going to Mars."

"Mars." Tina snorted.

"This is not a joke." Jean-Pierre looked wounded. "There really is going to be a manned mission to Mars. The people have been chosen, just not announced."

"But you know she's a woman?"

"No. I think she's a woman. I like to think she's a brave, strong, sexy woman, but everybody has their own image of The Traveler. Some people think he's a man, some people swear she's a girly man."

"A girly man?"

"That's what they call them in Haiti. A man who is becoming a woman."

"Why do they think she's a girly man?"

Jean-Pierre shrugged. "Why not?"

"Fair enough," Tina answered, and her eyes wandered back to the screen. "So, you earn miles, and then what? How do you know when you've won? And what do you win when you've won?"

"Nobody—"

"Nobody knows, right?"

Jean-Pierre nodded.

Tina tapped her index finger in front of the phone, now resting on the rattan coffee table between them. "I gotta say—this is kind of a boring movie. Do these videos ever have people in them? Or car chases? Or wild animal attacks?"

"No, never people, sometimes animals. But usually just squirrels or birds or the occasional cat."

"So, if there's never any people, The Traveler must just stick to the countryside. To the wilderness, really."

Jean-Pierre shook his head. "Actually, she's often in cities, often in the middle of the night when the streets are empty. I've recognized some of them — Montreal, Paris, Kingston — the Jamaica Kingston. But even in the day, she finds these spots — an alley behind an abandoned building, or the foyer of an old, rundown apartment building, or the far end of a subway platform, at the mouth of the tunnel — she finds these spots in the city that are empty, even if they're very small, even if the movie is very short."

"What's she got against people?"

He shrugged. "I don't know. Maybe nothing. I think she just wants us to be more curious."

"Well, that sounds good."

"It is good. It's very good. I watch this movie and I start putting together clues, like a detective. The shape of the mountain: Was it made by a volcano? The trees on the path: What kind of climate do they grow in?" Jean-Pierre glanced at her — seeking her approval? — and then laughed as a message floated up onto the screen from somebody named TiredPoppa saying, *Looks like my wife's garbage sculptures* and then another, building on his previous comment: *She makes mountains out of molehills.*

The Traveler abruptly shifted the camera angle, sweeping up from the forest floor to catch the frantic flight of a big black bird — a crow, maybe, or a raven — as it shot up out of a tree. They could hear its wings flap. Then the screen went dark.

Jean-Pierre picked up the phone, tapped the Back arrow, swiped down for a quick look at his other notifications, then set it back down on the table. He took a long swig of his Molson's, then thoughtfully spun the cold beer bottle between his warm hands.

"Have you ever guessed right?" Tina asked him.

"I never post my guesses." He tapped the side of his head. "I keep them to myself."

"Why?"

"Because they don't matter. The game doesn't matter to me. It's the surprise I like." He paused, still thinking. "I like to use my brain thinking about something besides how to earn enough to retire someday, or keep Peter active, or decide where to live after he's gone."

Tina shuddered. "Oh, I'm trying not to think about that."

"Do you have any family?" Jean-Pierre asked.

She shook her head. "I was an only child. I've got cousins—two I'm really close to, both in New York. But my parents are dead. No kids, no husband." Over the years she had said this sometimes with shame, sometimes with defiance, but now she said it with relief tinged only by a fading surprise. Her life would not go on forever, she'd come to realize, and if she was to fully inhabit it, she might best do that unencumbered by obligation.

"A beautiful lady like you?"

She waved the compliment away. Jean-Pierre was easily years younger than she was, maybe decades. Besides, at her age, she assumed that any praise of her looks was rote, mere kindness unfounded in fact. "I have a partner. Well, I've had several partners, but the one who was … who sort of still is my current love … Carl— he's an astronomer working in Spain—on a mountaintop in the Canary Islands, to be precise."

Jean-Pierre raised his eyebrows. "And you didn't go with him?"

"No. His research fellowship is for a whole year. There would have been nothing for me to do there, and I like to pull my own weight." He looked at her quizzically. "Sorry. I mean I thought we should take a bit of a break from each other so I could get back to standing on my own two feet." Again, he looked perplexed, and Tina laughed. "Jeez, I'm supposed to be the native English speaker here, but it appears that I only speak cliché." She took a deep breath, then exhaled. "I didn't want to be on vacation for a year. I wanted to be self-supporting. I wanted to have some more alone time to accomplish something."

"What do you want to accomplish?"

"That's the million-dollar question." She laughed. "I draw. And I'd like to help Peter write his book. That's an accomplishment, right?" She took another sip of wine. "And you?"

"Divorced. My ex-wife, Helene, she hated it here in Canada."

"Too cold?"

He laughed. "Exactly. I hate the cold too. I just hate being without work and without money even more. So," he said, shrugging, "she went back to Port Au Prince, and me and my son Jonathan stayed on in Montreal."

"Have you always done this kind of work?" She gestured vaguely around the living room.

"You mean handyman or helper?"

"Either, I guess. Both."

"In Haiti I was a laborer. You know, I dug trenches," he said, prodding the floor with a phantom shovel; "poured concrete" — holding his arms out in front of him, encircling an invisible cauldron, he strained and turned his arms sideways; "built walls." The pantomime continued with each task, and it was electric. Jean-Pierre was more animated than Tina had ever seen him. "And then I learned to be ..." He paused, struggling to find the word. "*Un arpanteur*, the guy with the tripod and the lines ..."

"A surveyor?"

He slapped his thighs. "Exactly! A surveyor. But it's a poor country, and we had an earthquake in my town that destroyed all the houses. So there was no building of roads and bridges going on, just clearing rubble. And by then, man, I was too old, and my back was too sore and my knees too ..." He slowly straightened and bent his right leg while making a creaking sound. "I didn't have a home there anymore anyhow, so I thought if I got to start over, why not do it in a different place?"

"Why Montreal?"

"Oh, my sister, she was there already, and she said she could get me a job at her place, the nursing home. And she did." He sat back in his chair contentedly and took another gulp of beer.

"So how did you find Peter, or Peter find you?"

"I was working privately nights and weekends for Alain. Alain Desjardins, he was a guy who buys and sells — a broker — he was a broker of art. Paintings, sculptures, but mostly photographs. He had a stroke and he couldn't walk, couldn't talk, really, but his mind, it was still sharp. Peter used to come visit him every few months right up until he died. He would buy a picture or two, and they would talk ... very, very slowly." He laughed, a deep belly laugh that Tina wanted to curl up in. "Man, they were long, long conversations. But they were friends."

"And when Alain died?" *Alan*, she called him, still feeling pretentious using the French pronunciation even after all those years in Canada.

"Peter asked me to come help him out here. Melissa gets on his nerves, and besides, she's in Toronto. And his other daughter—"

"Wait, Peter has another daughter?"

"Sandy. Her name is Sandy, but that's about all I know about her. I guess they don't get along." He shrugged. "Peter, he doesn't take kindly to personal questions, so I don't ask them."

That was true, Tina thought. He was a charming deflector, relentless in his own inquiries and disdainful of others'. "Sorry to interrupt," she said, briefly laying her hand on Jean-Pierre's arm. "So, when did you meet Peter?"

"About a year ago. I remember because Montreal was stinking hot, and I was glad to get out into the country. Jonathan, he didn't need me around no more, the money was good—better than I was making—and Peter, he's a good guy. So I said why not?"

"And the rest is history."

"Yes, Mademoiselle."

They fell into another companionable silence. Jean-Pierre asked her no questions. She used to see that lack of curiosity in others as a character flaw, but now she was grateful for it. Besides, she didn't think Jean-Pierre was uninterested, just an astute observer. And what she was signaling, she knew, with her book and her crossed arms and her forward gaze was *Not me. Not now.*

Jean-Pierre's phone dinged again. He glanced down at it, swiped a message away, then leaned back again. "It's so easy," he said with a laugh. "Poof, and it's gone."

"Are The Traveler's movies always live?" Tina asked.

Jean-Pierre looked startled. "I don't know. I've never wondered that before? It's a good question. But how could she fake it?"

"She could be sitting in her basement, watching old movies on her tablet, recording them, transferring the files to her phone, then streaming them to all of you."

"But why would she do that?"

"Why would she do *this*?" Tina pointed to the phone. "Just to mix things up? Or maybe just to remind us of how timeless some sights are, of how some experiences seem to live outside of history."

"Nothing lives outside of history," he answered sharply. "Us here, drinking our beer, sipping our wine, chatting, you know, talking about nothing much—someday somebody will look back on us as history. They'll say ..." He thoughtfully scratched his chin and then spoke in a robotic voice with a mangled English accent, "I wonder why these people, these primitive folk, used those funny phones. Why didn't they just think to one another? And those big metal things, those cars, why didn't they just fly like normal people?"

Tina laughed. "Point taken," she said, throwing up her hands in surrender.

"Shhh," Jean-Pierre suddenly held a finger up to his lips and pointed out the window. A doe and two fawns stepped delicately across the lawn, nuzzling the ground, capturing the remains of fallen apples. As they chewed, Jean-Pierre raised his phone and began filming them. After a few seconds, he slipped out the front door and made his way around to the back of the house, stopping a good distance downwind from the deer.

Tina watched him watching them, the silence not even broken now by the sound of Jean-Pierre's breath. This is so meta, she thought as she raised her phone camera to photograph him through the window. She couldn't help herself. He was so concentrated, so unguarded in that moment. Those were the kind of pictures she liked to take and regard.

A scrawny gray cat approached the family of deer and stopped, no more than five feet from one of the fawns. It squatted, its belly almost touching the ground, poised to leap. The fawn skittered backwards towards its mother, then stopped, torn between safety and the piquant crabapple just out of its reach. Jean-Pierre also inched away from the animals, the better to pan the scene. Then suddenly he stood, dropped his hands to his side, and looked up with annoyance as two quick blasts of a car horn broke the silence. The deer bounded off towards the line of trees adjacent to the house. The cat startled, stared after them, then turned and slunk back towards the road.

Behind her, Tina heard the front door open, then the sound of cans and bottles falling to the floor.

"Goddamnit!" Melissa muttered, both hands still on the handles of Peter's wheelchair, one holding what was now just the handle of a torn paper shopping bag.

Tina leapt to her feet. "Let me help."

"I offered," Peter sang out. "This lap is still good for something. But no, my daughter is an I-can-do-it-all kind of woman."

"Thanks, Dad. Really helpful."

Tina flashed Melissa a sympathetic smile as they both bent to pick up canisters of mixed nuts, tins of smoked mussels, and a miraculously still-intact bottle of Bordeaux rolling across the floor.

Jean-Pierre came in behind them, pushed Peter into the house, and helped him out of his jacket. "Welcome back, my man. Did you enjoy your weekend?"

"Oh, it was splendid. I learned that I am a role model to legions of young television journalists, all the pretty boys and girls."

Jean-Pierre smiled broadly. "Admit it. You loved it."

Peter bowed his head with disarming acquiescence. "I loved it." He raised it again and gave Tina an inquisitive look. "And you, my dear? Did you enjoy your break from indentured servitude?"

"I did." She smiled sweetly, thinking, *You canny son of a bitch.* "I got a lot of work done—some of it yours, some of it mine." She adjusted her armful of groceries and nodded towards the kitchen. "Let me just put these away."

"Oh, you can't just drop that line about your own work and then exit. I'm intrigued." He followed her into the kitchen, wheeled up to the table, and happily smacked both hands, palms down, on its burnished surface. "So, tell me: What are you working on?"

Tina silently berated herself. Why had she made that reference to her own pursuits? It was too soon; they were too embryonic. "It's really just the flip side of my work for you. You and I are focusing on the photographers and the external circumstances—"

"The facts," he corrected.

"Yes, the facts surrounding the photo. Was it taken where the photographer claims to have taken it? Is it truly documentary, or arranged in some way? Is the photographer's caption an accurate description of the photo and its context? But I'm equally intrigued by the subjects of these pictures."

"Of course." He looked at her with genuine interest. "But isn't the subject one of the facts?"

"Sure, in terms of who she is, or how old he is, or even whether the subject knows they're being photographed. But even in the posed shots—even when the subject knows and we know who that person is—the picture tells us nothing about that subject's internal state."

"The good ones do," he protested.

"Even the good ones—they make it easier for us to interpret, to project our own template onto their circumstances. But really, think about it. Think about *Migrant Mother*. We can see that she's emaciated, that her children are thin, that their clothes are ragged. Those signs tell us that this is a portrait of desperately poor people. But the rest of it— whether you see exhaustion, desperation, pensiveness, pride in that picture—that's all what you as the viewer bring to it. And I defy you— anyone—to tell me what that woman, what Florence Owens Thompson, was thinking and feeling in that moment, and in the moment before, and the moment after."

"Well, actually, I can," Peter said, almost apologetically.

She smiled. "Okay, bad example. I can too, because she gave interviews about the photo. But if she hadn't, or if we hadn't ever learned her name, we could only imagine her history."

She paused, but Peter didn't fill the silence. He just looked at her expectantly.

"So that's my little side project," Tina said. "I'm making drawings of photographs—family photos of my own, and drawings of the ones you're writing about. I'm trying to imagine the histories of these subjects, and to convey my best guesses as to what may have been passing through their minds in the moment that the shutter was snapped, and somehow make it evident."

Peter cocked his head. "How?"

"Through facial expression, body language—all the ways we normally read people."

"And why? Why are you doing that?" Peter's eyes didn't leave her face, and Tina suddenly remembered what he'd been like in his prime, in those on-air interviews when his curiosity was unbullying but relentless. He asked actual questions, as opposed to simply making statements for his guest to garnish. He created a dialogue, and assumed that his audience was smart and interested enough to engage and draw their own conclusions. He had been thrilling.

But this time he didn't wait for her answer. "Imagined history," Peter said slowly. "Imagined history," he repeated, swilling the words around in his mouth as if trying to figure out if they were still good or had turned to vinegar. "You mean fiction?"

She laughed, startled and embarrassed and relieved all at once. "Maybe. I'm going for truth, I guess, with or without the facts."

"Truth without facts," he said drily. "It's a tall order." He took a sip from the Thermos of ice water, his perpetual companion, that Jean-Pierre had silently placed in his hand. "But why drawings? After all, the whole point of photography was to more accurately display what drawings could only illustrate. You're an artist. Unlike a camera, you don't have to be literal. So why not use that powerful imagination you seem to possess?"

"But I am!" she retorted. "You can't sketch a face without imagining the thoughts and feelings that animated it. At least I can't. And my drawings aren't literal; I'm not trying to be the neutral recorder. Sometimes I end up just replicating the image in the photo, but more often, I find myself exaggerating some implicit emotion and altering the drawn image, highlighting its differences from the photo."

"But why not start from scratch, create something new?"

Melissa blew into the kitchen and began talking with no pause or preamble. "Before I go home, we've got to figure out the tax thing."

Peter laid a calming hand on his daughter's arm. "Relax. Sit. Stay for dinner. We'll take care of it." He looked up at Tina. "Big, weighty matters lie heavily on our shoulders. We have to decide the best strategy for evading income and property taxes." His eyes widened. "Oh, did I say 'evading'? I meant 'paying.' " Then he turned sternly back to Melissa. "And I really do mean 'paying.' Even at 35 percent, we'll be just fine."

Tina welcomed the interruption. She put away the groceries and thought about how to answer Peter's question. Why make a drawing of a photograph? With charcoal in hand, what compelled her to try to reproduce—no, recreate—the image that had been so precisely captured with lens and light? It has to do with perspective, she thought. The photographer's choices are invisible and unacknowledged. But I want to make my perspective—no, my effort, the effort that empathy requires—visible.

This wasn't the first time she'd taken to drawing photographs. During the SARS outbreak, recovering from the disease herself and largely holed up in their apartment, she'd spent weeks looking at pictures, her sketch pad and charcoals arrayed in front of her, ready for the impulse to strike.

At first it was the photos of deserted landmarks that attracted her—the gray, rain-slicked esplanade around the Eiffel Tower, barren; the Kaaba in Mecca, normally dwarfed by the pack of pilgrims circling it, standing alone, an elegant little black jewelry box in a bleached white square. Absent the people, monuments were rendered meaningless. She felt a sort of relief in drawing these barren cityscapes; she could see these buildings not as symbols, but simply as shapes made of darkness and light. Drawing became once again a purely technical exercise—a welcome one—where she didn't worry about how to interpret the image. It offered no clues to be read or misread.

The moment life was introduced, the drawing challenges became more complex. She looked at photos of mountain goats grazing in front of a Welsh church, standing in small, social clumps, their handsome coiffed heads pointed at each other, communicating ... what? Promenading down a lane past the closed pub going ... where? And the hordes of hungry monkeys in a Bangkok rotary, jabbering and wrestling over the paltry food scraps normally so plentiful—how should she feel about them? Without knowing whether she was witnessing combat or play, competition or communalism, without her own interpretation of what she was witnessing, she felt paralyzed.

A solitary seagull flying over the deserted Millennium Bridge in London epitomized motion versus stasis. She realized that she wanted to draw the viewer's eye to the bird, to the beating wings of life over the bereft city, but it didn't stand a chance of competing with the stretch of rippled steel, the curve of metal railings, pulling the gaze towards the dome of St. Paul's Cathedral, sterile and white against the sky.

Occasionally a person appeared in the photos she studied — the Pope, standing alone in St. Peter's Square; a featureless man traversing the long, elaborate shadow of a streetlamp in Milan, the concentric stone rectangles of the Piazza del Duomo empty and pristine were it not for the pigeons casting their own flurried shadows against the gray stone.

Then she moved on to the opposite — to photos of people congregating at festivals, in parks, at outdoor restaurants. There was no ambiguity here, just faces emanating hunger and joy. Those were the feel-good pictures, easily drawn.

But what to capture in the photo of the doctor, her face covered in a surgical mask and a plexiglass shield, her blazing eyes burning through the camera lens, radiating what? Exhaustion? Fear? Or maybe the furious grief a doctor feels when losing a patient? So many of the pictures she studied offered just eyes, portholes too small to see into anyone's soul.

Photography was a dialogue between the photographer and the viewer, Tina understood, as the subject's intentions and thoughts are unknown. She wanted to draw the people who were the object of study, to give them voice and agency. But she was fooling herself; she was no more objective than the photographer who framed the shot, adjusted the composition, dodged the over-exposed areas, burned in darkness to create better contrast.

As she laid out the fine hors d'oeuvres and poured the wine, whisked the vinaigrette and tossed the greens and sliced the beef tenderloin and sang snippets from *Camelot* and cleared the raku-glazed plates, she asked herself another question. Why now, after years of being an artistic dilettante without seriousness or discipline, why am I now spending precious off-hours trying to make pictures that nobody will ever see? Or perhaps more to the point, why have I avoided it for so long?

That night, randomly looking through photos from her shoebox of family snapshots to sketch, Tina realized that the answer — until now always the same answer — was fixed in some of the moments those pictures had captured. She pulled one out — a terrible picture of herself as she stood in front of Momma Maria's on Broadway, her face contorted in an attempt to smile, her middle and right index fingers holding up in a peace sign — more a mug shot than a family photo. But no wonder she was beseeching for peace. That had been one hell of an evening.

• • •

June, 1970, New York City

"Two hours ago you're handed your diploma — your high school diploma — and now you just announce you're moving to San Francisco?" her father had said with no preamble after ordering a beer for himself, a gin and tonic for Joan, and nothing for Tina.

She and her parents were sitting tensely around a linen-covered table at Momma Maria's for her high school graduation dinner. The argument had started the prior night.

Tina studied the menu with close attention, grateful for any reason not to have to look at her father's furious face.

"Dad, it's just for three months."

"You say that now, but once you're there you're not going to want to turn around and come back so soon."

"NYU will still be here, whenever I come back."

"So you're not planning to start college in the fall?! I knew it!"

"I didn't say that." Tina avoided his eyes.

"But that's what you're thinking."

Tina looked past him at the waiters bustling in and out of the kitchen behind him. But she startled when Bob grabbed her forearm. It hurt, and she was shocked.

"Look at me when I'm talking to you!" her father barked.

Seeing his hand like a clamp, hearing his own hectoring voice, her father released her and took a deep breath. "You're a smart girl. You're brimming over with talent. Why do you want to throw it all away?"

"I don't ... I'm not ..." It was oppressive, this love he had for her. She wasn't some kind of prodigy. Could he even see the real her, or just his idealized image of her?

"You weren't much older than me when you went off to the Air Force, Dad, and nobody said you were too young," she said instead. "Well, just like you, the people are going to make history, and I just want to be a part of it."

He rolled his eyes. "History happens every day, everywhere. All you've got to do is be alive, punum, and you're part of history."

"Oh, come on, Dad. You know what I mean. You had your war. My generation, we have our ... our anti-war."

Bob took a deep breath. "I understand. Hell, I sympathize. I'm on your side. I just don't understand why you have to uproot everything when we've got plenty of peace marches right here in the city. You could go to school, pop out between classes to chant some slogans, then go back to what you're supposed to be doing."

"But this *is* what I'm supposed to be doing! Learning doesn't just happen in a classroom! This isn't some extra-curricular activity, Dad, like Debate Club. It's not a hobby."

"Oh, but it is, sweetheart," Bob answered fiercely. "Being contrary is a hobby. That's what I learned after over twenty years of listening to my parents and older brothers fight bitterly—and always with shifting alliances—over whether they should have gone to Palestine or the United States when they left Germany in 1933, about whether there could possibly be a God who would allow such a thing as the Holocaust, about whether Dutch Leonard or Bob Feller was the best pitcher in baseball, about whether the Hitler-Stalin pact was a shrewd move to buy the Soviet army time to prepare or a craven, anti-Semitic act of isolationism—"

Joan placed a placating hand on his arm, but he wasn't done.

"—about whether the point or the flat was the better cut of beef brisket, about whether it was Great Aunt Dora or Great Aunt Myra who had married the gentile in Kiev, about whether the Midtown

Tunnel or the 59th Street Bridge was the better route to Seymour's Discount Warehouse." He paused to take a few gulps from the glass of beer that the waiter had just set down in front of him. "And what did all that passionate feeling buy them, besides the opportunity to feel wounded or superior? Who needed the chaos?"

That speech was probably the longest, most self-revealing monologue her father had ever offered. But at the time, Tina couldn't really notice that. This was probably the first time he had ever been really angry at her. To be so insulated for so long, she now wondered—was that a gift or a handicap?

"Last week you came home from work talking about how television can save the world," she had retorted, feeling her own surge of sour fury, "and now you're telling me I'm, what, too emotional? Too much of an idealist?"

"*One of my sons is a Communist,* my mother used to say, *one a Trotskyist, and one an atheist. But my baby boy, Robert—he's a realist.* Smartest thing she ever said. So listen to me," Bob said fiercely. "I don't subscribe to ists or isms."

Her mother tried to hide it, but Tina saw her shoot Bob an incredulous look.

"I don't!" he insisted, now to his wife.

Joan gazed back, impassively.

Bob searched Joan's face. "So you're really not worried," he said flatly.

"Of course I'm worried." She threw up her hands in exasperation. "Our daughter is hellbent on going to her hippie commune on the other side of the country, to do God knows what, with God knows who. But I'm trying not to be. She's a sensible girl, Bob. She's grown up in New York City and she knows how to take care of herself."

At the time, Tina could have wept with gratitude. Now she was stunned at how sanguine her mother had been ... or how unjustifiably trusting.

"I know, I know." Bob took a deep breath, trying to calm himself, but without much success. Beneath the table, his knee was jiggling. "But not everyone's as sensible as her."

"And shaking your leg and pulling at your ear lobe—"

"I'm not—"

"You are pulling at your ear lobe."

"—Won't make it better. I know," Bob finished.

"What?"

"Shaking my leg and pulling at my ear lobe won't make it better. That's what you were going to say, right?"

Joan smiled. But the smile left quickly as she faced her scowling daughter.

"Yes, I'm still here," Tina said. "But don't mind me. You guys can figure out my future all by yourselves."

"Tina!" her mother snapped. "Don't go acting like a child and proving me wrong!" Tina shrugged in a parody of faux innocence. "It's not that your decision is so objectionable—though I think it's foolish, I do. It's the sneakiness. You didn't just come up with this plan, did you?" It wasn't a question. "Instead of consulting with us, you just sprung it on us."

"I'm a high school graduate. I'm old enough to make my own decisions, Mom."

"Is that what you think adulthood is? Making unilateral decisions, furtively, with no consideration, no ... partnership?"

Joan's scorn was withering, and despite her best efforts, Tina felt tears spring to her eyes.

"That's not maturity. That's selfishness."

"Well, if I'm hiding things, I learned it from the two of you!" Tina suddenly felt that she might throw up.

"What the hell's that supposed to mean?" Bob demanded.

"Never mind."

"I do mind. What are you talking about?"

Tina looked down at her menu, tracing the letters of *Ensalata* with her fingertip. "You guys keep secrets from each other," she said, not daring to look at her parents' faces.

Joan's tone sharpened still more. "Yes, dear, what *are* you talking about?"

Now Tina felt stupid. Her father's midnight raids on the refrigerator were hardly criminal. ("I always need a second dinner on salad nights," he'd confided just a few weeks earlier when, coming home late from a concert, she found him sitting in a dark kitchen wolfing down a sandwich of chopped liver and pastrami on rye. "Don't tell your mother." When she was little, those were her favorite words.) Her mother's frequent and unreported tours of larger apartments that they might someday rent didn't seem momentous, even to her. And she hated fighting with them, hated the way it made her feel small and scared and ungrateful for their love, which threatened to drown her.

"Never mind," she said. "Nothing important."

"It sounded pretty important," Joan said, her eyebrow arched in that *Surely you jest* sort of way.

Just then the waiter—an ancient, beak-nosed man in a white shirt and black jacket—slammed down a basket of dinner rolls on the table. "Can I take your order?" he croaked, barely audible above the din of Friday night diners.

Saved by the Italian Penguin, Tina thought. Though her appetite had vanished the moment the argument began, she ordered her standard Fancy Dinner Out meal: a Caesar salad and fettucine Alfredo. Not to have done so would have felt like she was disappointing her parents still more.

She looked around the restaurant. The uniformed people ferrying plates to and from tables were a mix of old men and young women—some close to the end of their working lives, some just starting them. Was taking orders, ceremoniously grating cheese over other peoples' pasta, calling patrons "my friend" regardless of whether or not they were—was this the work that they chose, or had they even had a choice? The waitress at the next table—Tina would bet her life that she was an aspiring dancer. She had that pronating walk, like she was stuck in first position, and when she filled the water glasses at the far end of the table, she didn't so much bend as hinge, her straight back at a sharp angle to her waist. For her, this job was temporary, a holding action until her real life started. But how about the older guy, the plump man in his thirties or forties, who was now singing a boisterous *Happy Birthday* to a mortified kid across the room. His voice wasn't bad. Had he wanted to be an opera singer and failed? Or was he a man who liked people, liked food, and liked to sing—an intentional waiter who defied his parents' injunction to be a cop and had found his calling here at Momma Maria's? And the birthday girl being regaled, with her gleaming blond hair and flaming cheeks behind her splayed fingers, would she ever forgive her parents for making her, the apple of their eye, the center of strangers' attention? Or would she grow up to be a hermit meditating on some Tibetan mountaintop?

"Okay, so you don't want to talk about us," Joan now said, picking up where they'd left off. "That's fine. We'll talk about you. Clearly you've got a plan. What is it?"

"Take a plane or a bus to San Francisco—I have the money saved up for that—stay in a hostel until I find a commune to live in, get a job. ... It's really nothing out of the ordinary, guys. In fact," she said and paused, realizing this for the first time, "the point is to *be* ordinary, you know?"

"This is your ambition?" Bob asked, incredulous. "To be ordinary and accomplish nothing?"

"Of course not! There's plenty I want to accomplish ..."

"Like what?"

She didn't know how to answer. "Like change the world."

"Oh, that's all?" Tina had rarely seen her father sneer. It diminished him, which only made her feel worse. "You're smart, you're talented, you're one of a kind, and you want to throw away all your potential on a pipe dream?!"

"You've got the same dream, Dad!" That startled him and emboldened her. "And it's *my* potential, not yours."

"Of course! Jesus Christ, you think we don't know that?" Joan grabbed her linen napkin, balled it up in her hand, then threw it back down onto the table.

"Enough!" Tina threw up her hands, in both warning and surrender. "I'm sorry, okay? I'm not doing this to hurt you." Her face crumpled and she covered it with her mother's napkin, unable to hold back her tears.

Her parents' anger instantly dissipated. Both reached out, each petting one of her shoulders.

"It's okay, sweetie," Bob said. "And you're right. This is no way to celebrate your graduation."

Joan murmured her agreement.

"And besides, we don't want to get this fancy napkin all teary and snotty, right?"

Tina breathed a shuddering sigh, regaining her composure. She nodded, grateful for the ceasefire.

Their waiter returned for her favorite Momma Maria's ritual. Holding a small butter knife, he carefully swept the breadcrumbs off the tablecloth onto a little saucer. She loved the dull sound of the blunt-edged instrument traversing the table, metal against linen.

"You used to think he was collecting breadcrumbs for the pigeons in the kitchen," her father said.

"Are there pigeons in the kitchen?" Tina asked, horrified, but oh-so-grateful for the change in tone.

"Not as far as I know. But apparently when you were little I said something about there being some mighty plump birds behind those swinging doors ..."

Her parents smiled sadly at each other in shared memory.

Tina reached out to pet both of her parents' hands. "I'll stay in close touch while I'm gone," she reassured them. And as the Old Man of the Manicotti arrived with their appetizers, she acknowledged with fearful honesty that she could not promise to return to start college in the fall.

When they got home, stuffed and weary and quiet, Tina sat cross-legged on the cedar chest under her parents' bedroom window as they prepared for bed, just as she often did when she was young. Now that they'd acknowledged that she was grown up, she realized, she felt free to be childlike, at least for a night.

From her perch, she could see Joan standing in front of the sink, brushing her teeth for as long as it took Tina to wash her whole body. She watched Bob reach behind her to get a roll of Tums from the shelf. Then, as Tina assumed was the usual routine, he got into bed first.

As she watched her mother undress and hang up her capri pants, place the brown leather flats next to the black ones at the foot of their bed; as Joan half-folded her blouse before tossing it into the laundry bin and systematically applied Noxzema to her cheeks in small, vigorous circles, Tina thought she looked more frail than fierce. Her skin was more pellucid—it no longer glowed—and her arms were an asymmetric mix of loose and bony. She was aging, and it scared Tina. They counted on Joan to be the imperturbable one at home, to stay calm while Tina and Bob muttered and paced, to frostily put others in their place while they silently seethed. Her father managed things, but Joan managed them.

Or, now that Tina was leaving, him.

September 2011

They were wrapping up work for the day. Jean-Pierre came into the study with a glass of milk and a mint Aero chocolate bar for Peter, who took a blissful bite.

"Milk and chocolate," Tina said. "That was one of my father's favorite snacks too. He practically lived on Hershey's bars when they were making the first episodes of *Now and There*."

Peter paused mid-chew, then practically yelped, "*Now and There!* I remember now. It was the first episode, and I was sent to western Canada. Just a pup." He stopped, straightened his shoulders, and focusing on a point about a foot to the right of Tina's head, said in a slightly deeper voice, "It's a beautiful morning here at Stanley Park, in Vancouver, Canada. On this Sunday morning at 11 a.m., families are frolicking at the beach." Peter once again looked at Tina. "Or some nonsense like that. Everyday life, babies being born, people going to work—the whole idea was to show how we're all the same beneath the skin, which is, of course, ridiculous."

"In what way ridiculous?"

Peter looked at her, aghast. "Whether you believe in nature or nurture as the force that shapes us, surely you'll agree that some of us are smarter or stronger or more disciplined or more relaxed than others. Humanity is blessedly diverse, thank goodness. Otherwise we'd all be running banks or unclogging toilets."

"Of course people have different skills and interests and temperaments," she answered, already regretting that she'd tried to mine her boss's convictions. Below his certain, aristocratic countenance, there was clearly a lot of coal intermingled with the gold. "But don't you think there's a pretty universal set of needs and motivations that we all share? You know, Maslow's hierarchy? Shelter and food—physiological needs—love, belonging ..." She slowed down, counting on her fingers as she strained to remember the labeled pyramid on the blackboard in the one psychology class she'd ever taken. "Oh, esteem, and self-actualization. I'm missing one ..."

Peter sighed. "I acknowledge that we're all motivated to stay alive and be liked," he said with exaggerated patience. "Even, God help me, hugged now and then. As for self-actualization, I thought psychobabble like that died with the 1970s."

Right, because you never had to struggle to realize your ambitions, Tina thought. It's amazing how privilege lubricates the belief that since you were born from the head of Zeus, fully formed, everyone else must be also.

Then came her own nagging, needling rejoinder: Yes, but at least he had ambitions.

There was no point in continuing down this path. "Speaking of motivation," she said brightly, "what drove you to want to write this book?"

Peter peered at her, sheltering his eyes from the late afternoon sun streaming in through the window. "A man needs a legacy, doesn't he?"

Tina didn't know how to respond. After all, hadn't she just come to the same conclusion? Why else had she decided, after fifty-nine years, that she needed something to *show* for her life?

Silence suddenly draped the room, and for once, it was Peter who seemed uncomfortable. "*Now and There,*" he resumed. "Quite the logistical extravaganza."

"But you pulled it off."

"Yes, my dear, dozens of translators, about 10,000 frantic technicians and producers across the globe, and me. We pulled it off. An amazing bit of engineering with content so breathtakingly banal that nobody remembers it today, including me."

Tina felt a pang in her chest at Peter's breezy dismissal. She remembered her father's excitement, his conviction that he was doing transformative work.

•　•　•

July, 1969, New York City

She was complaining about the boring predictability of these stifling days and evenings to her cousin Elaine in their daily phone call.

"First I'll have to help my mother make a chicken salad for dinner. Because after all, it's Thursday. Chicken salad night. Then my father will get home and turn up the fan in the sweltering kitchen when we sit down to eat it, my mother will complain about the napkins flying off the table when he does, but still complain about the heat. Then they'll ask about each other's day, find something to say about each other's non-adventures, then turn to me and ask me about my last ten hours, as if today was in some momentous way different from yesterday."

But when they sat down for dinner that night, Tina's father disrupted the routine. After wolfing down a few bites of mustardy chicken and iceberg lettuce, and without waiting to be asked, he announced, "I had an interesting day." Joan cocked her head and raised her perfect half-moon eyebrows, signaling that she was now officially listening. "I got a call from a guy at the BBC in England, Lesley Lynley. He's cooked up this really bold idea for a live documentary, with segments emanating from and beaming to about 25 countries — on every continent except maybe Antarctica. It'll use all five communications satellites that are circling overhead" — he pointed to the ceiling — "and traverse every time zone in the world. It'll start with a ninety-minute broadcast, then if that goes well, become an ongoing half-hour series."

"Lesley with an ey or an ie?" Tina asked.

"Ey," her father answered impatiently.

She knew she was missing his point and took great pleasure in it. "Because I've never known how to spell it when it's a man's name. Of course I've never actually known a man named Lesley either ..."

"He's English. English men have names like Lesley."

"Wasn't there a Lesley in *Gone with the Wind*?" Tina asked her mother. She didn't know why she was trying to derail her father's story, except that she could.

"No—you mean the really passive guy that Scarlett was unfathomably in love with? Wasn't his name Ashley?" Joan answered. "Oh, but he was played by a Lesley. Lesley Howard."

"Lesley, Leslie - the spelling of his name really isn't the point of the story I'm trying to tell you," Bob fumed. "He's a producer at the BBC, and despite his funny name, I imagine that like so many of the Brits I met at the airbase during the war, beneath his smoking jacket and flannel pants, the guy's got balls."

Joan cast Bob a mildly disapproving glance.

"It's okay Mom," Tina sighed. "I know what balls are."

"Can I please—" Bob asked.

Joan pet his hand. "Go ahead, dear."

"What's so fascinating is the technology. The technology is revolutionary. In 1945, Arthur C. Clarke figured out that at the right elevation, it would take exactly twenty-four hours for a satellite to complete one orbit, essentially staying fixed in the sky of an entire hemisphere," he explained.

Joan looked at him blankly.

Bob lifted out one small, perfectly circular radish from the salad— as useless a vegetable as Tina had ever encountered—and slowly began spinning his dinner plate, while holding the radish a few inches away from it.

"See how the radish's position changes in relation to this chicken salad?" Then he held it directly over the center of the plate. "Same thing happens if the radish is too close. But—" This time he carefully positioned the radish over the edge of the plate, and circled it around the spinning plate once again—"put it into orbit at the right distances and the radish maintains a fixed location in relation to the chicken salad." He dropped his napkin and leaned back in satisfaction. "Well, the radish is the communications satellite, and this little bit of bird thigh and mayonnaise is New York."

"Why is this a big deal?" Tina asked after a lengthy silence.

"Funny you should ask. That was exactly my question. On the phone to him, I said, 'Let me ask you, Mr. Lynley …' And he said 'Lesley, please.' So I said, 'Let me ask you, Lesley, what's your mission? What are you trying to accomplish with this?' and he said, 'That's a fine question, Bob — may I call you Bob?' And I thought, Jesus, the Brits."

Joan rolled her fork through the air at him, urging him on with his original story.

"He wants to demonstrate that communication satellites can and should be used for benign purposes, to link up the world in real-time."

"Sure, but why?" Joan asked.

"So we can be less foolish and more aware. The idea is that if we can learn about and react to global news quickly, we'll be forced to understand our responsibilities to one another." Bob's voice rose half an octave, the words coming faster. "If we can make Americans see that Russians are just like them — that they go to school and to work and raise children and, if they're lucky, spend a sunny day out in the country, and vice versa — if we can do that, maybe we can inch our way to an armistice in the Cold War."

"And then we shall overcome?" Joan asked sardonically.

Tina watched her father flush, then answer in a wounded tone, "Well, maybe not in one ninety-minute broadcast, but you get the gist."

"I do," her mother answered with sudden and conspicuous kindness. "I do get the gist. And the gist is that this sounds like long hours and a lot of pressure."

Bob threw up his hands, then let them thud to the table. "Yes, Your Honor, it'll mean long hours for a few weeks. But, excuse me, it's demanding to revolutionize television."

"I'm not denying the importance of your work, dear," Joan said, unruffled. "I just don't want you to deny the importance of your health."

"Yeah, yeah—sleep, fresh air, healthy eating," he said, his voice rising in annoyance. "I'm not an invalid, for Christ's sake. And I didn't have a heart attack. It was just—" He stopped abruptly, then followed Joan's eyes as they came to rest on Tina.

"What are you looking at me for?" Tina demanded. "I didn't say anything." Then, after a pause, she forced herself to utter the frightening words. "Did you have a heart attack?"

"I just said I didn't!" her father answered, sighing heavily. "It was just a little angina." Then, smiling bitterly at her mother, "See what you started?"

"Well, if I started it, I guess I can finish it," Joan answered, her voice cold and clipped. She stood. "Tea?"

Bob shook his head.

Uncertain of whose side to be on, but certain that no more information was forthcoming, Tina began clearing the table. "I'll clean up," she said. "You go watch the news or something."

She hated this. Her parents rarely fought, but when they did, she felt completely unmoored, terrified that this apparent contempt for each other was how they really felt, and that the rest of the time they were just acting. Their family was too small to afford conflict. They were a tiny island, with not enough mass to absorb many shock waves.

She paused, then rummaged through the knives, spatulas, rubber bands, and screwdrivers in the Everything Drawer, emerging with a metal shish kebab skewer. She impaled the radish with its tip, then put the skewered radish back on the now empty table. Then she took down the cake platter from the cabinet over the toaster, removed an ice cream scoop and a roll of electrical tape from the Everything Drawer, and deposited a small sphere of chicken salad onto a clean salad plate. After setting the plate on the cake platter, she carefully taped the skewer perpendicular to the platter. After revolving the plate with one hand and the platter with another, she was satisfied.

Sticking her head into the silent living room, she saw her mother reading a copy of *The New Yorker* while her father leafed through *Popular Mechanics*.

"Can you guys come into the kitchen for a minute?"

They dutifully rose from their respective armchairs and followed her in.

"Ta-dah," Tina sang out with forced cheer. "A working model of the perpetual communications thingy. The radish connecting the world."

Her father broke into a huge grin. "What a work of art!"

Her mother cast her a quick, scrutinizing glance, as attuned to her motives as her father was blind to them. Then, as if to thank her for the gesture, Joan said, "We have to memorialize this before it rots. Don't move. I'm just going to get the Polaroid."

. . .

Late in the rainy afternoon, while Peter was napping and the pork loin was roasting in the oven, Tina retreated to her room and dug into her shoebox of photos. She found what she was looking for: a picture of Bob and her teenaged self standing behind adjacent kitchen chairs. Both are beaming with obviously false pride, their smiles unnaturally wide, as each stretches out an open hand to Tina's construction on the table. The cake platter is a bit blurry, as if it was in motion when the shutter was snapped. Behind them, dirty dishes are arrayed on the counter next to a table fan. Above the stack of plates, a cocktail napkin appears to be suspended in mid-air.

The kitchen must have been hot that night, she thought. Just like tonight. Normally the window fan was enough to cool her bedroom, but this evening it seemed unable to power its way through the heavy air. She longed for an air conditioner. And with a surprising pang, she longed for her parents, whose arguments about the need for one had been a regular feature of her summers at home.

She remembered when her mother had finally prevailed.

Her father had trudged into the apartment after a twelve-hour day, stripped down to his boxers and undershirt, and stretched out on the couch, sighing and sweating.

Joan, with irritated efficiency, brought him a glass of ice water, then stood over him. "Just don't get too invested," she scolded. "So far *Now and There* is just one show—90 minutes on a summer weekend when people are thinking about picnics and popsicles and having to go back to work the next day. They may be wishing there was an open Sears nearby so that they could finally, once and for all, buy a goddamn air conditioner for their stuffy apartment."

Bob smiled. "All right, all right already. When they have the Labor Day sales next weekend, so help me God, we will borrow your brother's car and drive out to Sears in Flushing and buy ourselves an air conditioner for the bedroom window."

"And maybe the living room window too."

"Jesus, you drive a tough bargain. Are you a social worker or a union boss?"

"Oh, I'm multi-talented," Joan cooed. "Music?"

Bob shook his head, too tired now to even speak. Joan repositioned the fan on the windowsill to blow directly on him, picked up her copy of *Clinical Social Work Journal*, and sat in the easy chair Bob usually claimed for himself.

Seated in the other armchair, Tina began sketching in the sticky silence. The floor lamp created a cone of light that covered her mother's head like a Chinese bamboo hat. Her father was spread over the length of the couch, his forearm over his eyes, his elbow jutting up at a right angle to his face, perched against the irritating bristle of the upholstery. The room was settling into darkness. Soon she'd need more light to draw, but she hesitated to make a move. These were living people so temporarily sunk into themselves that she could sketch them as she would a still life.

As her father softly snored, she studied her work. Not bad. She was pleased with how she'd captured her father's splayed knees and bony toes, her mother's tapered fingers on the page of her magazine. But she couldn't capture the sheen of sweat on her father's neck or her mother's arm. The trick was to refrain from drawing, to use what her eleventh-grade art teacher, Mr. Procaskinoff, had called the "negative space" and reveal rather than impose. But that required, what? Vision? Restraint? I don't even know, Tina thought, which is why I'll probably never be a great artist.

Will I ever be great at anything? Self-doubt snuck in like the last shards of light through the Venetian blinds. And if I'm not, what will my parents do?

• • • •

This reverie was doing nothing to improve her mood.

She turned on her computer and called Carl on Skype. He answered almost instantly.

"I didn't wake you, did I?" she asked.

"On the contrary," he said. "It's—" he squinted down at his watch—"it's just a little before midnight and I'm headed to work."

"Do you have time to talk?"

"Of course. Of course I do."

"So, have you been swimming yet?" Tina still couldn't get over the fact that Carl was spending his days on an island whose beaches he had yet to visit.

"No," he sighed, more with annoyance than embarrassment. "I've just been hanging out at the observatory. It's amazing. There's a whole little city up here—probably twenty astronomers, plus support staff."

"Sounds like a booming metropolis." That came out unintentionally snarky. "Sorry," Tina hastened to add, "I just mean it sounds less isolated than you've been at some other telescopes."

"You're right, relatively speaking," Carl answered cheerfully. But he was almost always jovial—that had been one of the things about him that drove her nuts. "Oh, and you'd love the caldera. We're so high that it's cloud-filled most of the time, like a giant steaming pasta pot made of hardened lava."

"Wow." She didn't know what to say. Why this sudden awkwardness? Dumb question, she scolded herself. You know exactly why. He's baffled and hurt, and you can't adequately explain your decision to stay behind to yourself, let alone to him.

"Do you want to give me a tour?" she asked him. Anything to break the painful silence between them.

He hesitated. "Well, it's midnight, so it's going to be tough for you to see much, especially with just my phone."

"I just meant your living quarters."

"Oh, sure, the dorm. Of course. Let me pick you up and show you around." His thumb briefly filled the screen, then his squinting face as he looked for the button to change the direction of the camera. Clumsy and self-conscious, he lacked all the skill that The Traveler demonstrated in her videos, images that forced you to see the ordinary as alien, the mundane as mysterious. "Okay, so here's my desk" — pristine as always, she thought; "the view out my window, which is actually pretty spectacular during the day; my bed" — unmade, a twin, she thought with foolish relief, not made for rolling around in; "and" — he zoomed in on a small night table — "here's you!"

She was looking at a framed photo of herself that he'd taken about ten years ago, on the sweltering July day when he moved into her Toronto apartment. In her Joan Mitchell "City Landscape" t-shirt (God, she'd loved that. Where was it now?) and a ghastly lavender culotte (What had possessed her to buy that hideous garment, let alone wear it?), she stood on the top stair, leaning like Sisyphus into a tower of moving boxes, arms outstretched, as if pushing them over the threshold. Her hair, frizzy and damp, flared around her face, and her look of faux strain hovered between a grimace and a sheepish smile. She hated being photographed and never mugged for the camera, and yet there she was, doing just that.

"What an awful picture! I look ridiculous — more ridiculous than usual. Why did you bring that one?"

"Because it was the beginning of our life together."

"Of our life *living* together," she corrected. "I mark the beginning as the day we met in Alaska — ten years ago, not nine."

Now Carl turned off the camera on his phone and just spoke to her.

"Every morning after I finish work I get some toast and orange juice in the dining hall, come back here to catch up on news and email, pull down the shades against the gorgeous blue sky, and climb into bed. Then you're the last thing I look at before I go to sleep."

"I do love you," Tina said. It was the one true statement she could muster right now. She didn't look at his picture every night or even think of him every day since he'd left. She'd felt suspended in space and time, waiting for the next episode of her life to reveal itself, knowing Carl was in the wings but out of her line of vision.

Finally Carl said, "I've got to get to work."

"Hi ho," Tina softly sang.

"So I'm going to sign off now. What's the thing Peter Bright used to say at the end of his broadcasts? Something about stories? End of story?"

"Right ..." She lowered her voice, intoning "And those are *today's* stories."

"Goodnight, Canada."

October 2011

Boiled wool. That's what the child's hat appeared to be made of in the
photo that Tina was sketching. Or maybe I'm just remembering my
winter hat, she thought, the one my mother made me wear when I was
that age. She'd hated the red woolen bonnet with its ridiculous ear
flaps. It scratched her scalp and smelled like pickled eggs. It had no
shape, and when Tina tried to give it one by folding up the hem or
wearing it pulled down more on one side than the other, Joan
intervened. God forbid she should look unstylish.

Tina studied the original print — number eight of ten — of Mara
Vishniac standing on the sidewalk. While black and white photos
usually lent intensity to the image, this one was just colorless and
bleak. It was not artfully composed with its subject at an odd angle or
interestingly framed by a crumbling archway or wooden window
frame. No candlelight shone up to illuminate Mara's face and no
sunlight streaked across it. The only vibrancy in this picture was the
Art Deco zigzag of men's shirt boxes and collars displayed in the store
window to Mara's left.

Roman Vishniac had taken this picture of his daughter in
November of 1933. Tina imagined that it was a Sunday, an especially
gray and damp day even by Berlin standards. I need color, she
thought, to capture the grayness. She pulled out her case of oil pastels
and started over on a new sheet of paper, laying down a steely blue at
the bottom of the page to create the impression of snow crusting the
sidewalks, then applying gray over it and scumbling the two.

In the photo, Mara stood on a block of mostly shuttered stores on
Uhlandstrasse, where the building façade between each glass door

was plastered with posters. Vishniac had positioned her sideways next to a painted image of two children—a stern-looking blond boy about his daughter's age and his brown-haired little sister. They gazed out reproachfully at passersby, and below them was a slogan that Peter had translated on an index card attached to the print: "The coming generation accuses you!"

She wouldn't try to depict the contents of the posters, Tina decided. She'd use cross-hatched lines to evoke the size and density of them, then create abstract lettering that would convey their hectoring tone. She pulled out her India ink set and started experimenting with different nibs, applying slashes and dots of ink within the borders of rectangles meant to evoke the signage.

Then she turned her attention back to Mara, drawing her from the feet up. As in the photo, she aligned the child's head with the bottom third of a giant poster saying "The Marshal and the Corporal. Fight with Us for Peace and Equal Rights." President von Hindenburg's face looked tired and sagging, but Chancellor Hitler's looked frozen and bright. Draw them? She thought not, daunted by both the challenge of creating a picture within a picture and the misery of studying those two wretched mugs. But the language—that, she could use. Using a font she invented on the spot, she made "fight" and "peace" the only two legible words.

Mara's head was cocked. Was she quizzical? Defiant? Or just plain miserable? Did her father treat her to a hot chocolate when their work was done? Because this photograph was, after all, Vishniac's work, and his daughter a prop in the scene. Tina understood why. If stopped by the SS and asked why he was taking these pictures, Vishniac could blandly answer that he was just taking snapshots of his daughter out on their Sunday stroll together. It was the only way he could document Berlin's transformation, shoot pictures of swastika banners and flags waving cheerily over bustling merchants and women pushing children in prams, of phrenology shops and massive campaign posters, of marching Brown Shirts and stiff-armed saluting pedestrians.

Tina paused. What if she documented the whole day, frame by frame, each containing a sketch of Mara posing amidst the symbols of the Third Reich?

She looked for the other prints from 1933 but found only one more of Vishniac's daughter. This time Mara stood feet together, hands behind her back, her head slightly higher than that of a mannequin's head next to her in the store window. A lock of waxy hair curled over the face of what looked like a sculpture of a teenaged boy. It was not the usual ghostly faced lump of papier mache; its features were well formed. His eyes were wideset, his nose short and straight, and a faint smile shaped his waxy lips. Two semi-circular calipers adorned his head like an airy, fancy hat, measuring the diameter from one temple to the other.

Phrenology shop, Peter had scribbled on the index card affixed to it. *Sign = "Nurture your Race!"*

Mara's gaze was steadfast, perhaps even a bit curious. Did she know that the stores lining this damp, barren block had once been owned by Jews? Did she know that she and her Jewish friends and dogs of any faith were now barred from entering them? What had her father told her as he stood a few feet away, his Leica lovingly enfolded between two chapped hands, staring down at the view finder, his head bent as if in prayer?

Tina heard the squeal of Peter's tires and looked up as Jean-Pierre wheeled him to the study door. She quickly closed the sketch pad and returned the pastels and ink bottles to their respective boxes. She didn't want Peter seeing her art. She wasn't sure if she wanted anyone to, but certainly not this arrogant, opinionated man. He'd object to her choices. *Her* choices.

"Am I disturbing you?" Peter asked automatically, clearly indifferent to her answer.

"No. I'm just indexing the Vishniac photos you want to use."

Peter gave his aide a quick nod. Jean-Pierre pushed Peter to sit beside Tina at her desk, then took a seat in the massive leather wingback chair next to the window.

Squinting at the photo displayed in front of Tina, Peter said, "No need to spend time on that one. That one's legit. That whole Berlin series from the early 30s is legit. It's the later stuff, the *Vanished World* photos, that have been manipulated."

"Wait a minute." Tina challenged her boss. "The story that was told about the pictures—when they were taken and what was happening in them—that may have been distorted, but the images themselves weren't altered."

"They certainly were," Peter answered icily. "Get the book. The *Vanished World* book. Get it."

Tina stood leisurely, and walked with exaggerated slowness to the bookshelf, exchanging a quick commiserating look with Jean-Pierre as she passed him. Increasing pain and fatigue exposed a different Peter than the man she'd first met a few months earlier. She'd come to recognize those times—generally late in the day—when his casual charm sagged like a loose pair of socks and some innate imperiousness asserted itself.

She pulled down a worn copy of the photography book that had adorned her parents' coffee table, and that of most American Jews who had coffee tables circa 1960, and handed it to him without comment.

"Thank you, dear," Peter said, now chastened. He rifled through it, past the pale faces of stolid peasant women, past the luminous white beard and challenging gaze of the old rabbi, head resting on hand, hand resting on cane; past the boisterous scrum of boys, some in caps, some in the black hats and payot of the Orthodox. He paused briefly to study the black, beseeching eyes of a little girl beneath a tousled pelt, huddled in blankets, a dingy wall adorned with lurid painted flowers behind her. "Since the basement had no heat, Sara had to stay in bed all winter. Her father painted the flowers for her, the only flowers of her childhood," he read, and sighed heavily.

Then he flipped to the final spread. "You see this?" He turned the book around to face Tina. She'd studied this image dozens of times before. On the left side of the spread, a grizzled man in a cap peeked out from a small rectangular opening in a metal door, gazing down the street to his left. His puffy eyes dominated his gaunt, bearded face. On the right, a small boy in a ragged woolen jacket and oversized cap pointed down the block.

Peter turned the book back to face him and read the caption. "The father is hiding from the Endecy (members of the National Democratic Party). His son signals him that they are approaching. Warsaw, 1938." He looked up at her. "Scary, right? Tragic. And it gets worse." He closed and reopened the book, this time going to the index with additional commentary on the first few pages. He held up a forefinger, commanding Tina's attention. " 'The *pogromschiki* are coming,' " he read with dramatic urgency. " 'But the iron door was no protection.' " He slammed the book shut. "The roles reversed. The father hiding while his little boy serves as scout and protector."

"Yes," Tina said with a nod. "It's tragic. And so ominous."

"And such nonsense."

"What?"

"The pictures — the one on the left and the one on the right — came from two different rolls of film!" Peter crowed. "They were probably shot in different towns, and earlier than 1938."

"Why do you say that? How do you know?"

"Because Vishniac was commissioned by a Jewish charity to photograph Jewish poverty in Eastern Europe. All of those pictures that made their way into *A Vanished World*, they were taken between 1935 and 1938. And they were propaganda photos. The Joint Distribution Committee — they're still around today, I think — hired Vishniac to document the lives of rural, Orthodox Jews. They wanted pictures that would tug at the heartstrings of urban, secular Jews, that would move them to donate money to help out their poor country-bumpkin cousins."

Tina was puzzled. "To help them emigrate?"

"No, no, this was before the war. To help them eat, for God's sake! To fund schools and clinics and soup kitchens. It was the European Jewish equivalent of the American Farm Services Administration. Why do you think Roosevelt's administration sent Walker Evans and Dorothea Lange and Arthur Rothstein and that whole crowd to migrant farmworker camps and dustbowl towns and the hollows of West Virginia? Because rural poverty was so much more compelling to urban dwellers than the beggars and bums they rushed past every day on their own city streets."

"Are you saying they were staged?"

"No, not staged," Peter said. "Just selective. The poverty was real, the anti-Semitism was real, the boycotts of Jewish businesses—he didn't make that up. But the pictures weren't used for their original purpose. Between the time they were taken and the time they were shown in New York City, the world had changed. Genocide had become a bigger problem than poverty."

"So instead of the pictures being used to raise money for rural peasants, they were shown to drive support for Jewish refugees?"

"Exactly."

"So what's so wrong with that?" she asked, then almost cringed from the impact of Peter's glare.

"Public relations should be called by its name. Public relations is not photojournalism. One manipulates, the other merely documents."

Tina, accustomed to speaking equivocally, to thinking equivocally, was put off, as always, by his certainty. "Is the line of demarcation really that clear?" she asked slowly.

"Of course," he snapped. "You don't see calls to donate money beneath a photo in a newspaper or a magazine ... or at least you didn't when there were still thriving newspapers and magazines."

"But that's just a function of where the picture appears, isn't it? Not why it was taken."

Peter was momentarily silenced. He sighed heavily, then said, "You can't lie."

"Of course," Tina answered, feeling, not intoxicated, but shaken at having scored so quickly and decisively in this battle with her boss. "If Vishniac or his editor said the picture was taken in ... I don't know, Bucharest, when it was actually taken in Warsaw, or that it was taken in 1939 when it was actually taken in 1936—if they intentionally misled, well, that obviously crosses the line. No, what I'm struggling with is the question of intent. Does it really matter whether the photos of Eastern European Jews were taken for the Joint Distribution Committee or the *New York Times*? Whether they were meant to document pogroms or Nazi genocide? Either way, these were people who were oppressed and endangered."

"Like my people," said Jean-Pierre. Tina and Peter both looked at him in surprise. "Nobody cared about Haiti before the earthquake, and nobody cares about it anymore. But in the days—maybe the week or two after the quake—when people saw the pictures of our tumbled-down cities, of the little boy dragged from the rubble, they felt something. They were—what do you call it—aroused. They gave money to the Red Cross and Medecins Sans Frontieres. And it was the pictures on the news that made them do it. Not the facts, the pictures. So why do I care who paid the photographer?"

Peter slumped, gesturing vaguely towards Tina's water Thermos on the desk. "Can I have some of that?" He looked suddenly pallid and clammy.

She stood, alarmed. "Are you okay?"

"I'm fine," he snapped. "I'm thirsty, not dying."

Tina and Jean-Pierre silently studied Peter as he sipped, his hands shaking. His window of equilibrium is so narrow, Tina thought. Just a slit. Carl would have explained it to her in some other more scientific terms. *It's hard to maintain homeostasis as we age,* he might have said. But having now spent a few months with Peter, Tina saw his travails much more vividly than that. By the time you reach his age, the mere act of living is like plodding your way across a glacier, she thought, always cold, always at risk of slipping. And when you do, it's like falling into a crevasse. The descent was so deep, the return to the surface so laborious. Thank God her parents had died young and she'd been spared from witnessing their decline.

The color gradually returned to Peter's face. He took a few deep breaths, leaned back in his chair, and looked around the room, studying the bookshelves dense with volumes of photographs, histories of world wars, biographies of politicians, and one high shelf housing tall, slender collections of botanical prints. "Did you ever read Susan Sontag?" he asked Tina casually, as if nothing had happened.

"I'm embarrassed to say I haven't."

"She said that photography had advanced well beyond its original purpose, which was to more accurately chronicle what is. She said that photos have *become* the reality, that we consume pictures like gum drops and often experience the reality that constitutes the image as a letdown. I think she's right, and it scares the hell out of me. So, when I hear people like you or my daughter talk about 'intent' or even worse, about everybody constructing their own goddamn narrative, well, it just cements my conviction that all we've got, all we can count on, are facts."

"I've never heard Melissa talk about narrative," Tina mused.

"Not her. Sandy."

"Your other daughter?" Tina cast Jean-Pierre a look over Peter's head. He cupped his hand to his ear, signaling his interest in hearing more.

"Yes," Peter answered brusquely. Tina wanted to draw him out, but Peter's "Don't ask" signal was flashing brightly. So she stayed silent as he pulled the laptop computer towards him and with surprising speed and dexterity, typed in a URL. "He loved kids," Peter continued. "Vishniac. He took thousands of pictures of kids. And now —" he pointed to the computer screen— "here they are, here and forever, all the courage and the risk sapped out of them. That's the thing about the digital world ..." He trailed off, and Tina once again anxiously checked his face and posture. He seemed so labile this morning. But he was fine, she realized, just lost in thought.

"Were those the last pictures he took in Europe?" Tina asked.

"Oh no. The Joint Distribution Committee sent him back after the war to document the Jewish displaced persons camps." Peter flashed a twisted smile. "Lots of pictures of kids from that assignment too. And now the Holocaust Memorial Museum, they've posted them all, with an invitation for anyone still living to identify the subjects. See?"

He pushed the computer to Tina, who saw a page of small black-and-white images, some high-contrast and clear, some bleached and faded. They were photos of prints, each with a blurry black border framed by the clear white borders of the photographic paper. She began scrolling through them. In 1935, on the narrow streets of Bratislava, children ran; on Warsaw's cobblestones, they sat and played checkers. In a Berlin Children's Home in 1938, they gathered in circles, playing bells and triangles, and hit tambourines with their sticks. At charity-sponsored summer camps for impoverished Jewish children in Poland, they tipped their chins towards bowls of porridge, clutching spoons in small fists. At the Colony for Frail Children in Vilnius, Lithuania, they sat outdoors in rows of wooden chairs, their stiff white cotton gowns and shaven heads toasty in the sun. In 1938, expelled from Germany, they crammed themselves into basement apartments in a Polish border town and stared, pale and waiting. Four years later, outside New York's Jewish Children's Home, some who had made it out of Europe stood, feet apart and solidly planted on a sunny lawn, looking hearty and bronzed. Five years after that, some who had stayed in Europe and survived gathered outside the transit bureau in a Displaced Persons camp in the American sector of Berlin. These children were taller, mostly teens. They gazed directly into Vishniac's camera. Their minds were not on tambourines or porridge and dodge ball; they awaited transit papers to Palestine or the United States.

Every time Tina thought she was reaching the end of the collection, another 20 pages worth of pictures would be loaded. Most were group shots of children in pairs or trios. But some were individual portraits, one so striking and pure that Tina stopped swiping and zoomed in. A little girl—probably no more than five years old—stood ramrod straight on a stone sidewalk in a checkered dress, looking up at the camera. The child's thick dark hair was a wacky mess, parted jaggedly and flying skyward at odd angles as if grabbing for clouds. The girl's half-smile and the look in those dark eyes—unguarded, curious, absolutely delighted—was breathtaking. Behind her, only partly visible in the frame, was a small toy truck or cart.

Roman Vishniac photographed this girl in Mukacevo, Czechoslovakia, circa 1935–38, the caption read. *She is one of the many people curators hope to identify by making Vishniac's work available to the public.* Tina scrolled down the page. *We invite you to view his full collection—spanning the prewar and postwar period—on the ICP website to help us make further identifications. If you recognize a person or a place, click the link below the photograph to generate an e-mail to Museum and ICP curators.*

"I wonder if anyone's claimed her," Tina said, showing Peter the picture.

"What makes you think she's still alive?" he challenged.

Tina was stung. "You're right, of course. She probably isn't. But born in 1931 or 1932, maybe, she'd be younger than you, and you're still kicking."

"Hardly kicking, dear," he said drily. "And unlike little Helga or Sala here, the closest I got to Europe during the war was an army base in London, Ontario."

"But look at her," Tina insisted, only half-playfully. "No child this—I don't know, this luminous—could have been snuffed out."

"Please," Peter answered, not trying to hide the contempt in his voice. "You know better than that."

"You're right. I do know better than that." Chastened, she gave the computer back.

Peter chuckled. "Your imagination is extraordinary," he said. "And so misdirected."

Tina willed her voice to be simply inquiring. "What do you mean by that?"

"Nothing offensive, dear. I just mean that instead of imagining the lives that real people might have led, instead of turning their histories into *stories*—your marvelous mind would be better applied by investigating and documenting the truth."

"Are you saying that stories are inherently untruthful?" She leaned in, as always infuriated and intrigued by her elegant, opinionated boss.

"I'm saying that they're subjective. Everyone thinks their suffering is unique, their misfortunes are unprecedented. They infer motivations and harp on them—'He just wanted to be seen as generous,' or 'She just wanted to be needed'—instead of assigning weight to concrete actions. Everybody's so busy appropriating facts to fit their own narratives—such a degraded term—that they lose sight of the real history." His cheeks reddened, his tapered fingers clutched the arm rests of his wheelchair, and Tina could feel, but not understand, his rage.

"But ..." She spoke cautiously now. Philosophy was never her strong suit, and more to the point, she wasn't sure that's what they were really discussing. "Isn't history defined after the fact? I mean, isn't it just the agreed-upon story about what happened, made up well after the facts have unfolded?"

"Made up?" He straightened his shoulders, triumphant. "Thank you, dear. You've just proven my point." He turned to Jean-Pierre. "Shall we proceed to breakfast? There's nothing like a good argument to work up an appetite."

"Scoring in the last minute." Jean-Pierre extended his hand to Peter in a fist bump, and much to Tina's amazement, Peter returned it. "Good job, my man." He winked at Tina over Peter's head, released the brakes on Peter's chair, and wheeled him out of the room.

Tina hated that faux brotherly solidarity, that schoolyard competitiveness. She didn't know whether to abhor Jean-Pierre in that moment or admire him for finding ways to boost the self-esteem of a failing old man.

I need a walk, she thought, and after grabbing her lightweight fleece from the coat hook by the door, she headed down to the river. She kicked the leaves as she shuffled down the lawn, but found less solace than usual in their rustling sound.

The air was too warm for the autumnal light. She was too hot with her jacket on and too cold with it off. The water had the gray sheen of winter, but not the frigid calm. She was hungry for something but for the life of her didn't know what.

She stopped her aimless striding and sat down on a rock to check The Traveler's latest video log. It was a murmuration of birds, thousands of them making breathtaking patterns against a dusky sky. They swooped and swirled, forming a swift, fluttering mobius strip, then morphed into a round cloud, then a cylinder, and all the while, still managing to go somewhere, even if their destination wasn't clear. Starlings! That's what these birds were—tiny little animals that alone were defenseless and cold. But together, they created warmth. *Hiding in the collective*, Tina could hear her father say, not about birds but about her and the choices she'd made.

But was that true? The starlings flew in such tight formation, she'd learned, that when one moved, whether to dodge a falcon or catch a wind current, it affected at least seven others, and each of those seven had the same rippling impact. Like a mass of snow becoming an avalanche, like water becoming steam, these assemblies of birds were systems on the edge, ready to be completely transformed in an instant.

Tina knew how that felt. And she admired The Traveler's eye and steady hand, so alert and able to capture such transient glory.

When she got back inside, she tracked down the email address of the photo curator at The Holocaust Memorial Museum.

Dear Ms. Cohen, she wrote:

I am a photographic researcher, studying and documenting some of Roman Vishniac's work. I would like to be of help in identifying and locating the unknown children in his archive, particularly the child shown photographed in Mukacevo, Czechoslovakia between 1935-1938 and shown on your website's landing page for The Roman Vishniac Collection. I have access to numerous academic libraries, and friends in leadership positions in the Combined Jewish Philanthropies whose assistance I can enlist. Please let me know if and how I can be of service.

Then she hit Send before her natural reticence could stop her. She felt foolish, but when she saw the picture of that unidentified child, something in her stirred. Call it curiosity, call it purpose, or call it, as Carl probably would, distraction—she was determined to find that child, to learn what was in her head when that photo was taken. How else to bridge the gap between individual and icon, to understand the person and not just view the subject?

"Once an aristocrat, always a goddamn aristocrat," she said of Peter when she and Carl Skyped later that night. "He's smart and funny and can be very sweet, but God, he can be such a bastard sometimes."

"Sorry you're having such a tough time," Carl said.

Did you get that line from *Empathy for Dummies*? Tina thought, instantly irritated. But she held back the words, knowing that it was Peter, not Carl, who she was really mad at. But it was also true that Carl didn't know what to do when she was angry. Fury, it seemed, was simply not included in his emotional repertoire. That was one of the things about him that annoyed her.

She inhaled and exhaled deeply, willing herself to calm down. "I've missed you in the last few days."

He grinned. "Lucky for me. Out of nowhere?"

"No, it's just that spat with Peter." So much for deep, cleansing breaths. "Honest to God, his arrogance is insufferable sometimes. And it made me think of you."

"Because my arrogance is insufferable?"

"No," Tina said with a laugh. "That came out wrong." Tina gazed at Carl's puzzled, boyish face. She needed his happiness in the throes of uncertainty. She wanted to lay her head on his chest, to feel him stroke her hair with one hand while holding *Science* magazine as distantly as possible from his far-sighted eyes in the other, reading and sighing with contentment as another theory in the canon of 20th century physics was blown up.

Tina had recognized Carl's curiosity, his unique delight in being proven wrong, almost the moment she first met him ten years earlier.

• • •

August, 2001, Skagway, Alaska

Tina boarded the overnight Skagway-to-Ketchikan ferry, and though it was 10 p.m., the August sun was still skimming the horizon. She was on the return leg of a camping trip in Alaska and the Yukon. Her friend Marnie had flown back to Toronto, but Tina, with time on her hands and an as-yet-unsatisfied desire to see orcas in the wild, decided to take a more meandering route. She'd driven from Whitehorse, capital of the Yukon territory, back into Alaska, down to Skagway.

A hundred and ten years earlier, this town had been the embarkation point for the Klondike Trail. Desperate men and women had hauled tools, provisions, and sometimes their own pack animals, up and over the White Pass to Bennet Lake. There they'd build rafts or boats to float across the lake and down the Yukon River to the Klondike gold fields in search of the fortune that would justify their hardships. And their suffering was immense. Over 80,000 people had passed through Skagway during the Gold Rush, and the White Trail was littered with the corpses of fallen travelers, dead from starvation and exposure, and horses that had stumbled and gotten sucked into the three-season mud. In a Skagway Museum photo from May of 1898, a single-file line of small black figures snakes through a valley, snow-covered mountains jutting up on either side of them. If she hadn't read the caption, Tina would have thought she was looking at refugees, not adventurers.

Now that mountain trail was overgrown; the stakes that marked the path and held the ropes that climbers clung to had rotted into pulp. But the threads of the lives that had passed through this town had been woven into legends of the Gold Rush that adorned every poker chip, napkin, storefront, and restaurant place mat in this kitschy but still rough-edged town. Walking down the boardwalks lining either side of the main street, Tina had felt like she was the only woman there who wasn't a waitress or a hooker, and she was glad to put it behind her. This trip down the Inside Passage, first to Ketchikan, and from there to Vancouver, would, she hoped, be the perfect end to a stunning trip.

When the sun finally went down, she stretched out in one of the dozens of reclining chairs filling the lower deck. The murmurings of the couples and families around, even the clanking and groaning of the boat's engines, soothed her. The ferry was for natives, not tourists, and in this democratic din, parents were singing their children to sleep, the navigator was studying the tide charts, and below deck, she imagined that mechanics were softly swearing at the motors and pulleys and crankshafts that kept them all afloat. Tina knew nobody, but they were almost all strangers to each other and in that way all belonged.

So the next day, as they milled on the top deck watching the eagles soar overhead and first hearing the fizz, then seeing the tapered spout of an Orca, conversation was easy and free. And when a man spotted a moose swimming through the frigid water toward the boat, he kindly offered up his binoculars to anyone who wanted a closer look.

"Jeez, I hope it doesn't get too close to us," Tina said, peering through the lenses at the goofy long snout gliding towards them. "I don't want it to drown in our wake, or get cut by a propeller." Years earlier, in Florida, she'd gone swimming in an inlet frequented by manatees, and seen the massive scars in their elephantine hides as they'd silently passed below her. She'd hated motor boats, hated the blithe damage they inflicted, ever since.

The owner of the binoculars—a tall, lanky man with silver-flecked, bowl-cut hair, like a prematurely gray child in a Norman Rockwell painting—reassured her. "He's not headed towards us," he said. "That's just an optical illusion. He's headed to that island over there." He pointed at a disc of rock and cedars hundreds of yards away.

"Why would a moose go swimming?" Tina wondered, lowering the binoculars. "I mean, I know it's summer, but it's not like it's hot outside."

"They like the salt water," the man said. "It kills all the bugs that take up residence on moose. Or mooses. I'm not sure which."

"Kind of like a spa treatment," Tina mused. "Exfoliation, free of charge. I wonder if there's a masseuse on that island, awaiting the moose with a bathrobe and some herbal tea."

He laughed. "I'm afraid that I know more about moose than about spas, and I know practically nothing about moose."

Tina raised the binoculars to her eyes again. What an endearing, absurd-looking animal. Floppy ears, a long, flat face parallel to the water, with nothing on it until you got to its almost piggish snout, and a huge rack of antlers that sat on top of its head, prongs up, like her Aunt Bertha's coral ashtray. But its eyes, large and brown, shone as it paddled through the icy water. "It looks so earnest," she said to the man, "like a kid who's just learned how to swim."

"Oh, he's got a ten-point rack," he said. "He's no kid." The man stuck out his hand, and Tina hastily pulled the binoculars off from around her neck. "No, I wasn't asking for them back," he said. "I was just trying to introduce myself. You know, shake your hand. It's stupid, right? Such an antiquarian tradition."

"Oh no, my mistake." She transferred the binoculars to her left hand and stuck out her right. "It's nice to meet you. I'm Tina."

He shook her hand. His fingers were pleasantly cool and his palm felt weathered but smooth. "I'm Carl."

Then, of course, they fell into an awkward silence, one that Tina gamely but lamely broke by asking about the eating habits of moose. Carl answered with an ease that led her to suspect he was a local, a scientist, or both. She turned out to be half-right. He lived in Toronto (Whoa girl, she had to tell herself) and was an astronomer.

"I just come up here to play with radio waves," he said almost bashfully. "You know, bombard the ionosphere with high-frequency waves to see what happens. My real specialty is dark matter."

"It's interesting. I hear your voice and see your lips move and know you're speaking English, and yet I haven't understood a single word you just said." Am I flirting, she wondered with surprise? I do believe I am.

He flushed. "Sorry, yeah, I'm still learning how to talk to normal people."

She laughed. "Oh, well, don't waste your efforts on me, then."

But to her great pleasure, he did. They talked all morning, and when the boat docked in Ketchikan, they got their packs and met up on the pier so they could explore the town together. The houses tucked into the hills were made of brightly colored wood, the streets were lined with totem poles, most new and richly hued, but some faded, spindly, and towering. When they walked through the small town park and followed the trail to Ketchikan Creek, they found a fast, narrow river clogged with molting salmon tunneling up stream, their once shiny skins now dissolving in their final, frantic race to die in their home waters.

Carl was the youngest of three, she learned, the only son of a math teacher and a national parks administrator. He'd lived all over Canada as his father moved from one assignment to the next, and since he was rarely in one place long enough to make friends, he'd learned to rely on his sisters, his books, and his own curious mind for all the companionship he needed. On long, demanding hikes, his mother taught him how to use a compass and triangulate to find his way through dense Northern woods. His father taught him how to read the stars and memorize the names of constellations by reciting the stories they signified. "And my sisters taught me how to cook anything with just one pot and some corn meal, and how to change diapers on their I-Wet-Myself dolls," he told her.

"Did you change many real diapers?" she asked over coffee in the Ketch-if-you-Can Cafe, despising her own coyness as the words came out.

"Are you asking if I have kids?"

"Yes," she said, mortified. "In the stupidest possible way, that's what I'm asking."

"One, a son named Keenan," Carl said, smiling fondly. "He just graduated from McGill and is about to start a new job as a high school math teacher next month. He's a good kid."

"And your wife?" Tina asked with a sinking heart.

"Jane, my long-time ex-wife, is on the astronomy faculty at McGill. We were only married for about two minutes, just long enough to conceive Keenan. Then she got a post-doc at Cambridge and I got one at Berkeley and we split up when he was six months old."

"Was that difficult?"

"Nope," he answered. "As easy as falling off a log ... though that actually isn't so easy. No, I mean it was hard only seeing Keenan a few times a year, but Jane and I both felt relieved to get out of the marriage."

Their waitress—a pierced, tattooed Native American girl who couldn't have been older than fourteen—hastened to the table, as if summoned. "Can I get you something else?"

"No, I ... um, pie. Do you have any pie?" Carl asked. Tina watched a blush rise from his tanned neck to his stubbly cheeks.

"Apple and wild Alaskan blueberry."

"Oh, great," he said with obviously false enthusiasm. "Can I have a slice of blueberry pie, please?"

"Sure thing."

"I don't even like pie," he muttered as she returned to the kitchen.

Jimmy Stewart, Tina thought. He reminds me of Jimmy Stewart, with that aw, shucks modesty that she normally found so corny at best, disingenuous at worst. But in Carl it seemed authentic. "So, tell me about dark matter. What is it?"

"Well, everything I'm going to tell you is a guess, since we don't really know. But the speed with which galaxies are spinning suggests that there's something out there that we can't see, something that's exerting significant gravitational force. And that's what we call dark matter."

"You mean like a black hole?"

"Good question," he answered, and Tina felt ridiculously proud of herself. "Sort of but not quite. Unlike a black hole, dark matter doesn't interact with light. It doesn't emit it or absorb it. And it isn't a discrete, autonomous object like a black hole."

"So what is it?"

"That's the million-dollar question. It's more like a web, or a root system, something that seems to fill some of the spaces between galaxies."

"Like that giant fungus in Michigan?" He looked at her blankly. "Oh, somewhere in northern Michigan they found that all of these dainty mushrooms on the forest floor were actually all part of this thirty-acre fungus that's about two thousand years old and weighs about a hundred tons."

"Cool."

"Or those quaking aspens in Utah. They found—I don't know— forty or fifty thousand trees that share a single root system. It's amazing—they all turn colors in the fall at exactly the same time. So what on the surface looks like 50,000 separate entities turns out to be just one." He was listening intently, she saw, but his face showed little more than polite bafflement. "Sorry. I tend to trip off ..."

"Oh please, don't apologize. I do exactly the same thing." Tina relaxed. She'd thought for a moment that she was losing him. "So, to answer your question, we don't think dark matter is a single entity— it seems to be scattered all over the universe. No, it's more like the ground that everything else stands on, that determines what moves where."

"But if a galaxy's spinning faster than it should, how do you know if that's really true, or if you were wrong about how fast it should have been spinning in the first place?"

"Because sometimes our predictions about their rate of spin are right. Most of the time, in fact."

"But maybe they're just unpredictable, like people. Galaxies. Just when you think you know one, it goes off and joins a rock and roll band ..."

"Or maybe people are like galaxies. Maybe we think we're autonomous, self-directed creatures, when actually our trajectory is determined by large, invisible forces."

"Are you a conspiracy theorist?" Tina asked with a smile. She needed him to know that this was not a hostile question, even though it sort of was.

He shuddered. "God, no. Reality is weird enough."

The waitress set the bill and a dry sliver of pie in front of Carl. Its crust was as shiny as her cheeks. They both stared at the wafer-thin triangle of dough.

"Enjoy!" Tina said cheerily.

Carl took a desultory bite. "It's like a stale Fig Newton," he said after chewing briefly but laboriously. "I hate Fig Newtons."

"You can just mash up the rest with your fork," Tina said, "and it'll look like you ate some of it."

Carl obediently pressed the sides of the tines into the rigid crust, sending the pie skittering across his plate.

"Riddle me this, Starman. What's dark matter made of? Is it hot or cold, thick or thin? Like this blueberry pie or like something humans would eat?"

"We don't know if it even can be cold or hot, or if it can form complex objects like blueberry pies. We're still in the early days of trying to map its topography, but as best we can tell, it's clumpy in places and has long, skinny tendrils in others."

"I love how you talk," Tina blurted. "I mean I love the specialized language that astronomers and physicists use—tendrils and clumps and quarks and—what is it?—charmed quarks. It's like wine connoisseurs talking about wine as ashy or grassy, only you're talking about the universe."

"Wine connoisseurs are more authoritative than we are ... and I suspect they get invited to more parties." He smiled, and deep crow's feet radiated out from his gray eyes.

"So, you can't see it, you don't know what it's made of ... you just infer that it's there?

"Can you see gravity?"

She nodded. "I get it. But at least we can feel gravity. Our senses tell us it's there, and we can prove it in an instant. But your work can take a lifetime, right? And you may never know if you're right."

"Yup," he said cheerfully, reaching for his wallet.

"Or worse, what if you work on this for thirty, forty years—your whole professional life—and then someone proves you wrong?" She felt a sudden anxiety for this man who she'd only just met.

He stood, put on his jacket, and left payment and a generous tip on the table. "Then, great. If someone proves me wrong, that'll meant that they've learned something new, that science has advanced. And then I'll get to make up another story."

He held open the café door for her, then followed her out onto the sidewalk. They were halfway down a steep hill. Below them, a different boat than the one they'd come in on was tethered to the ferry dock. And up the hill, behind Carl, a small glacier, slushy and breathtakingly blue, poured down a mountain. The air was tangy with salt and cold and Tina felt more invigorated than she had in years.

They split from each other just long enough to board the ferry that would take them to Vancouver and to deposit their bags in their respective rooms.

"Room" was a stretch, Tina decided as she stood at the door—it was more like a closet, not much wider than the single bed it held. She unpacked her toiletries and looked without regret at the unopened copy of *War and Peace* that she'd planned to read on the boat. She applied some lipstick for the first time in about three weeks—Passion Fruit. How apt, she thought. Then, with a toddler's wide-legged gait, she lurched down the rolling, bucking hall of the ship to the cafeteria.

Carl bought them two cans of Molson's Golden ("No charge for the plastic cups," the cashier trilled as she rang them up. "Alaskan hospitality"), and they went back outside to study the scenery. The sky was gray and the evening air was colder than it had been the night before. They pulled two deck chairs close together, unzipped the sleeping bag Carl had brought on deck to drape over themselves, and continued talking. They would be in Vancouver by the next morning, and Carl seemed to feel the same urgency that Tina did to … to what, she wondered? To sleep together that night? To forge a strong enough bond to ensure that they'd see each other again when they returned to Toronto?

"And you?" Carl asked with no preamble. "Husband? Kids?"

"No and no. I had a few long-term relationships that just kind of fizzled out, first when Richard and I realized that our coupledom was bringing us nothing but boredom and irritation, then when I hit middle age and Sean wanted a newer, turbo-charged model."

"I can't understand how any man would feel that way about you," Carl said, fiercely, she thought.

"Oh, I can," she answered, though her heart was melting in gratitude. "I got sadder as I got older."

"About what?" He took her hand under the sleeping bag, as if they were an old married couple, as comfortably as if he'd been doing it daily for thirty years. His hand was so warm.

"About the loss of my parents. About missing my chance to have kids."

"Didn't Richard want them?"

"No, and in those years I didn't either, for all the usual reasons. I didn't want to give up my freedom, as if being able to go to a gallery opening at midnight was what made my life worthwhile. And I still had this belief—the same conviction that had led me to skip college and go to San Francisco when I was 17—that my tribe was somewhere out there, that I'd find my community rather than have to hatch it."

Carl looked at her, head cocked.

"You remember how we thought when we were young and idealistic and outliers in the Reagan years, right? The world had enough children with no homes, the answer was to live collectively, to pool our resources, not to fragment and skulk off each to our own little house in the suburbs."

"I'm embarrassed to say that by then, my family had finally landed in a little house in the suburbs of Winnipeg, and I spent those years in our finished basement, reading science books."

"Well, I was a true believer, a drum majorette for the counter-culture. And I clung to those beliefs, to that life, well past its expiration date."

"I don't believe you're as cynical as you sound," he said quietly.

Unthinkingly, Tina lifted his hand to her face and kissed the tops of his fingers. He sharply turned his head. She was shocked by what she'd just done, but willing herself not to stop now, she leaned over the chair's plastic arm rest and lightly kissed his lips. He responded in kind and she sighed inside, a big, rich release.

"You're right," she said. "I'm not cynical, not even now. What I thought then, what I held onto so hard—it was juvenile. But it wasn't wrong. I still believe in mutual aid, in the idea of from each according to his ability to each according to his need. Maybe it's the result of being an only child, but I'm still looking for my larger family."

"Your stand of quaking aspens?" His mouth twitched, as if he were trying not to grin. But what she saw in his face was tenderness.

"Yeah, man, my cosmic destiny," she answered in a stoned voice, self-mocking.

"Well, I know a thing or two about the cosmos," Carl said, now smiling broadly. He pulled her toward him, leaned toward her, and kissed her deeply.

She sank into the warmth of his lips and tongue, and felt the back of his hand, still holding hers, now nestled like a precious cameo between her breasts.

And as they lay on her narrow bed later that night, the smell of diesel fuel wafting up through the seams of the metal floor, she understood the urgency she'd felt earlier in the evening. She'd been swimming upstream for so long.

• • •

Carl's curious voice brought her back to the present. "So, what did you fight with Peter about?" he asked.

"Oh, about the nature of truth …"

Carl arched his eyebrows. "That's a pretty big topic. Your boss thinks he's got a monopoly on that?"

Tina felt suddenly protective of Peter. She remembered a story he had told her soon after she'd started working for him. Early in his career as the nightly news anchor, he got to interview the newly elected head of the Liberal party, a man he'd admired from afar for years. "He seemed like the last principled man in politics," Peter had said, "a guy with integrity who practiced what he preached — respect, rationality, progress — true liberalism. Anyhow, a few minutes before we go on air, I go to the make-up room just to introduce myself and welcome him to the broadcast. I walk in just as the guy's taking a gulp from his pocket flask. Then he puts it back in his pocket and — he doesn't see me, doesn't know I'm in the doorway — as the make-up girl is applying some color to his face — he's clammy as hell — he reaches up with both hands and twists her nipples like they're radio dials. Just like that, out of nowhere, just because he could. So I knew then, and I know now," he told her with a bitter sort of pride, "that you have to look for the facts that contradict the image."

"No, Carl, not a monopoly" she said. "It's just that he's lived most of his professional life before Photoshop. You can't be a journalist for as long as he has without believing that everyone has ulterior motives and something to hide, everyone's bending the facts to fit their story, whether or not they know it."

"Is that what you believe?" Carl sounded startled. "I never thought you were such a cynic."

"I don't know if it's cynicism or realism. And I sure don't know what I believe." She sighed, tired of her mental jumble and frustrated by these false starts in her conversation with Carl. "He's got another daughter," she said abruptly.

"Who?"

"Peter. It turns out he has another daughter. I've been here three months and this is the first I've heard of her. No pictures, no mention of her name. It's a little weird."

Carl shrugged. "Maybe he's just a private guy. And when your kids are no longer kids, when they're grown-ups leading their own lives, they can become more like old friends."

"Really?"

"I mean you still love them, they're still an integral part of your history…" Carl was struggling for words, but Tina couldn't tell if that was because his ideas were elusive or his feelings were. "They're just not a part of your daily life anymore, and maybe less central to your future. I mean, how often do I talk about Keenan?"

Tina cast her mind back and came up almost empty. "Good point. But that's because your relationship has evolved. With Peter and Sandy — I don't know — I just get the feeling that something's been erased."

"I'm sure you'll find out in time," Carl soothed.

"Don't placate me," Tina snapped.

"That's impossible." Carl smiled gently. "You are unplacateable."

Tina's annoyance dissolved as quickly as it had appeared. "I'm sorry. Enough about me. I'm fine. Everything's fine. How about you? Have you shone any light on dark matter?"

"You used that line last month, and the answer is still no. Slow and steady, though …"

"… wins the race. I know." Tina leaned in closer to her own screen, as if that would somehow let her speak more intimately.

"Yikes! You're all nose now," Carl said.

She sat back. "Sorry. I forgot that I'm on camera too, not just you."

"So, what did you want to tell me so up close and personal?"

"Mostly just that I love you. This separation is helping me realize that whatever's impeded me from — I don't know, from acting, from committing to my own work and following through on it — it isn't you. It was never you."

"So that's a good thing, right?"

The moon—overhead in Brockville, reclining in Carl's sky across the Atlantic—illuminated a bit of stubble on his cheek and the corner of his mouth. "Yes, my love, that's a good thing."

For a time, Tina heard nothing but silence and the faint hooting of an owl. Then Carl said, "That's the sound of me smiling."

November 2011

"Dinner's on me," Marnie said as they sat down. The French bistro-style chairs, with their rounded seats and wooden backs, were even less comfortable than they looked. But the amber liquor bottles over the bar, the gleaming copper espresso-maker atop it, and the large, rush-filled brass planters imbued the room with warmth.

"That's very sweet, but don't be ridiculous. This place isn't exactly cheap."

"But I *am* ridiculous," her friend answered happily. "And besides, you only turn 60 once."

"Thank God," Tina muttered. "It's freaking me out."

"Fear not," Marnie reassured her. "As a much older, somewhat wiser 61-year-old, I'm here to say that 60 really isn't so different from 59. You'll feel a tad stiffer in the morning and find yourself drinking tea after dinner no matter what the temperature is outside. You'll discover your glasses on your forehead no more or less frequently than you did before. You'll finally understand why your grandmother ate only bran cereal. And you'll find yourself surprisingly at peace with getting senior discounts on your subway pass and movie tickets."

"Promise me that we won't start having dinner at 5:30 and in bed by 9:00."

"I can only commit to the first part," Marnie answered solemnly.

"Will I start endlessly reminiscing?" Tina asked.

Marnie looked up from her menu and gave Tina a penetrating look, alert as always to her unspoken thoughts. "You haven't so far," she answered.

"Not out loud, but I've found myself plunging into memories — like dropping through a trap door — at the most unexpected moments."

"What kind of memories?"

"Oh, all kinds of stuff. Mostly episodes from my childhood, memories of my parents." She paused and gazed out the window. It was good to be back in Toronto for the weekend, good to be distracted by the noise and odors and signs and parade of people. Out on the sidewalk, dinner-and-playgoers were bundled up, leaning into the damp November wind. How does she ambulate in those heels? Tina wondered as she watched a tall, slender woman in stilettos and fishnet stockings scurry into the lobby of the Princess of Wales Theatre. And more to the point, why? She turned back to face her friend. "Nothing dramatic or dementia-like. Nothing to worry about. I've just been thinking about them more lately — since going to Brockville, I guess — than I have in a very long time."

"Well, you're taking care of a man old enough to be your father."

Tina nodded. "True."

"And you're turning 60."

"Yes." Tina sensed that Marnie was driving at something, she but didn't know what. "And ...?"

"Wasn't your father 59 when he died?"

Tina startled. "You're amazing! How did you remember that?" Marnie just shrugged. "Yes, he was. So you're saying ..."

"I'm saying that I've read that a lot of people struggle at the point that they start to outlive a parent."

"I wouldn't call it struggling," Tina answered slowly. "More just ... re-examining. I mean, my dad died ... what would it be ... over twenty-five years ago, and my mother's been gone for over a decade. So it's odd to be suddenly thinking of them so often. And my time in San Francisco and Vermont, even when you and I met in Montreal — doesn't that feel like another lifetime?"

Marnie sighed. "That's how everything before yesterday feels to me now. Immediate and incredibly distant at the same time."

A waitress came to take their drink orders. As Marnie chatted with her about the cocktail options ("Remind me — what's the difference between Aperol and Campari? Will both of them make my mouth pucker?"), Tina studied her friend's face. As they aged, the two were becoming the inverse of each other in the flesh, not just in personality. Tina had "filled out" (as her doctor had delicately put it), starting to stray across the border between slender and solid. She'd developed her father's jowls and her mother's furrowed neck. Marnie, in contrast, had cantered down the trail from firm to gaunt, her high cheekbones and large, almost bulging eyes looming over the rest of her bony face and frame. But the uncanny blend of defiance and insight that had drawn Tina to her in the first place—that had endured.

"You know, my best years started when I met you," Tina blurted out, then felt herself blush. She rarely expressed her affection so directly. ("You should have been an author," a writer friend had once told her. "You show but never tell.")

Marnie snorted. "That's because you left Richard around the time you met me." But Tina could see gratitude in her friend's lingering smile.

Tina nodded. "And after all those years, it turned out to be so easy." She paused, then corrected herself. "I think I may have left Richard *because* I met you. Swapping him as a lover for you as a friend—God, was it twenty-five years ago?—was one of the smartest things I ever did."

Marnie raised a clenched fist. "Yeah, I'd say you traded up."

April, 1984, Montreal

Despite all those years with Richard, breaking up turned out to be easy.

When Tina got home to their third-floor walk-up on Durocher, the first thing she saw was the morning's dishes still stacked in the sink, and Richard's political science students' term papers strewn across the small, porcelain-topped table.

Richard lay on the couch, his feet up on the frazzled arm, one big toe poking through a hole in his hiking sock, reading *The Hitchhiker's*

Guide to the Galaxy. On the color television he'd recently acquired at a moving sale, *M*A*S*H* played at a barely audible volume. "Hey, Tiny," he said cheerfully, using his own nickname for her, one that she hated. "How was the Yellow Door?"

"I wasn't working at the Yellow Door tonight." She heard herself answer with the same tight, controlled exasperation that her mother sometimes used on her father. "I was working at the gallery opening."

"Oh, yeah. What's the show again?"

"Martha Rosler. *House Beautiful: Bringing the War Home.*"

"And she is ..."

"A collagist, famous for her anti-war photo montages. You've seen some of them; she Xeroxes them to be used as flyers. In fact, a bunch of them used to be on the wall at the Montreal Council to Aid War Resisters' office."

"And they are ..."

"Good. They're good, Richard, and rather than my describing them to you yet again, maybe you want to just go to the gallery and see them yourself."

Richard let his book drop to his chest and raised both hands in mock surrender. "Sorry. Just demonstrating interest."

Not really, Tina thought. Just going through the motions of conversation. "It's been a long day," she said instead. "I'm tired and hungry and cranky."

"I saved some leftover pea soup for you on the stove."

No, you just didn't clean up after yourself. "Thanks." She ladled out a bowl of the now-rigid soup, mealy and dense, and began leafing through the show catalog, which she was only now getting to see in its final, printed form.

Rosler's montages weren't in the least bit subtle. They were a head-on assault on comfort and complacency. In one, a New York Society doyen stands in front of a fireplace in a floor-length yellow gown and glimmering beaded jacket. She smiles graciously beneath her honey-brown bouffant. Her dress matches the plush golden sofa and gleaming table lamps. Behind her on the mantelpiece are two giant candelabras, and between them, hanging in an ornate frame, is a black-and-white photograph, sharp in its contrast and crystal clear, of a dead

Vietnamese woman, her head listing to the right, her crooked hands collapsed on her chest like broken wings.

Grotesqueries collide, Tina thought, amplifying each other.

She turned the page to a faintly colorized image of a young housewife, a portable vacuum cleaner strapped to her shoulder, holding its wand up to a heavy damask curtain. She is cleaning the drapes. Outside the window, in black and white, stand two helmeted soldiers in flak jackets, cigarettes dangling from their mouths. They are in a trench, the sandbags piled chest-high around them, on a break from the killing.

The next page: an airy modern living room, with a white shag rug, chic armchairs, a glass coffee table, and beyond this room, a sun porch in which you can see a delightful bamboo catbird seat suspended from the ceiling. In the foreground, a black-clad Vietnamese man with panicked eyes carries in his arms the scalded, half-naked body of a child.

Rosler had chosen to place these images of carnage in rooms— comfortable domestic interiors. This was, she readily admitted, propaganda, intended to arouse consciousness of what it meant to witness what the media had taken to calling "the first living room war." But what about the Vietnam photos she'd pasted in? Was it accurate to call them "propaganda" when the atrocities they chronicled were real?

These pictures were so powerful that rather than inviting closer scrutiny, they made you look away, Tina thought. How had Rosler felt when she made them? Sorrowful? Enraged? Professorial?

Until the past few years of taking art classes and working in a gallery, Tina had never thought about art as a means of making a statement. In her life drawing class and in the sketches she made outside of it, she didn't consider how her work would be seen. She was fully focused on the person she was drawing, as if by capturing the hitch in this man's shoulder or the crow's feet radiating from that woman's eyes, she was somehow connecting to them, trying to get inside their skin and experience the world as they did.

"That's naïve," Marco, her teacher, had said when she gave voice to that ambition. "It's presumptuous. The only truth you can know is how *you* see them."

Maybe he was right, though she hoped he wasn't.

Richard rose from the couch and snapped off the television. He sat down across from her at the cluttered table and stretched out a hand to rub her right shoulder.

It was a sweet gesture, Tina reminded herself, even if a spontaneous massage just as she was raising the soup spoon to her lips was not exactly helpful. She forced herself to smile.

"Do we have any plans for the weekend?" Richard asked.

"I do."

Richard cocked his head and jutted out his chin, his all-too-familiar signal for *More, please,* whether for more information, more food, more attention.

"I'm doing some street art," Tina continued. "Legally this time."

Two weeks earlier, at 2 a.m., she'd driven to the railyard in Montreal West with two fellow students from the Museum School. While she stood guard and tried to illuminate their work with a wide-beam flashlight like the useless old lady of thirty that she was, her companions—both a decade younger and way cooler—adorned the side of a CNR freight car. Standing and pacing in the damp dark, she felt an adrenaline-fueled mix of fear and elation. Denise sat on Hugo's shoulders to spell out RAGE in brilliant red letters, then below it, with wide sweeps of their arms and at lightning speed, they created freeform, abstract images of the city—silhouettes of people's upper bodies on a crowded Metro platform, piles of rubble and rebar, a garish fireman's pole around which a skinny nude had draped herself, and emerging from this visual chaos, looming over it, the cross atop Mount Royal.

Or at least that's how it looked to her as she panned with her flashlight when Hugo tersely said "Finished." Tina was amazed by the athleticism it took to create this mural, the assurance and vision required to paint it. The metallic chirp of crickets, distant sirens, and the clang of a bead striking the inside of each can of spray paint they shook—this was an utterly new soundtrack.

But probably not one she was likely to hear again. As she drove back to the student ghetto—within the speed limit, signaling every turn despite the empty streets—Hugo and Denise chattered and smoked and smooched. As much as this illicit guerilla art-making had served as an aphrodisiac for them, it had exhausted her.

When she'd gotten home and climbed into bed, Richard woke enough to say, "Hey, whatcha been doing?"

"Breaking the law."

He ruffled her hair. "Good for you," he said contentedly, like a proud father, then resumed snoring.

No, she knew herself well enough to recognize that graffiti art was a form of expression for people younger and angrier than she was, just as slam dancing was their sport. Still, the exhilaration she'd felt working in frantic partnership with them—the portion of it that wasn't pure fear—was something she wanted to experience again.

But on Sunday, outside an abandoned, decrepit garment factory, standing with an orderly group of art students, volunteers, and a representative from the Canada Council for the Arts, what she felt was a placid, almost childish contentment. Cans of spray paint and buckets of acrylics were arrayed on the sidewalk in front of them. The wall they faced already had the outline and annotation for a paint-by-numbers portrait of Jackie Robinson, who had played for the Montreal Royals before making it to the big leagues. An organizer distributed little reference cards to the gathered volunteers, showing which number corresponded to each paint color.

"All we need is an Easy Bake oven to play with when we get tired of painting," murmured a spiky-haired woman next to her, picking up a pristine paintbrush.

Tina laughed. "Yeah, and a wood-burning set."

Her companion turned to her, astonished. "I *loved* my wood-burning set, and I've never met anyone else who even had one!"

"Karma."

"Is that your name?"

"Sorry, no, my name is Tina. And you?"

"Marnie." She stuck out her paint-smeared hand for Tina to shake. "But my dog is named Karma."

"What a great name! When he's good—he?"

Marnie nodded.

"When he's good, you can say 'Good Karma,' and when he's not, you can say 'Bad Karma.' And either way, people will think you're some kind of mystic."

"When I'm actually some kind of half-assed dog trainer."

They continued chatting as they painted, occasionally crossing the street to get a more zoomed out view of their work. Robinson's life-like face, painted in shades of gray, was beaming, and the multi-colored, translucent ribbons of orange, green, and blue enveloping his head and torso lent an even more festive quality to the image.

"It *almost* looks joyful," Tina said.

"In a pasteurized, commercial sort of way." Marnie finished her thought.

"Maybe that's inevitable when you've got a group trying to create a single work of art. I mean making visual art ... it's not like being in a band. Maybe it just doesn't lend itself to collaboration."

"No maybe about it," Marnie answered with the certainty that Tina would grow to both love and resent.

They fell into a brief silence as they studied their handiwork.

"Definitely commercial," Marnie announced. "It looks like packaging for kids' candy."

"Exactly. It reminds me of the art on the Pop Rocks bags."

"Or Fizzies."

"Fizzies!" Tina clasped her companion's skinny forearm in her hand. "Marnie," she said solemnly. "This could be the start of a beautiful friendship."

It was.

Marnie was the chef at a vegetarian restaurant just a few blocks down Mountain Street from the gallery where Tina worked, and the two of them began meeting up for a walk or a drink a few nights a week. When Marnie learned that her boyfriend, Guy, was sleeping with her step-sister ("and routinely stealing my cigarettes, too!"), Tina was the first person she called. And when Tina, in a screaming row with Richard over whether the Parti Quebecois represented, as he claimed, "a national movement of resistance against English hegemony" or, as she argued in relative ignorance and blind fury, "a group of cultural nationalists as bigoted as those they claim to object to;" when she barely cut herself off before calling Richard a "fucking moron" — it was Marnie's couch that she slept on for the following two weeks.

"It's not about politics," she'd explained to Marnie over a Sunday morning hot chocolate. "All these years I actually thought he was superior to me. He's principled, he's smart ..."

"He's a parasite."

Tina nodded. "That too. But I let him feed on me. Why do I do that?"

"You like to be helpful," Marnie answered dryly.

"That's me. Richard's Little Helper. It's so ... Victorian!"

Marnie grabbed Tina's wrist. "You're not going back to him, are you?"

"God, no." She hadn't realized that until she said it. But having uttered the words, her shoulders relaxed and her jaw loosened. No ambivalence, no fear. Just relief.

"So, what do you want to do?"

Tina raised her hands, perplexed, then let them drop.

"I mean, I love you, sweetie, but I imagine you'd like to have your own bed, and I'd kind of like my couch back."

It's time to move, Tina thought. When in doubt, plunk yourself down in a new setting. Apartments, doctors, jobs, friends — you have to start from scratch every time you move, and it takes months to rebuild a life. Months when, outside of work, that's all you get to focus on.

"Let's go to Toronto," she said. "Easier winters, more people to meet, more jobs to be rejected from ..."

"Just like that?"

"Just like that."

Together, they moved to Toronto, rented a tiny house, and hung the ubiquitous but beloved poster of a large fish peddling a tiny two-wheeler ("A Woman Needs a Man like a Fish Needs a Bicycle") on the sliver of wall separating their two bedrooms. (In time, the poster would be autographed by the procession of boyfriends that frequented that home over the course of the next ten years, then tossed in the trash without regret when the two of them finally moved, each into her own apartment.)

Their lives were similar, though not their temperaments. Both juggled jobs at the intersection of arts, food, and event planning. But when Marnie got home from work, she would happily spend the evening venting about the fools she worked with and rhapsodizing about the few who weren't. Tina was content to listen and doodle, making sketches of the scenes that Marnie described, and occasionally suggesting a counter-perspective to Marnie's binary version of encounters and events.

After one such bitching session—in which Tina gently suggested that perhaps the stress of trying to keep his restaurant afloat accounted for Marnie's boss's short temper more than some intrinsic misogyny did—Marnie lost it.

"Why do you always adopt someone else's perspective?" she demanded. "I'm your friend. You don't even know Harris. Why can't you just take my side?"

The question, angry and plaintive, stopped Tina in her conversational tracks.

"I don't know," she said after a long silence. She saw her friend's rigid face relax, disarmed by her admission. "I guess I always assumed I could be more useful to people as a dispassionate observer, as someone who could help people see each other's point of view."

Marnie snorted. "Dispassionate?!" She leaned over the kitchen table where they sat drinking hot toddies and maternally petted Tina's hand. "Sweetie, you may be Ms. Fence Mender, Professional Placator, but you're hardly dispassionate. You just don't own your passions." Then, after a pause, "No offense."

You know me so well, Tina thought but didn't say. "None taken," she answered instead. Then, almost gaily, "There I go again."

That night, as she lay in bed listening to the solemn hoot of nearby trains, she decided that she was more grateful than annoyed by her friend's sharp observations. Marnie's declarations pierced the armor she'd worn so long that it felt like skin, and when they did, it felt more like a tickle than a jab. What a relief it was to be known and still be loved.

. . .

"Maybe someday before I die I'll figure out what my cocktail is," Marnie now said. "But probably by the time I do, I won't remember it."

"I think it's great that you still have some self-discoveries to look forward to," Tina said. "And I'm only being half-sarcastic."

"Hell, yeah. I've only scratched the surface of my scrawny soul. I still don't know what I like to drink, who I'd like to sleep with, whether it's worth getting snow tires for my car, what I stand for beyond momentary pleasures ..."

Tina chuckled. "Well, at least you know what you want to be when you grow up. And you're doing it."

"Yeah, it's odd, because I don't remember ever saying to Mrs. Fletcher—she was my first grade teacher—I don't remember ever telling her, 'When I'm a big girl I want to be a vegetarian caterer for ladies with too much money and too little drive.' "

"Drive?! Is that what they're lacking? Ambition?"

Marnie took a tentative sip of the ruby red concoction that the waitress had just set before her ("Enjoy your Aperol That!"). She furrowed her brow, took another sip, and smiled broadly. "Excellent! This may be it." Then realizing she hadn't answered Tina's question, said, "Oh, they've got plenty of social ambition. No, I mean drive to push themselves, to do anything really hard."

Tina tamped down a surge of ... what? Annoyance? Resentment? "Not everyone wants to run a marathon, Marnie. And even if they wanted to, not everyone can."

Marnie pulled back her head, obviously stung. "I know that. I realize that we distance runners—oh, who am I kidding—we former distance runners, are a weird little cult. I just meant that these women don't like to fail. And you're never going to do anything hard if you're not willing to fuck up or be imperfect in some way."

"And by you, you mean …" Tina deliberately let her question trail off.

"Oh, not *you*, sweetie. I mean 'one.' "

"Phew."

"Of course, if the shoe fits …" Marnie blew her a kiss. "I kid, I kid."

"Does it?" Tina asked, suddenly wildly uncertain. "Does the shoe fit?"

Marnie put down her drink and reached across the table for Tina's hand. "You've always chosen the hardest path. I don't know what you thought was at the end of it, but …" She paused and lifted her hand from Tina's to pick up one of the cornbread slices that had just been placed in front of them. "What I mean is …" she said, looking down as she systematically buttered every square centimeter of it, "you've always been a free spirit, and free spirits don't get free rides." Then, apparently pleased with her own word play, she rewarded herself with a giant bite.

Tina recognized the move. She was practiced in it herself. With unnerving skill, Marnie had given the comforting answer while dodging the question.

The next night, back in Brockville, Tina rifled through the shoebox of pictures until she found what she was looking for— a photo that had been taken on her father's birthday.

In the picture, Bob is sitting on a couch, its teardrop pattern of blue, teal, and orange illuminated by the glare of an overhead light. On the coffee table in front of him is a chocolate-iced cake with a single candle and the number 43 spelled out in raspberries, so she must have been about eighteen when it was taken.

It was so long ago, but that night flowered from her memory.

• • •

November, 1969, New York City

After Bob's favorite dinner—beef Stroganoff—they'd decided to take a digestion break before birthday cake. Tina shooed her parents out of the kitchen while she cleaned up. When she joined them in the living room, Joan lay curled on the couch, her feet in Bob's lap. She was snoring slightly, little sound bubbles puffing out from her slack mouth.

Pointing to her sleeping mother, her father raised a silencing finger to his mouth. Tina quietly sat down in the cracked leather armchair that filled half the living room. On the television, secret agent Maxwell Smart was nattily dressed in suit and tie, self-important, and laden with gadgets. Sitting on a park bench, he peeled the sole off his right shoe to reveal a telephone and cradled the shoe phone on his shoulder.

"Hello, Control Central? This is Agent 86. Stand by to execute Checkpoint Action Plan on Harvey Satan."

"Harvey Satan." Bob shook his head. "Subtle as always," he said quietly.

"Are all our agents at their proper checkpoints?" Smart asked. "Good," he responded after a moment. "I'm putting you on hold and switching to my wallet." He flipped open his billfold and made a call to Agent 99 from his wallet phone.

"Imagine a phone small enough to fit into your pocket," Bob murmured to Tina. "It could be great. It could be hell."

Meanwhile, Smart was back to his shoe. "Hello, Central," he said. "I'm switching to my eyeglasses. Put a hold on my wallet but keep my shoe open."

"Spectacles. Of course," Bob muttered as Smart took a pair of glasses out of his shirt pocket and began speaking into the lens.

As Bob chuckled, Smart removed his tie and tried making a call from that. "Hello …. Hello … Hello" Smart called. He let go of his tie.

"He'll go back to the shoe," Bob predicted.

"What?" Joan startled awake.

"Control Central, what's the problem?" Smart demanded of his shoe. "Oh, my tie is busy? Then put me on my handkerchief, Extension 4."

"Nothing," Bob said, waving away Joan's question, then took a swig of beer.

A phone started ringing, and Joan sat up.

"Don't worry. It's on the television," Tina told her.

"What do you mean? It's on the coffee table."

"Not *our* phone," Bob said, smiling broadly. "Jeez, Who's on first?"

"What?" Joan demanded.

Bob started to laugh. "No, What's on second."

Smart put Control Central on hold and fumbled to answer his belt. "Hello, Central? Cancel my handkerchief, hold my glasses, cut off my shoe, and see if you can get that guy off my tie."

"What are you talking about?" Joan demanded.

Bob exploded in laughter. He helplessly roared as Smart removed the garter holding up his socks and placed yet another call.

Joan stared at him, bewildered, then at Tina, who was now laughing with, or maybe at, her father.

"Oh Jesus, oh Jesus, this isn't even that funny," Bob whimpered, wiping the tears from his eyes. "I'm just—oh, thank God, a commercial—I'm just …"

"You're just what?" Joan asked as she walked to the television to turn down the volume.

"Oh, boy." Bob heaved a big, unsteady sigh. "I'm probably just overtired."

"Well, you're certainly overworked."

"The one follows from the other, dear," Bob said, his composure regained.

"There's no need to get smart with me," she answered, stung.

"To Get Smart?" Bob asked incredulously, starting to giggle again.

Joan histrionically rolled her eyes. "You know what? I won't even try to have a grown-up conversation with you right now." She turned the volume back up, ruffled the thick crescent of grayish brown hair rimming the back of Bob's head, and gave him a maternal peck on the forehead.

"That's very wise of you," he answered, grabbing her hand and kissing her palm. "Hmmm…" he said. "Glycerin and dish washing detergent. Intoxicating."

As bad as it was when they fought, Tina felt almost as uncomfortable when they made up.

Her mother lay back down on the couch and placed her feet in Bob's lap to be massaged.

"Oh, that is just the spot," Joan purred as Bob pressed his thumb into her instep.

Tina waved her finger at her parents. "Not in front of the children," she scolded. Tina's appreciation of her parents suddenly flipped to impatience. That happened a lot these days. Like someone whipping off a mask to reveal another face, she found the familiar suddenly annoying. Still, it was her father's birthday. She had to rein it in. "Are you ready for your presents?"

The previous day, she'd taken the A train down to the CBS Building on West 52nd. Sure enough, the gift shop had *Get Smart* posters, pens, fake shoe phones, and the kind of hat that Maxwell Smart wore with a plastic cylinder that rolled down from the brim. They called it the Gas Mask bowler, which was stupid since the clear vinyl looked nothing like a gas mask. But it could provide protection from the rain, and Tina knew that her father would be tickled by the compact construction of the thing. It was exactly the blend of gag and practicality that he would love.

Now she brought out the cake and her gift from the kitchen. Bob's reaction didn't disappoint. When he unwrapped the hat, he looked vaguely puzzled, smiled, and dutifully put it on. But when she pointed out the small pull tab on the brim and pulled down the vinyl enclosure, he guffawed and bent down to see his reflection in the glass of the television screen.

"This is really neat," he declared. "Really neat. Like a beekeeper's hat, only stylish. And it'll come in handy, too."

Tina was pleased that her gamble had paid off. "Better than an ashtray with my handprint, right?"

"Oh, nothing is better than that. But this is special in a different way."

Joan flashed Tina an approving smile, then took two packages, elegantly wrapped in pleats of blue and white tissue paper, out of a shopping bag that had been hidden in the hall closet.

"For you," she said. Bob fumbled to receive them, clearly struggling to see through the breath-fogged veil.

Tina yanked on the pull tab and, as promised, the plastic sheath retracted like a window shade, back up into the brim of the hat. "You can take it off, Dad. It's okay."

He removed it, gulping air. "I can't wait until it rains," Bob said. "I can walk to the train in my own wearable umbrella."

Tina suddenly felt like a fool, making a gift of something that, realistically, was good for nothing more than a one-time laugh. And when her father literally purred upon opening the first gift from Joan — a Bill Evans solo piano record — and immediately started leafing through the pages of the book about the moon walk, she felt like a dumb little kid.

How do they do it? Tina wondered. How do they find so much feeling between just the two of them? Of course, they loved each other — she understood that — but how could just one or two other people make up so much of anyone's world? Wasn't it suffocating? And, thinking once again of the fragility of her father's heart, wasn't it risky?

December 2011

The weekend before Christmas, Melissa and her husband, Michael, came to celebrate Peter's 90th birthday. Peter and Melissa spent the darkening afternoon holed up in Peter's study preparing tax records, Jean-Pierre and Michael watched a golf tournament on television, and Tina cooked and read in front of the blazing fireplace.

When they sat down to eat, the dinner conversation was wide-ranging, touching on everything from the fine points of microbrewing to the ambiance in the CBC newsroom during the Cuban Missile Crisis. Everyone wolfed down Tina's coq au vin, praised the roasted root vegetables and wilted greens, and groaned at the prospect of dessert. On the break between courses, Jean-Pierre looked up other December 18th birthdays.

"You are in some serious company, my man," he told Peter. "Joseph Stalin. Ty Cobb. Brad Pitt. Steven Spielberg. Keith Richards. DMX."

"DM who?"

"He's a rapper. DMX. Mr. X to you." Jean-Pierre's smile was broad, a facial emoji to make sure Peter knew he was joking.

"A toast!" A surprisingly intoxicated Melissa tapped her wineglass with a dessert spoon. "To Dad. A man with Stalin's sunny disposition and Ty Cobb's good looks."

Peter looked at his daughter quizzically. "Thank you? Or I beg your pardon? Or should I offer you a hot cup of coffee and a cold shower?"

"Oh, for heaven's sake, Dad. Once a year I get a little tipsy. No harm, no fastball."

"No foul," her husband corrected. It seemed to Tina that this was the first thing Michael had said all night.

"No farm, no howl, okay?" Melissa clearly didn't welcome his intervention. "Anyhow, seriously, Dad. I wish you a happy birthday and a happy year and happy memories of people gone by." She stood and held up her glass. "To you! And to my late, great mom!"

Peter nodded in appreciation.

Melissa remained standing. "To Tina, for a wonderful meal! To Jean-Pierre, for taking much better care of you than I ever could!" Then, looking right past her husband and out through the snowy window behind him. "To my sort of sister, wherever the hell she is."

Peter smiled tightly. "That's all the toast I can handle in one night. But thank you, dear."

"But wait! There's more," Melissa shouted, gaily imitating a late-night infomercial. "What's a birthday without presents?" She walked carefully to the whorled maple sideboard, picked up a tightly wrapped red package, and handed it to her father.

He tore the wrapping off with gusto and opened the Hudson's shirt box inside. "What a lovely sweater," he said after a pause. "Mohair, isn't it? And my favorite shade of blue." Tina heard shades of his television anchor voice—cordial, welcoming, and turned on and off as easily as a light switch.

"I know," Melissa said, sinking back into her chair. "Another sweater. But what do you get for the man who's got everything?"

"Your presence is gift enough, even without the presents."

Tina had the feeling that they'd had this exact exchange many times before. She felt a twinge of sympathy for Peter's striving, ungainly daughter. Showing love for her own father had never been so effortful, even if their relationship had been just as fraught.

Jean-Pierre walked to his winter jacket hanging on a hook by the door to the deck and reached into its pocket. He returned to the table with a round object enfolded in white tissue paper that was pulled together by a ponytail holder and adorned with a taped-on swirl of thin, multi-colored ribbons. "The gift is classier than the wrapper," he said as he handed it to Peter.

He opened it. "Oh my, it certainly is." Peter beamed at Jean-Pierre, then softly passed his gift of a baseball from hand to hand. "Andre Dawson," he mused, studying the signature on the ball. "Four hundred home runs, 300 stolen bases, and what—eight knee surgeries? Ten?"

"Twelve," Jean-Pierre answered. "They say if he hadn't played on the cement, you know, the fake grass—"

"Artificial turf," Peter corrected.

"—the artificial turf in Montreal, he would have better knees and a hundred more stolen bases."

"I believe that," Peter said solemnly. He reached up, shook Jean-Pierre's hand, briefly, tenderly placing his own left hand on top of it. "Thank you very much, Jean-Pierre. I shall treasure this."

Tina stood. "I'm afraid my present is a lot less durable. It's homemade, in fact. Let me get it for you."

She walked into the gleaming kitchen and returned holding a rectangular sheet cake. Its black and white icing formed a picture, a crude replica of Joe Rosenthal's 1945 photograph, *Raising the Flag on Iwo Jima*. The stars that Tina had dabbed onto the flag looked more like polka dots, and the coarse grass on which the men's feet were planted looked like a jagged pile of auto parts. But she was pleased with how the dark chocolate swirls evoked the scrum of soldiers, and especially proud of the swirling and misty vanilla sky. Planted into one end of the cake was a long toothpick with a small paper flag. On it, Tina had lettered, *The picture may have been staged, but the chocolate, vanilla extract, eggs, flour, and butter are all real. Happy Birthday.*

Peter clapped his hands together in delight as she set the cake down before him. "Did you do this yourself?" he asked.

"Well, it sure wasn't done by a professional."

He leaned over to study her creation more closely. "This is extraordinary," he said. "I had no idea you were so talented."

Flustered, Tina reached for the knife.

"Wait, wait." Jean-Pierre put a hand on her arm. "Let me take a picture before you cut into that."

"You want to take a picture of my picture of a picture?"

"I do. It's a chef-d'oeuvre, a what do you call it ..."

"A masterpiece," Peter said. "A buttery, sugary masterpiece, and I'm very grateful."

"It was my pleasure," Tina said, uncomfortable with all of this praise, conscious of Melissa and her taciturn husband glumly sipping their wine, spectators at what should have been their own party.

The next morning, Melissa joined Tina as she stood in the kitchen unloading the dishwasher. In the six months that she'd been there, this was probably the first time the two of them had been alone together.

Tina offered Melissa some tea. "Earl Grey, right?"

"You've got a good memory," Melissa answered, startled. "Do you remember what I take in it?"

Tina shook her head ruefully. "I'm not that good. Do I get to stay anyhow?"

Melissa flushed. "Sorry, I didn't mean to make this a test. Whatever would be fine." She paused, flustered. "Milk and sugar, actually. Really strong tea with milk and sugar."

"Coming up."

"My husband tells me I turn every conversation into grand rounds, you know? Testing people instead of just talking to them. Like at parties, he'll say I'm more prone to ask, 'What's Mrs. Smith's history' instead of, 'How's your mother?' That sort of thing."

"I didn't notice," Tina lied. "Besides, I like the Socratic method." She poured the hot water into the cup, and arranged some grapes, crackers, and slices of gruyere on a small serving dish. "Remind me — what's your specialty?"

"Cardiology. The electrophysiology of the heart. Not your vanilla ischemias, not coronary artery disease — I'm not going to be the one lecturing you about trans fats or triglycerides — speaking of which, thanks. This cheese is delicious." She stuffed a gruyere-laden cracker into her mouth. "No, my specialty is arrythmia. Defibrillators, not stents, are my implantable accessory of choice."

Tina had never heard her speak with such uncomplicated happiness. "I understood only about half the words you just used, but it seems as though you love your work."

Melissa blushed. "Sorry, I tend to get carried away. But yes, I do. I do love my work."

"Did you always want to be a doctor?"

"No, I only started to think about that during my last year as an undergrad, when I realized how hard it would be."

"How *hard* it would be?"

Melissa looked confused. "I'm not saying I'm a masochist. I just mean that I knew all these guys applying to med school and not a single woman, and I thought there was something wrong with that. But if it hadn't been for male chauvinism, I would have been a librarian. That's what I really wanted to be—someone who could hide in the carrels and read books."

"So, you rise to challenges," Tina said. "Good for you." She felt kindly towards this awkward, domineering woman who now seemed so willing to show some vulnerability. She wanted to reciprocate. "I've spent my life avoiding them."

Melissa gave a small, grim laugh. "Yeah, well in my house there was nowhere to hide."

They fell into a brief silence. From the sun porch came the faint sounds of Jean-Pierre's morning exercise regimen with Peter. Tina had watched only once as Jean-Pierre helped the elderly man to his feet, maneuvered him into a stance between two parallel bars, then sidestepped his way down the length of them as Peter progressed, each arm taking its turn bearing the bulk of his weight as he threw one withered leg out in front of him, then the next. What tenacity, she thought. Is he investing all that energy, subjecting himself to all that pain, just to hang on? She wanted to know how it felt to have such drive, just as she never wanted to witness this painful process again.

"There you go," she heard Jean-Pierre say encouragingly. "Almost halfway now."

"He is one determined man, your father," she said to Melissa.

Melissa looked toward the sun porch. "Yup." Then, focusing her gaze on Tina, she asked, "Is your father still alive?"

"No, he died when I was pretty young, when *he* was pretty young. He was fifty-nine."

"Really," Melissa said with great animation. "What did he die of?"

Tina found Melissa's gracelessness endearing. "Sudden cardiac arrest. Some kind of arrhythmia. He just dropped dead on the subway — well, not literally dropped. They told us he was sitting. He would have gotten a kick out of that; I imagine him describing his own death, saying, 'Sure, I died during rush hour, but at least I had a seat!' Anyhow, it was sudden."

"Interesting. Have you ever been screened for WPW or cardiomyopathy?"

"I don't think so. But since I have no idea what you're talking about, I can't be sure."

"Oh, these are genetic conditions that can cause arrhythmias, though WPW is rarely fatal. Still, you may want to know if you're at risk."

"If I was, could anything be done about it?"

Melissa looked startled. "Good question. Many patients don't think to ask that question."

"Well, I'm not a patient. At least not at the moment. And I think I'm conscious enough of my own mortality without needing to pile on." The words came out more sharply than she'd intended. "But thank you for asking."

"Well, I'm just interested in matters of inheritance. As you may have noticed, my father and I are nothing alike. He's arts, I'm sciences. He's sophisticated, my tastes are plain. Honestly, if we didn't both have unusually long digits and hate the taste of cilantro, I'd swear we weren't related at all." She paused. "It's actually pretty amazing that we get along as well as we do."

Touched by her candor, Tina wanted to offer some disclosure in return. "Oh, I think it's probably harder to get along with someone who's just like you. My father and I were like that, very similar. We both got annoyed by the same qualities in each other, we both dug our heels in around the same sorts of issues. We weren't like fire and water. We were like fire and fire."

Melissa nodded. "Fire and fire. I like that. Did you fight much when you were a kid?"

Tina rifled through her most accessible memories. She remembered nothing but contentment as her father sat on the edge of her bed at night and told her improvised, not-too-scary ghost stories about the Adventures of Nosey and Naughty, replete with the sounds of creaking doorways and cracks of thunder. She easily summoned the thrill she felt as her father held her under her arms as she treaded water in the deep end, then let go, his face beaming as he cheered, "You're swimming, all by yourself!" She could hear his helpless, high-pitched laugh as they'd watched *The Pink Panther* while she curled up, mortified, in the seat next to him in the movie theater. The occasional moments of embarrassment—that was as bad as it got when she was a kid.

Even in high school, when she increasingly neglected her homework and instead spent her time organizing anti-war marches, picketing in support of the farmworkers, and listening to music with her friends—even then, she and her father rarely fought. He was increasingly absent, consumed by work. But when he was home, their dinnertime discussions were more earnest than contentious. He worried about her grades, of course, but she felt that he was on her side.

"No, it was really only when I left home that we started butting heads," she told Melissa.

•   •   •

August, 1970, San Francisco

"Don't bother trying to borrow a car," Bob told Tina on the phone the night before his trip to San Francisco. "I'll get myself from the airport to your apartment."

"So, listen, Dad," she said carefully. "You're more than welcome to crash here. But I've got to warn you—the lodgings aren't exactly luxurious. There's kind of ratty couch you can sleep on, or if one of my roommates isn't sleeping at home, you might be able to score a mattress on the floor. But, you know, it's, like, loud here, and kind of smoky, so you might be happier at a hotel. But really,"—she was now tripping over herself—"you know, if you want to stay here it's cool." She really, really hoped she'd succeeded in discouraging him from staying with her. She wasn't sure that she could take the embarrassment of having her father there. Or, to be honest, the prospect of seeing her home through his eyes and wondering what the hell she was doing there.

"Don't worry. I'm staying at the Stanyan Park Hotel, courtesy of ABC. Want to just meet me there?"

Relief. "It's a deal. I'll come straight from work."

The next day, when she met Bob in the hotel lobby, she was still in her sludgy brown Waffle House uniform. She'd thought of bringing her normal clothes to work and changing before picking him up but decided against it. He had to see her as she was in the world, not as someone extraordinary, but as someone plebian and proud of it.

"This is the job you put off college and moved across the country for?" he asked after enfolding her in a hug.

"This is the hello you give me after we haven't seen each other for a month? Jesus, Dad."

He held up his hands in surrender. "You're right, you're right. That's a lousy greeting. Let me start over." Bob put a hand on each of his daughter's shoulders and stepped back to examine her. "Front looks good," he said gruffly. "Turn around, please."

Tina spun so that her back was to her father.

"Back looks fine. Face me again, please."

She obediently turned back.

"Now turn your head to the left and cough," he instructed, quoting the army doctor who figured in so many of the jokes that he had told over the years.

She laughed. "Daddy!"

"Some things never get old, right?"

"So, listen," Tina said, "I figured we'd walk back to my place so I can change, then you can take me out for a great dinner. Who's paying—ABC or you?"

"Me, I'm afraid."

"Okay, bread and water it is." She took her father's arm and led him out the door. "Seriously, it's like New York here. Lots of delicious, cheap Chinese and seafood. And they've even got Mexican and Thai food."

"I don't think I've ever had Thai food. Let's go for that."

Bob tamely followed Tina out to the street.

"Where to?" he asked.

"My apartment, just a couple of blocks from here. But Dad, please—no inquisitions. No debating my roommates. This isn't New York, and they're not your kids."

Outside his hotel, on the corner of Haight and Stanyon, Haight Street was clogged with pedestrians, cars, and the occasional psychedelically painted Hippie Hop Tour Bus. Conversation was almost impossible as Tina led him through throngs of young people in white cotton shirts, Peruvian vests, long skirts, halter tops, and bandanas. Panhandlers sat leaning against storefronts, some jittery, some barely awake. Two guys played bongos on the steps of the United California Bank.

"It's like Central Park," Bob yelled to her over the din, but she just smiled, then tugged on his sleeve to keep walking.

The sagging, peeling but fancifully painted Victorian houses lining Masonic Avenue looked nothing like the brownstones back home. But inside, they were similar, with splintery floors and dingy lighting, reeking of pot and cooking onions. Tina hadn't really noticed the odorous squalor until now, when she was seeing her home through her father's eyes.

But Bob seemed perfectly comfortable as he sat on the beanbag chair in the living room, chatting with housemates.

Katherine ("Call me Kat") was the den mother, a poet who cleaned houses. Peggy worked at The Head Shop down the street and was never going back to "that ticky-tacky little Candyland village in Minnesota where I grew up." John, who grew up in Oakland, helped his father paint houses, volunteered at the Free Clinic, and wanted to be a doctor, though he'd never gone to college. "At this rate, the only place I'm likely to go is Canada," he told Bob. "Or jail."

It was Randy, a polite kid from Nebraska who was just there for the summer before starting at CalTech in the fall, who was most interested in talking to her father. No surprise there. Apparently, *Popular Mechanics* afficionados could sniff each other out in no time.

"You work for ABC Sports?" Randy asked eagerly.

"I do. In fact, I'm here to scout out the broadcasting facilities at Oakland Coliseum. We've got three or four Raiders games on the schedule come fall."

"Cool. Yeah, they're going to be fantastic! Daryle Lamonica, Fred Biletnikoff — they've signed all these amazing guys. They mean business." Tina had never seen Randy so animated.

"I'll take your word for it. To be honest, I pay more attention to how to cover the field than to who's on it."

Randy sat up straighter. "Well, yeah, sure, of course, you're a professional, not a fan, right?" Tina could have sworn that he'd lowered his voice by an octave, too "You've got to worry about the angles and the audio and the signals and whatnot."

Tina could tell that her father found his floundering endearing ... the way he used to find hers.

"Well, just between you and me," Bob confided, "This year we'll be experimenting with something pretty new. We plan to show one or two slow-motion replays of key plays at half-time."

"Far out! You mean like if somebody fumbles the ball ..."

"Yeah." Bob nodded solemnly. "If somebody fumbles, or makes a great catch but maybe both feet weren't in bounds. Or even if there's some question as to whether a guy makes a first down ..."

"Outta sight! And tackles! Man, if we could see somebody like Willie Brown tackle some dude running right at him, like just fucking crush him, man ..."

"Football," Peggy said scornfully. "Football and technology, violence and machines. They go together like, I don't know, like ..."

"Like Benzedrine and Coca-Cola?" Kat suggested helpfully.

"No, more like, I don't know, hamburgers and hot dogs," Peggy replied. "All products of the war machine."

"Yeah, but you've got to admit, pretty delicious," Tina said. Managing her father and her roommates ... it was like juggling watermelons, but harder.

"I admit no such thing," Peggy answered. "What I think is delicious is not killing animals or harming the earth."

Randy rolled his eyes at Bob and Bob winked back.

"You boys talk among yourselves," Tina said airily, waving her fingers at the two of them in an imitation of her Aunt Carol, one her father was quick to recognize. "I'm just going to change out of my work clothes."

She went into her bedroom—a former walk-in pantry off the kitchen—and emerged a couple of minutes later, now in her other uniform of bell-bottomed jeans, a white peasant blouse, and an army jacket.

Her father struggled to rise from the beanbag chair. "Well, if you'll excuse us," he said, "Tina and I are off for a peaceful dinner."

Tina pointed out the sights—the radio station, the free clinic, the day-care center where her friend Karen worked—as they ambled to a restaurant on Fell Street.

They were seated by a window, handed huge but sparsely populated menus, and Bob ordered a beer for himself. "You can take sips of mine," he promised.

"So?" Tina asked.

"So they're nice kids."

"We're not kids, Dad. We're all working, paying taxes even, except for some people who are withholding them to protest the war."

"Excuse me. They're nice young adults. And some of them are even going to college."

"Here we go ..."

"Tina, sweetheart, I'm not trying to pick a fight with you. I'm just trying to understand you."

"What is there to understand? I don't want to be a robot, that's all. I know you like machines, and that's cool, but I want to ..."

"You want to what?"

"To be a human being."

Bob spread his arms, mystified. "That's wonderful. I love human beings."

He was such a sweetheart and such a dolt, her father. "What I mean, Dad, is that I don't want to just get an education, get a career, get ahead. I want to learn, sure, but I want—what I mean by being a human being is that I want to create something, you know?"

"Well, you do. You create beautiful paintings. And sculptures, like that curvy soapstone thing in our living room — I love that."

"I don't just mean things, or even art. I'm just a dabbler, anyhow, not a real artist." The sooner he got over his conviction that she was destined for greatness, the better. Maybe she'd become a better artist — she hoped she would — but she sure wasn't going to get there fueled by her father's extravagant expectations. "No, I mean a culture, or at least a commune, a place where people all contribute what they can, where we pool our labor and our earnings and build something bigger and better than ourselves."

"From each according to his ability to each according to his needs?"

"Yeah, something like that."

"In my day, we called it Communism."

Tina scowled. "Please don't start with the labels, Dad. I'm not talking about a bunch of us waving red flags and saluting missiles and goose-stepping around Union Square."

"Okay, okay. Believe me, darling, I'm the last person to red bait you or anyone." He took a swig of his beer. "Listen," he said, trying again. "You think I don't sympathize with your ideals? I do. Of course I do. Where do you think you got them from? But to change the world, you have to be in it. You can't just say 'Me and my friends, we're going to go off and start our own separate society.' "

"Why not?"

"Why not, she asks me. Because you're trying to turn back the clock, and time just doesn't work that way. People like their pre-sliced bread and their televisions. They want machines to go places faster, and telephones — princess telephones and maybe eventually even cordless ones — for when they can't. And that doesn't make them evil people."

"No, not evil, but maybe shallow. Maybe when you're materialistic enough, you just stop thinking. Or thinking enough. Maybe when all you think about is consuming —"

"May I take your order?" a waitress asked.

Bob and Tina exchanged a look and burst out laughing.

Bob went first. "Since chicken curry is the only thing I recognize, I'll have that."

Tina studied the menu, finally opting for something called Pad Thai.

When the waitress left, Bob clapped his hand on top of his daughter's. "Listen, do you remember the UFO craze a few years ago, when people were seeing flying saucers over Michigan and upstate New York?"

Tina nodded.

"How did you feel while that was going on?"

"Excited, I guess. Maybe a little scared, but mostly excited."

"Did you believe that these were really UFOs, creatures from another planet dropping in for a visit?"

They were back into a familiar groove, tossing questions and answers back and forth as if they were playing catch in Central Park. "I don't know. I didn't know what to believe. But lots of people I know thought they were real, that aliens were coming to save us before we blew ourselves up with nuclear bombs."

"At the network, we covered that story. We sent a guy out to Michigan and he talked to some farmer who saw the glowing discs in the sky, and the flashing lights—the whole megillah. Now the government said that what this guy saw was swamp gas—just some glowing farts in the sky—and they implied that maybe he'd been hitting the corn liquor a little too hard. But the farmer insisted that he saw what he saw, and lots of people corroborated his story. They said this light streaked across the sky, then slowly came vertically down into a field in—I forget, Dexter, I think it was, Dexter, Michigan—then took off again. And the sheriff, who, believe you me, was no Martian-loving freak, he thought there was a government cover-up going on."

Tina was puzzled. "Okay. So why are you telling me this?"

"Because there were lots of competing stories! The farmer thought we were under attack. His new hippie friends, they thought that intelligent life from outer space was going to come rescue us from ourselves. The sheriff thought the government was lying to us, as usual, hiding the truth about an alien invasion. But the fact was that this shitkicker guy in Wisconsin—"

"Michigan."

"In Michigan—this guy saw a new generation of communications satellites, two of them the very satellites we used in the *Now and There* broadcast. So he wasn't nuts—he really did see something, just not a UFO. And the sheriff was half-right too. The government really was covering it up because they didn't want the Russians to know just how far we'd come with this technology. And even your hippie friends—hell, in some ways they were the most right. I mean, these weren't aliens who were going to rescue us from our worst animal instincts. The opposite, in fact. These satellites—by letting us connect with each other, quickly, with incredible clarity—well, that's the infrastructure that's going to save us from ourselves."

"Infrastructure?" This was the longest, most coherent speech she thought she'd ever heard her father give. Usually he distracted himself with "which, by the way's" that sent him off onto endless tiny detours.

"Like tunnels, roads, bridges, phone lines, the power grid. These are all society's connective tissue."

She was listening hard, but she was baffled.

"Look," Bob continued. "You said you wanted to build a culture, right? A more peaceful, cooperative society."

"Right."

"So, this work that I do—this technology that your friends like to sneer at—it's the infrastructure for that culture. It's what will make it possible as the population gets bigger and bigger and the world gets smaller and smaller."

"But Dad, you're not out here in San Francisco to create some sort of telepathy network, some sort of, I don't know, compassion grid." She felt him listening as intently to her as she had to him. "You're here to help ABC sell more ads for a fucking football game."

He looked gut-punched, and for once, had no comeback or correction.

Tina felt stricken. She never knew she could hurt him. Just as she tentatively reached out to pat his hand, the waitress arrived with their dinner.

Not knowing what else to do, how else to show him that she loved him, Tina slowly ladled out the rice and the curry from the serving dish onto his plate. She artfully planted a sprig of basil like a flag atop the mound of food. "Like the cherry on top of the sundae," she said gently. "Remember?"

• • •

"You started fighting as grown-ups?" Melissa now asked. "That's usually when parents and children stop fighting … or so I've read."

"Yeah, well, I was living in a commune in San Francisco and he was worried that I was sacrificing myself to others, and I thought he was just a materialistic striver, and he thought I was just running away and rationalizing it all with some Age of Aquarius mumbo-jumbo, and I thought he was a closed-minded, paranoid product of the Cold War, and he thought I was ignorant, and I thought he was smug, and … well, you get the drift."

"Actually, I'm not sure I do," Melissa said, "but that's just me." Her self-deprecation was disarming.

"What's just you?" Michael ambled into the kitchen, stopped to stand behind his wife, and, with a formality that she found bizarre, extended his hand over Melissa's shoulders to shake Tina's. "How was your night?" he asked her. "Did you sleep the sleep of the righteous?"

"I slept the sleep of the sleepy. And you?"

"I had a magnificent sleep." Michael rubbed his hands together, then briefly thumped his wife's shoulders. "There's nothing like country air to knock you out at night and make you hungry in the morning."

They must have had sex last night, Tina thought. It must be a rare event. There was no other explanation for Michael's boisterous bonhomie. That, or he's a doofus.

Of course, both could be true. *The two are not mutually exclusive*, she could hear her father say with relish. That was one of his pet phrases. *Correlation does not imply causation* was another.

Her mother had been the better educated of the two. With a bachelor's degree from Vassar and a master's in social work from Barnard, she was the one who read *The New York Review of Books* over their Sunday breakfast while Tina's father read the sports page or

Popular Mechanics. But even at a very young age, Tina could see how much Bob admired Joan's intellectual grace, how he thrilled to it as if to the sight of a gorgeously colored tropical bird. And when he did read books—Tina remembered *Microbe Hunters* and, later, the first-edition hardcover of *Cosmos* as being two of his favorites—he'd incorporate words and ideas from them that became his temporary templates for how to explain practically every phenomenon.

"Yes, Humphrey is a Democrat *and* a sell-out," he'd patiently argue with Joan's brother. "The two are not mutually exclusive."

"Yes, lots of college dropouts are smart," he'd said to Tina more than once, and with far greater urgency. "But that doesn't mean that if you're smart, you must drop out, or that abandoning your education will make you smarter. Correlation doesn't imply causation."

"You know," Tina said to Melissa now, "I don't know anything about your family." It was only as the words came out that she realized that this massive house—with its Tom Thomson originals of frozen northern landscapes and Dorothea Lange prints, its framed letters from Leonard Cohen and Prime Minister Pearson, its vaulting ceilings and concealed electronics and neat row of autographed baseballs, each on its own Lucite pedestal—this lived-in museum was barren of any signs of family or friendship. Her childhood home had been the opposite; the narrow central hallway of their apartment on West End Avenue was lined with photos—formal black-and-white portraits of both sets of grandparents, the elders sitting in chairs, their children surrounding them like a wreath; her parents' wedding dance, in which her mother's elegant, sharp features seemed softened by the nearness of her father's young but still slightly doughy face, already etched by smile lines flaring out from his eyes; scalloped-edged snapshots of Tina and her cousins at the beach, blowing out birthday candles, playing guitars in Central Park.

But the only family photo she'd seen here was a small, pewter-framed picture of Grace, Peter's late wife, sitting on his desk, next to the computer monitor. "I've seen that portrait of your mother, but that's it. She looks like she was—was?—a lovely woman."

"Yes, was. She died when I was ten and Sandy was six. Ovarian cancer."

"I'm sorry."

"Water under the bridge. She was a very nice lady, though. Very kind."

"And Sandy? She's your sister, right? Where's she?"

Melissa grimaced. "That's the million-dollar question, isn't it."

Tina raised her eyebrows.

"She took off when she was nineteen and hasn't been back since. I don't know where she is or what she does or if she ever married or has kids ... I don't know anything except that she's alive. And I only know that because she sends me a birthday card—a physical card, if you can believe that!—every year."

"Is there a postmark on the envelope?"

Melissa shrugged. "I guess. Once I noticed it was from Vancouver, once from somewhere in Indonesia. But never a return address."

"Forgive me if I'm being intrusive, but last night, you called her your 'sort of' sister."

"Well, like I just said, she hasn't really been in my life—certainly not in my father's life—for most of her own. And you know, she was already four and I was already eight when she was adopted, and it's amazing how much your sense of family—of who is 'like me' or 'mine' versus 'not like me' or 'not mine'—well, I think it's almost hard-wired. And look at us. My father and I, we're so pale we're almost ghostly, while Sandy, she was dark-skinned and broad-cheeked, even for a Cree."

"A Cree?"

"Cree Indian. Oh shit, I realize that I'm probably sounding like some sort of racist, and I'm not. She was my sister, for Christ's sake. But I don't think she ever felt that way, like sisters, like part of our family—not when she was four and shipped to us in Toronto from some remote reserve in Alberta."

"Was she an orphan?"

"I honestly don't know much about her background. I just know that my parents, being enlightened, liberal do-gooders, decided that bringing one new person into the world was enough, especially when there was such a glut of needy, impoverished Black and Brown kids. Sandy was going to be the first of several kids that they were going to adopt. But then my mother got sick—soon after they got Sandy—and that was that." Melissa studied her now-tepid tea, then took a sip.

"Goddamnit!" Tina heard Peter yell from the sun porch. Behind Melissa's shoulder, Tina saw a large purple medicine ball slowly roll into the living room.

"My fault," Jean-Pierre said soothingly as he padded out to retrieve the errant ball. "It was a bad throw." He cast a look towards them in the kitchen—apologetic? Long-suffering? Tina wasn't sure—and then returned to Peter.

"If you don't mind my asking," Tina barreled ahead, "Was there a falling-out between your father and Sandy? I'm just curious, because frankly, he's practically never mentioned her."

Melissa laughed grimly. "Yeah, I guess you could call it a falling-out. You could call it a feud, in fact … though not really. A feud implies something that both parties are participating in, right?"

She stopped and looked inquiringly at Tina. Oh, this isn't a rhetorical question, Tina realized.

"Right."

"So it's a falling-out, because Sandy just severed all contact with my father." Melissa pulled back her hair from her horsey face and into a ponytail.

"Why?" Peter was difficult—irascible sometimes, certainly arrogant—but not fundamentally a bad person.

"Why?" Melissa repeated, as if this was the stupidest question imaginable. "This kid is, I don't know, removed from her birthplace, from her own family, and brought to Toronto so that she can assuage the conscience of two people who, it seems to me, weren't actually guilty of anything in the first place except being white, maybe, and comfortable. So, you know, that's traumatic enough, and then her adoptive mother up and dies on her. And meanwhile, all the kids she knows treat her, not meanly, but like a pet, you know? Like a stray cat or dog wandering through the neighborhood. And so then, then …" She apparently heard her own voice rising in anger and paused, then resumed in a whisper, "When she has the temerity to express some resentment, to ask Dad why the hell he put her in this position, he gets offended."

"I guess he felt hurt?"

"Sure, yeah, hurt, but also insulted. Here he was, trying to do something good—that's how he sees it, anyhow—and all he got for his efforts was the resentment of an ingrate."

"But he's not a stupid man, your father. Surely he could see why ..."

"Of course he could, but he felt like his good intentions should have been given more weight. And when she got to college and started studying history, when she started talking about societal this and systemic that ..."

"When she started talking about the narrative of colonialism," Peter said, silently gliding into the kitchen and inserting himself into the conversation as if he'd been there all along, "When she started ranting about assimilation and the denial of her legacy, etc., I lost my patience."

"But Dad, you can understand—"

"That's not what we set out to do, and we never denied her Indian ancestry or forced Sandy to do anything except brush her teeth and comb her hair and make her bed, same as you. As far as her mother and I were concerned—Grace, I mean, my late wife—as far as we were concerned, we were adopting a motherless child whose father was rarely around, a poor, malnourished little girl who deserved better. Period."

Peter and Melissa locked into each other's gaze. Then Melissa scraped her chair away from the kitchen table and stood. "Toast?" she asked the room, and opened the bread drawer.

Peter reached into the right pocket of his gray flannel pants and brought his hand out empty. "Where's my wallet?" he muttered.

"What do you need a wallet for?" Melissa asked with what sounded like genuine curiosity. "You never leave the house. You certainly never leave the house alone."

Her question, her tone, gutted Tina. Show some respect, she thought. But looking at Melissa's face, she saw no malice there, just the perplexity of the doggedly rational thinker.

Fortunately, Peter didn't seem to have heard her. His left hand emerged from his other pocket and he hoisted his handsome leather wallet triumphantly. Then he unzipped it, peered into its folds, pulled out a small color photograph, and held it up in front of Tina's eyes.

A topless little girl with long black hair and straight bangs covering her eyebrows leaned on her straightened arms, looking out a tall, vinyl-framed window. Tan lines on her neck and arms delineated where a tank top normally covered her willowy frame, and her chest and belly had a yellowish tint, as if she'd bathed in mustard. Her eyes were wide, her mouth half-opened, as if she was about to say something. The dark brown, muddy stucco below the window was swirled and rough, but the thick, painted-red band that ran horizontally beneath the windows made it a handsome wall.

"This was her," Peter said. "This was Sandy a few months before we got her. The social worker from the Bureau took this picture and sent it to us." He turned the photo around and studied it, tapping it with his left index finger. "Look at the light in those eyes. Such brightness. We knew we had to have her."

Melissa turned from the counter and came to stand behind her father. "I don't think I've ever seen this before," she said.

"Sure you did. Grace and I showed it to you many times before Sandy arrived. You'd ask to see it. 'Show me my sister,' you'd demand, your feet planted apart and your hands on your hips like, I don't know, like Mighty Mouse meets Eva Braun."

"I had no idea you carried around a picture of her."

"And of you," Peter said hurriedly, for once apparently sensing that his daughter might have feelings and those feelings might be hurt. He pulled out another photo. "See?"

Melissa briefly looked at a rectangular, standard-issue school photo of a ten-year-old girl in a white blouse and blue tunic before handing it back to her father. Tina saw it only fleetingly, but Melissa's high, rectangular cheeks and slightly furrowed brow were recognizable even then.

Peter took one more look at Sandy's photo, then tucked both pictures back into his wallet. "Of course, I've no idea of what she looks like now."

On the Sunday mornings of her childhood and young adulthood, Tina's family kitchen—the room where most conversations happened—had a rich and salty smell. It was the comforting and bracing center of the house, her native land of milky coffee, lox, and scrambled eggs. Here, on this bright, frigid morning on the banks of the frozen St. Lawrence River, the kitchen smelled of porridge and multivitamins, of grains and iron.

Tina pulled her fleece jacket tight around her and zipped it up, eager for warmth.

New Year's Eve

"It's overcast. Hell, the sky is like a dome of French Canadian pea soup up here," Carl said a few nights later, "so we can talk as long as you like. I'm not going to be able to see anything except you and a series of bad poker hands." He was stretched out on his bed, holding the laptop up in two outstretched arms, providing Tina with an aerial view of his bleached face.

"You look so pale," Tina said. "Is that the camera, or is that you?"

"It's me, I think. Remember, I live the lifestyle of a vampire, only without the bloodsucking."

"The next time I see you"—and she felt a pang to realize how far off in the future that would be—"I'd better be sure to remove that garlic I've been wearing around my neck."

"Ah," he asked, only half-joking, "is there someone in Brockville you're trying to keep away?"

"No, Peter's about 20 years past making passes and Jean-Pierre's not my type," she lied. With his taut belly, his slow but radiant grin, his appreciative attention to her, his unforced comfort with himself, Jean-Pierre was disturbingly her type.

"I'm glad to hear it." Carl relaxed his arms, bringing his elbows down next to him, and his face filled the screen.

Tina studied it like a passing landscape she would see only once. "What's with the stubble? Are you lazy, or growing a beard?"

"I don't know yet. Happily, the two aren't mutually exclusive." Carl stroked his cheek. "Do you like it?"

"I don't know yet. Happily, I don't have to get scratched by it." She smiled, so comforted to fall back into their familiar bedtime banter. How often did she echo his words? How often did he echo hers? "I can just admire it from a distance."

"Too much distance."

"Too much." Tina shook herself. This conversation was off to a melancholy start. "So I've been playing Nancy Drew," she said with forced cheer.

Carl's face looked blank.

"Nancy Drew, Girl Detective?" she continued. "She drove a maroon roadster?"

"Sorry. Another gap in my cultural education."

"Anyhow, I saw this photo of a child taken in Czechoslovakia, sometime in the mid-1930s, a little girl about five years old, and the light in her eyes, the beam of her smile — she was just electrifying. And below the photo was a caption from The Holocaust Museum saying that they were trying to identify the people and places in some of the pictures in their archive, including this one."

"And you decided to solve The Mystery of the Nameless Child."

"Aha! You *do* remember Nancy Drew."

Carl smiled sheepishly. "It just came back to me the second you started to talk … my sister's row of books with yellow spines."

"Yup, that's them. Personally, I preferred the Hardy Boys. Their adventures were more, I dunno, adventurous. They seemed to do more and be in peril less."

"But back to the little girl …"

Tina paused. "I'd love to know what happened to her. At least I think I would. I don't know what would be worse — to find out she'd been killed in a concentration camp or survived, had a bunch of kids, and become a bitter, overbearing hausfrau stuffing her family on blintzes and brisket." Tina paused, then, overcoming her embarrassment, said, "So I've been trying to find her."

"How?"

"Completely unsystematically. I placed ads with her photo in *Forward* and a Jewish newspaper in London, and sent a letter and copy of the picture to a friend who works for the Combined Jewish

Philanthropies in New York. Oh, and to the two rabbis I could locate in Warsaw." She felt herself blushing. She stood up from the dainty cherrywood writing desk in her bedroom. "Want to see my sketch of her?"

"Of course!" Carl sounded surprised, and Tina realized how rarely she showed him her work. Perhaps because she felt presumptuous calling it "work"?

She turned her computer around so that the webcam faced out her window. "Here, look at this gorgeous sunset over the St. Lawrence while I get it."

Tina pulled her portfolio case out from under the bed and unzipped it. Her sketch of the child was on top of the growing pile. She squinted at it, held it up, then dropped it. She had missed the mark. The details were good—the child's crazy hair, the jigsaw of cobblestones behind her, the radiant dark pools that were the little girl's eyes—but the overall effect was, what? Hagiographic? It looked like a picture made in tribute, or in memoriam. It lacked immediacy. Looking at her own drawing, Tina didn't see what she'd recognized in the picture—an exuberant child who'd stopped mid-flight to pose for a photo, standing ramrod still as she'd been taught. This charcoal child didn't look like she'd resume running the second she heard the click of the shutter.

She went back to her desk. "Never mind," she told Carl. "It's not ready for prime time."

"I don't care. I'd love to see your work in progress."

"Not yet."

Carl looked hurt.

"Sorry, I didn't mean to snap."

"What was it about her that grabbed you?" Carl asked.

Tina shook her head slowly. "I'm not sure. Her vitality, I guess. It was somehow so incongruous with her anonymity, with her absence."

Her bedroom was turning dark now, the last of the sun's rays disappearing below her windowsill. In the dusk, the expensive but austere Scandinavian furniture gave her room an even more monastic feel. Tina didn't like it. She wasn't big on penance. She hurriedly turned on the desk and bedside lamps, then sat in the small

Marimekko club chair, comforted by its rounded back and enclosing arms.

"So, you're looking for a Czech child who may well be dead by now."

"Well, I'm not really actively looking for her," Tina said, now wanting this conversation to end. "I'm more just curious …"

"Still," Carl said. "Do you think …" He paused.

"Do I think what?"

"Well …" Tina's screen was suddenly filled with Carl's nightstand and ceiling as he swung his legs over the side of the bed and sat up. "Do you think this search has anything to do with Tom?"

Tina felt her neck tighten. "You know, I hate it when you get all psychological." She spoke lightly, but meant it. "You have the IQ. Let me at least have the EQ." Carl looked puzzled. "The Emotional Quotient."

Carl wasn't playing along. "You know better than that," he said quietly.

Tom. She'd learned about him less than a week before becoming an orphan.

•   •   •

March, 1994, New York City

"I sometimes wonder if he looks like you," Joan said towards the end of a long, gray day, her first or second at the hospice. She had been drifting in and out of delirium — babbling happily to some friend from her childhood, Tina assumed, about mixers and jitterbugs, then crankily insisting "No. No, I'm not."

"You wonder if who looks like me?" Tina asked, to comfort herself with the illusion of conversation, not because she was expecting a lucid answer.

"Tom."

"Who's Tom?"

"Your half-brother, Tom!" she answered irritably.

Tina felt suddenly breathless. Joan was clearly in her right mind, at least in this moment. "My half-brother?"

Joan gave her a piercing look. "Oh, my," she said. "Did we never tell you?" She closed her eyes and centered her head on the pillow.

Tina silently willed her mother to stay with her. "Did you never tell me what?"

"I was sure he told you," Joan said, her voice increasingly wispy with each word. "Silly man."

"Mom." Tina laid her hand on Joan's emaciated forearm, trying to be firm but not painful. "Mom, do I have a half-brother?"

"Of course you do, dear."

"Whose son is he? Yours or Dad's?" How could this be? She felt almost panicky.

"Birmingham," Joan mumbled. "Or Manchester? It was Birmingham or Manchester, he told me. Or the other one. Leeds? Liverpool?" She was getting agitated.

Tina took the now warm facecloth off of her mother's forehead, soaked it in the cool water in the basin on the nightstand, and reapplied it. "Calm down, Mom. Can you tell me ..." Where to begin? "Is Tom your son?"

"Of course not!" Joan snapped.

"Okay, so he's Dad's son. Where does he live?"

"He's gone, dear," Joan said woefully. She was all over the map. "Your father's gone."

"No, not Dad. Where does Tom live?"

"Leeds? Liverpool?" Suddenly she began to sing, like a hoarse and wizened bird. "In Hartford, Hereford, and Hampshire, hurricanes hardly happen."

Tina smiled, tears suddenly coursing down her face. "*My Fair Lady*. I remember, Mom. That song's from *My Fair Lady*."

"What's next?" Joan asked vaguely. "In Hartford, Hereford, and Hampshire, hurricanes hardly happen ..."

"The rain in Spain?"

"No," Joan cried suddenly, her eyes flying open. "Glasgow. After the war, Tom and his mother moved back to Scotland, to Glasgow." She was back.

"Do you know them?" Tina asked. "Tom and his mother, do you know them?"

"No, of course not. I didn't know your father then."

"When?"

"During the war. I mean, I was here. I was knitting, terrible, terrible scarves for the boys. Oh, and hats that sat on their heads like meatballs."

"So Dad was married to someone in Scotland during the war?"

Joan shook her head, with difficulty at first, but then she kept shaking it, a pendulum motion that she couldn't stop. "No, not married. He offered, of course. Such a gentleman, such a gentle man, your father."

"Mom, are you saying that Daddy had a girlfriend and fathered a son named Tom?"

"He sired him. He sired a son." She suddenly grimaced. "Jesus! Pain!"

"Here Mom," Tina said, thrusting the button to the morphine pump under her mother's translucent thumb. Her skin, always fragrant and soft, now had the limp, velvety texture of a rose petal. "Press this."

"Why do I have to do everything?" Joan wailed.

Why indeed. Against the rules, Tina pressed the button, and within seconds, Joan's face relaxed.

"Do you know Tom's last name, Mom?"

Joan's brow furrowed. "Tom is his name. What's his game?"

"I'd like to meet him. Do you know where I can find him?"

"Somewhere over the rainbow," Joan sang. Then she resumed shaking her head. "No, no, no, wrong. Wrong. On the street. That's where you'll find me on the street where you live."

"Do you know his last name, Mom? Please."

Joan said something, but her consonants were now slurred, the words fused and incomprehensible. Then abruptly, she stopped. Her breathing slowed, and the movement of her sparrow-like chest was barely visible.

She spoke only once more. Sometime around dawn, she opened her gold-flecked, hazel eyes wide, clenched Tina's hand, searched her exhausted face, and said, "Thank you, darling."

Then, when Tina finally left her room to take a short nap, Joan died.

"You know how she hated making a scene," Tina told her cousin Elaine on the phone later that day, her voice clogged with admiration and grief. "She was in control until the end."

• • •

That had been seventeen years ago. Tina missed her mother at unexpected moments—when looking at German expressionist paintings, when seeing a stylish, undeniably smart female politician on television, or in the morning, quietly drinking really good coffee, which Joan had taught her to love. But she didn't really grieve for her. Her mother had raised her, loved her, advised her, and sent her out into the world in the hope that her daughter would be as self-contained as she herself was. Tina felt as if she and Joan each loosely held the tasseled end of a silk scarf. Their bond was cool and smooth and strong. There was nothing jagged in her adult relationship with her mother.

But when she heard about her Bob's other child, well, it was just another shard of unfinished business with her father. What in the hell did he think he was protecting her from? How could he not have known how desperately happy she would have been to have a sibling?

The mystery was partially solved a couple of weeks later, as Tina and Elaine cleaned out her parents' apartment. She was emptying the bottom drawer of the night table on Bob's side of the bed. It was like an archeological dig in there, with layers of subway tokens, receipts, handkerchiefs, and ancient, half-eaten packs of Tums and Rum Butter Life Savers. But the drawer jammed as she tried to close it; an envelope had fallen halfway out the back of it. Carefully, she fished out a wispy blue airmail envelope addressed to her dad—forwarded first from an

Air Force base in London, then from one in Mississippi. She hesitated for only a second before opening it.

Dear Bob, Tina read.

Congratulations! You're a dad. I found out I was pregnant just before you went back to America, and Tom was born in July. He is a happy, healthy boy. Martin came home from a POW camp in Italy, minus one leg and a bit worse for the wear, but Tom brings him much joy. We got married as soon as Martin was released from hospital, and he has adopted Tom. He wanted you to know you had a son, but that's it, once and done. We have moved to Glasgow and are carrying on with high hopes for the future. Please do not respond to this letter or ever try to get in touch with Tom. No need for him to know Martin's not his real dad. I wish you a happy future, and more children that you can call your own. ~Cheers, Gertie.

Cheers. For some reason, that sign-off just slayed Tina. Of course, she didn't know how this Gertie should have signed a letter like that. *Sincerely? Regards?* Not *Love.* You probably don't say *Love* when you're announcing that you've married someone else.

Why had they kept Tom a secret from her? *Because there was nothing you could do with that knowledge,* she could hear her father answer. *It's not like we could find him or get to know him. What good would it do you to know?* But on some level, had she known all along, tried to fill a gap that she sensed but didn't understand? That's magical thinking, Tina scolded herself. But still, she now wondered if her father's protectiveness—no, not that, but his commitment to his own vision of her—was rooted in a fear of not knowing her well enough.

For the first few years after Joan's death, Tina's drawings were almost exclusively self-portraits. "I know it's crazy," she'd told her friend Marnie at the time, "but it's as if I'm making a police sketch of myself. I think I half-hope that Scotland Yard will show it on TV and put it on the front page of British newspapers asking people to come forward with the names of men named Tom who look like me."

But over the years, her aching curiosity had diminished. Would it really change her life if she knew whether some guy out there had good teeth but bad knees like her? Loved arugula but hated zucchini? Never knew his father but wished he had?

Now she looked at Carl looking at her. A huge, gaudy Spanish fan with the wingspan of an albatross hung on the wall behind him and next to it, hanging from a hook, a pair of red and gold castanets.

"You got some souvenirs," she chirped.

"I did," he said, "and I'll tell you all about them if you really want to change the subject."

"I do. Your life is much more interesting to me than my own right now." *Bob and weave*, she remembered her father telling her after she'd had one especially merciless taunting from the mean girls in sixth grade. *You've got to learn to stand up for yourself, sure. But sometimes it's better to just bob and weave*. Was this what he'd meant?

"Well, since the sky is unreadable, we went down the mountain into town tonight."

"Who's we?" Tina asked casually. God, she hated feeling this noxious spurt of jealousy in her throat.

"A couple of other astronomers; you don't know them. Louis and Vera. Anyhow, we went to town and acted like total gringos. We went for tapas at a place that got three stars in the moderately priced restaurants section of the guidebook. We went for hot chocolate at the place next to it that had signage in English, German—not even in Spanish—and took a million different credit cards. And then we went to a club that advertised Authentic Flamenco Dancing—three shows a night!"

"Were there any Spaniards there?"

"Just onstage. The audience was all tourists—mostly Chinese and Brits. But the dancing and the music—holy cow! It was authentically amazing!"

"What was so amazing about it?"

"The ferocity. The women dancers moved with incredible speed, and the men playing the guitars and this huge, bearded old guy—he looked like a malevolent Santa who dyed his beard and eyebrows with shoe polish—they yelped and howled. It was eerie—like hearing a pack of coyotes. It literally made my hair stand on end."

As Carl went on describing the show with his usual blend of nerdy enthusiasm and academic precision ("They were playing in some crazy meter, like nine/eight time, and the mode—I think it may have been Phrygian!"), Tina found herself tuning him out. Her attention kept drifting back to the sketches that lay at her feet. Her confidence seemed to be lying there too.

"So what do you think?" Carl was asking.

"What?"

"Earth to Planet Tina."

"Jeez, I'm sorry. I just spaced out for a minute."

"I can see that. It was screamingly obvious." Carl's cheeks flushed. "I'm sorry if I'm boring you, but you did ask."

"No, you're not boring me. It's just ..."

"I mean, it's not like we're talking every day. And it's not like I'm surrounded by bosom buddies up here."

"I know, sweetie, and ..."

"So if you're distracted, fine. Just don't ask me any goddamn questions if you're not interested in the answers."

His anger, so rare, aroused her own. "Look, I'm sorry, all right? Stop being so petulant."

"Petulant?!" His voice rose indignantly. "You're the one being ... I don't know ... rude."

"I'm not rude. I'm from New York." The words—her father's oft-repeated rejoinder—were out before she could even choose them.

Carl's eyes widened and the storm left his face as quickly as it had inflamed it. "No, you're not rude," he said ruefully. "You're just a nut."

"Yeah, but I'm your nut."

They smiled at each other.

"Tough to crack," Carl said softly, "but so worth the effort."

January 2012

Are you looking for me? read the subject line. Tina's finger was on the Delete key when she noticed the name of the sender. *Not SwingingSingles*, not *RetirementSecurity*, not *Harder_Longer*, but an ordinary human name. Irena Stempl.

She opened the email.

Dear Tina Gabler,

I believe I may be the person you are interested in. My picture, a photo of me when I was six years old and living in Mukacevo, is on a website. The lady at the Australian Jewish News, Mrs. Norma Needleman, sent me your message wondering who I was. That's who I was. I am now Mrs. Irena Stempl and I live in Melbourne, Australia. Up until 25 years ago I was a ticket taker on the tram. Now my rheumatism is too bad to punch tickets or write messages. My son is typing this.

Sincerely,
Mrs. Irena Stempl

Tina quickly opened the page on the Holocaust Museum website that she'd bookmarked. There she was—that crazy-haired, grinning little girl standing ramrod straight in her checkered dress. *Mukacevo, Czechoslovakia, circa 1935–38.* Did she look like an Irena? Like an Australian public transportation worker? How could this be?

She went back to the message and clicked on Reply.

Dear Mrs. Stempl,

Thank you so much for your email. I am so happy to be able to put a name to a face. I am a photography researcher, and an admirer of Roman Vishniac. The childhood picture of you that he took was …

Electrifying? Compelling? English was not Irena's native tongue.

The childhood picture of you that he took really captured my attention, and I would love to learn more about your history and the history of that photo.

As you can imagine, I have many questions for you.

When did you leave Mukacevo?
How did you get to Melbourne?

She paused. Were these questions too dry? After all, she wanted more than the facts. She wanted the story.
Tina deleted the last two bullets and replaced them.

What do you remember about Roman Vishniac taking your picture?
When did you leave Mukacevo?
How were you affected by World War II and the Holocaust?
How did you end up in Melbourne?

She hesitated again, then added:

Did your family survive?

Tina deleted all of the questions. They were too much for an email. Irena's story should be elicited, not demanded, unraveled through leisurely conversation, not a bulleted inquisition.

As you can see, I'm very curious to learn more about your life and about the circumstances surrounding that photograph. You were certainly an adorable little girl.

Tina's finger again hovered over the backspace key. This was too cloying. But on the other hand, she really was an adorable little girl.

Australia is awfully far from where I live in Canada, but perhaps we could talk on the telephone, or online? If so, please write back and tell me how to reach you.

I very much look forwarded to hearing from you and to speaking with you.

Sincerely,
Tina Gabler

She hit Send, then fired off another message to the photography curator at the Holocaust Museum, to let her know that the subject in one of their photos now had a name. Then, too wound up to sit in front of the computer, she walked out into the living room. It was empty and quiet, as was the kitchen. These days Peter woke early, feverish to work, but ran out of gas by mid-morning and had taken to napping. He would summon Jean-Pierre at around 11 a.m. and get wheeled off to his bedroom. Once Peter was transferred to his bed and swaddled in the pastel blue and green mohair blanket that his mother had made for him sometime in the middle of the previous century, Jean-Pierre would sometimes go back to the study to chat with Tina. But more often he set off in the van on his mysterious errands.

She padded silently down the hall to Peter's bedroom. The door was slightly ajar, and she pushed it open just enough to see him lying still as a desiccated twig, his white head barely distinguishable from the pillow supporting it.

He opened one eye.

"I'm so sorry," Tina said. "I just wanted to see if Jean-Pierre was in here with you."

"Why?"

"I was thinking of going out for a walk."

"Stop thinking and just do it," Peter said, letting his eye close again. "I don't need a minder with me every minute."

"You're sure?"

He raised one elegant hand and weakly waved her away.

The sun was bright and the temperature frigid. Tina dressed in layers—long underwear, jeans, t-shirt, sweater, anorak, hat, mittens—before setting out. Thankfully, their neighbor Leo had shoveled the steps from the house down to the river the previous day, a generally useless activity, given that nobody but her would venture down there in late January. But here she was, grateful for the gritty sand beneath her boots as she descended, jabbing a ski pole into each step to steady herself.

The river seemed to be frozen solid, with bald spots between the snow drifts revealing mottled, milky ice. She'd seen enough snowmobiles zipping across its surface to feel confident that it would hold her weight. The gusts of Arctic air were stinging. But it was exhilarating as she developed a rhythm in her stride and heard the brittle, wind-whipped snow crunch under her feet.

She was glad to be away from Peter, whose physical decline was increasingly visible by the day. He was still thinking clearly, but as they discussed what photos to include in the book, or whether the photographer's decisions had been polemical or purely aesthetic, he had less and less energy for explaining or persuading. His passion was degrading into mere irritability. And who could blame him, the poor, wracked man.

A lone cedar angled out from the white-covered rock jutting up from the ice, and she saluted it as she strode past. The American shoreline was now closer than the Canadian one she'd left behind. Welcome to the United States, she thought. Welcome to the past.

But whose? Though she still had family in New York, her fraying tie to the city as home had finally broken when her mother died. She still enjoyed going back, of course, just as she appreciated visits to San Francisco and Montreal and even the site of her old commune in Enosburg Falls—all the places she'd lived in for so many years. But these trips felt like tourism, not homecomings. She'd notice the changes in the skylines and storefronts, observe brick and glass and faux clapboard on country roads that had once offered unobstructed views of meadows, all with a detached wonder at the pace and alienating quality of change. And when in those places, she'd vaguely recall herself as a child or a young woman—not how she looked or behaved, but how she saw—and feel the same puzzlement. More than puzzlement: loss.

How could I have been so much more self-involved back then, she wondered, and yet so much more observant?

Just then a snowmobile appeared from behind a small stand of trees in front of her—one of those tiny islands that had no name—and practically cut in front of her. Its loud, grating buzz had been inaudible only seconds before. Funny how the wind could blow sound away as if it were a thought.

Tina looked around her. No people. No birds. No boats. Just spiky branches and laden evergreens, drifting snow, and an icy blue sky adorned with tall, rimmed clouds. The cold, thin air gave the landscape a hyper-realistic quality. It's like the difference between high-definition video—crystalline and precise—and the warmth of film, she thought. And then, with a start—I've fallen into precisely the habit of mind that Peter warned of. *Reality has come to seem more and more like what we are shown by cameras,* she had typed for him only that morning, quoting Susan Sontag.

Though it was still just mid-afternoon, the sun was noticeably lower on the horizon and Tina felt the sweat she'd worked up turn into cold, penetrating damp. She looked ambivalently at the New York shoreline ahead of her—probably still a good fifteen-minute walk away. She'd been at Peter's for six months now and had yet to make it across the river. But today would not be the day.

She turned and headed back, feeling suddenly tired and even colder. Was this what Irena's journey out of Czechoslovakia had been like—a dark, wintry trudge, but without any knowledge of where or how it would end? She'd have to ask her when they spoke.

About twenty yards ahead of her, a man in a woolen duffle coat sat on a stool holding a fishing line. He looked up when he heard her approach, and waved. Tina took this as an invitation to stop and talk. As she got closer, she realized that the fisherman was Leo, the guy who ploughed Peter's drive and shoveled his stairs.

"Any luck?" she asked.

"No," he answered. "It's too cold for them."

Tina realized she'd never thought about what fish did in the wintertime. "Do they hibernate?"

"Actually, it's not true hibernation. Just a sort of torpor," Leo explained, rolling the word "torpor" around in his mouth like the whiskey in the flask clipped to his belt. "They swim, but slowly. And I could drop a lure or a big, beautiful piece of rotten meat right in front of them and they wouldn't bite."

"Why not? Why would they pass up an easy meal?" Tina asked.

"Because their digestion shuts down in the cold. What little energy they've got goes into motion. Even if they did eat something, they'd just puke it back up. Pardon my French."

Tina smiled. "No worries." She studied Leo's blue lips and wind-burned cheeks. A latticework of broken blood vessels in his nose gave it a strangely delicate look. If ever there was a classic handyman in appearance as well as skills, Leo was it. "So, if the fish aren't biting, why do you stay out here in the cold?"

Leo grinned, and Tina realized that he was missing diagonally opposed canine teeth in his upper and lower jaws, giving him a jack-o-lantern mouth. "Oh, you know, to think ... to drink. It's a relief from back there." He jerked his head towards one of the more modest houses on the Ontario shore. "No distractions." He reached into his pocket and pulled out an iPhone with a pair of earbuds plugged into it. "I come out here to study." Tina raised her eyebrows and tilted her head. "I've been learning about Greek mythology," Leo continued, "but I'm taking a break from that now. Decided I needed to try to understand my wife better. So I've been listening to this." He held up his iPod so Tina could read the name of the audiobook that was playing: *Men are from Mars, Women are from Venus*. "Ever read it?" he asked.

"I remember reading about it," she answered, trying to keep the surprise out of her voice, "but no, I've never read the actual book."

"Well, believe you me, it's fascinating. Turns out that I'm probably wrong about most things I figured she wanted."

"Like what?"

"Oh hell, you know, like showing my appreciation by buying her big presents at Christmas and her birthday — the 26-cubic-foot side-by-side with the built-in icemaker, a gift certificate to that Painting Bar place for her and a bunch of her friends, a dandy bracelet one year — when it turns out that women prefer your small but frequent tokens of affection. Am I right?"

At a loss for words, Tina found herself shrugging her shoulders and rotating her head, torn between nodding and shaking it.

"Or taking a time out, you know, a time away by myself or with a few buddies when I've got something on my mind or making me blue. Well, it turns out she'd rather I talk about it."

I'm with you, Tina thought. "Interesting," she said.

"So here I am, talking about it." Leo started to laugh, a deep wheezing that sounded like a cold engine trying to start up. "Yup, I'm talking about it. Just not with her." He laughed louder now, slapping his overalled knee.

"Well good for you," Tina said, "working on your relationship like that. You're a great example for your fellow men."

"Hell, I don't care about my fellow man," Leo's guttural laughter quickly turned into a coughing fit. Then suddenly quieting, he said, "I just don't wanna get stale, you know. I don't want to end up like these guys," he said, pointing down through the hole he'd drilled, "stuck under the ice, just swimming round and round in slow circles. Life rewards the living, or however the hell that saying goes."

"Truer words have never been spoken," Tina answered with mock solemnity. "I'll let you get back to it, then." She waved a mittened goodbye.

Another stereotype bites the dust, she thought. If she'd ever bothered to imagine Leo's life before today, she would have pictured him watching curling on television, spending Sundays and Tuesday nights with his bowling league, having desultory meatloaf dinners with his wife, and looking forward to his annual trip to Vegas.

We're so ready — *I'm* so ready — to impose my made-up story on everyone I see, she thought for what felt like the hundredth time since she'd come to Brockville. But really, we know so little from just looking.

Tina picked up her pace, striding faster and breathing harder. She was anxious and wanted to be back in the house before the sun went down. She yawned and her cheeks cracked in the cold. She realized that her neck was aching from looking steadily down. She looked up; she needed to get her bearings.

The lean-to on the narrow point of Refugee Island was just a few yards away, its roof covered in snow but its bench apparently dry and inviting. It would be so good to stop and rest for a bit. But on the far horizon, she saw that the light was on in Peter's bedroom. Either Jean-Pierre had gotten him up and Peter would be antsy to work, or he still hadn't returned and Peter would be stuck in his bed, helpless and enraged. In either case, she had to keep walking.

Her boss was still alone when she reached the house, reading quietly in his bed. Tina helped him up and into his wheelchair, then rolled him to the kitchen for a cup of tea.

Hunched over the gleaming table in that brightly lit room, he looked half the size he'd been just six months earlier, when she'd come to Brockville for the first time. Shriveled and wan, Peter looked like a dying man.

"How about a little beef consommé?" Tina suggested. "Or some rice pudding? Something with some protein, or fat ..."

"That'll put some flesh on my bones?"

Tina shrugged, trying to convey a sheepishness she didn't feel. "Busted."

"I'm afraid it's a vain effort, my dear. I was scrawny before I was lean ..." He paused for breath, then covered his infirmity with a sip of tea. "And as I age once again into childhood, I shall be scrawny again."

"Are you quoting someone?" Tina asked.

"Oh, just paraphrasing The Sphinx. Walking on three legs in the afternoon. Or at least I would be if I could walk."

"Have you been to see the doctor recently?" Tina asked, feeling stupid as the words came out.

Peter cast her a scornful look.

The front door opened, then slammed, and Jean-Pierre entered the kitchen bearing several shopping bags. Grateful for the interruption, Tina stood and took a bag from him. When all the bags were arrayed on the counter, Jean-Pierre began unloading them, one item at a time, in a sort of striptease.

"Socks," he said, waving them slowly in front of Peter's face. "Gold toes, mid-calf, wide band—just the way you like them."

"Bravo." Peter's voice was weak.

"Denture cleaner." Jean-Pierre held one box of tablets in each hand in a parody of a snake oil salesman. "So you can dazzle the ladies with your smile." Without commentary, he left the large package of adult diapers in the semi-transparent bag and moved on to the next one. "Two six-packs of Molson's Golden, the pride of Canada." He held one in each large palm and raised them both up over his shoulders like bar bells.

Peter nodded approvingly.

"And—the piece de resistance—two large Cadbury Dark Chocolate bars. Manna from the gods."

"Bad for the figure," Peter scolded.

"But good for the soul, no?"

Jean-Pierre's smile was hearty and broad and, it seemed to Tina, genuine. He was a guarded man, but a kind one.

"So, you weren't off visiting your secret girlfriend?" Tina asked, appalled to hear such coy, flirtatious language coming out of her mouth. After all, she wasn't looking for a romantic or even merely sexual relationship with him. But intimacy, some sort of private knowledge—that, she was hungry for.

"Well, if she's secret, I can't tell you, can I?" Tina nodded, surrendering to his logic. "I am a restless man," Jean-Pierre said after a short silence. "So sometimes I go for a drive, or for a walk. Or I go shoot baskets at the YMCA. But my secret girlfriend—she's in Montreal, so I only see her about once a month."

"Ah, so she does exist."

"Marie, yes, she exists." He smiled crookedly. "Like your astronomer. They both exist, but at a nice, calm distance." He inhaled deeply, then blew out a long, slow exhalation. "They give us room to breathe, no?"

"Your astronomer?" Peter asked. "I wasn't aware that you had a personal astronomer. Not even an astrologer."

"Well, we're not together right now ... obviously. Carl was, maybe still is, my boyfriend, but—"

Peter raised his eyebrows. "Boyfriend? Is he fourteen?"

Tina laughed ... but only a little. "I know, I know. There's just no good word for grown-up mates who aren't spouses. 'My partner' sounds like we're in business together ... or gay. My common-law husband is a bit of a mouthful. And besides, Carl does have a certain boyishness."

"Where is your Carl?"

"At an observatory in Spain. He got a research fellowship there, and I didn't really want to be an academic wife with too much time on my hands, and since I was sort of at loose ends anyhow, it seemed like this would be a good time to make a change."

"You realize, of course, that you said nothing of substance after 'too much time on my hands.' Loose ends? Make a change?" Peter paused to take a breath, then expelled it angrily. "What, really, are you talking about? I'm old, and sure, it's obvious that I'm running down, a goddamn trickle from a hose." He smacked his palm weakly on the arm of his chair. "I don't have time for these vagaries!"

Tina was too stunned to filter her words. "I wanted to accomplish something for once in my life, to do some work that wasn't eaten or recycled or erased. I wanted to have something I'd had a part in making to show ... "

"But the book isn't yours," Peter said flatly. "It's mine."

Tina pushed back her chair and strode to the stove, her back to the men. She was goddamned if she would let Peter see the tears in her eyes.

Jean-Pierre lay a big, silencing palm on Peter's shoulder. "Tina's your helper, man. The lady works hard for you."

"I know," Peter snapped. Then, after taking another sip of tea, he quietly repeated, "I know." Raising his voice to Tina, who now stood behind him, he said, "I'm sorry dear. I truly am. It's just that you've been here six months now and this was the first I've heard ... I'd just hoped that I'd become a bit more than your boss ..." He drifted off, then announced, almost happily, "I liked being a father .... Which is a bit surprising, since I wasn't very proficient at it."

Proficient, Tina thought. *No wonder you weren't.* But his openness, his longing, touched her. She turned and sat back down across the table from him. "Well, I was a bad daughter," she said, resisting the impulse to cover his hand with hers, "so we're a perfect match. And I'm sorry I wasn't forthcoming. I'm just a naturally private person, and the status of Carl's and my relationship right now is a bit ambiguous."

"Most things are, my dear," Peter said, smiling wryly, "as you yourself are so fond of pointing out to me."

"Touche." Then, after some hesitation, Tina asked, "Does Sandy know that your health isn't great?"

"You mean that I'm wasting away?" Peter snapped. "Let's not mince words, shall we? Life is way too short for that, especially mine." Tina forced herself to keep her gaze on him, unflinching. "I don't know if Sandy knows," Peter finally said. "I don't care if Sandy knows."

"She might care."

Peter, whose back had been slowly curling like a wave, forced himself upright. "Yes, well, she's got a peculiar way of showing it. But what do I know? I'm just an old colonizer. Maybe biting the hand that feeds you, fleeing the hand that feeds you, is some Cree tradition about which I'm woefully ignorant."

Tina held up her hand in warning, not knowing what to say, but sure that she didn't want to hear more of that.

Peter spared her the need to say anything. "Tomorrow I want to start the chapter on Rothstein," he said, all business.

"That'll be fun," Tina said, by now familiar with the controversy regarding the authenticity of some of Rothstein's work.

Peter once again let his shoulders sink, too tired to fight anymore.

• • •

Two weeks later, Tina met Irena. She looked like a peasant. The vibrant, gorgeous child who made her crumbling street look like the most exciting place on earth was unrecognizable in the visage of this 81-year-old woman. Through the dithery webcam, Tina saw a face that was broad and deeply creased. The eyes that squinted out from the papery lids were a brilliant blue.

"I thought your eyes were brown," Tina burst out, wondering if this woman was an imposter.

"Why? They've always been blue," Irena answered irritably.

"In the picture … of course it's a black and white image, but still, your eyes there are like coal."

Irena snorted derisively. "I've never seen blue coal."

"Of course," Tina said hastily. "My mistake. So how does it feel to be famous?"

"Famous?"

"You know, on a website and in a book of pictures that's been read by hundreds of thousands of people." *Shut up, Tina,* she scolded herself, horrified by the inanity of her own question.

"The same as always," Irena answered.

"Had anyone ever recognized you before?'

"What, from the book?" She looked at her son—himself an old man in a sweater vest and a plaid shirt—and rolled her eyes. "Not from the book."

"From something else?" Tina asked, enriching Irena's apparent confusion with her own.

"From the bus!" Irena answered, still impatient, as if Tina had asked her something blindingly obvious, like the color of a carrot or a purple cabbage.

"What were you doing on the bus?" Tina decided she'd just go with the flow.

"Punching tickets, like always." Again, she cast an exasperated look at her son, as if to ask why she was wasting what could be the last day of her life with this idiot.

This conversation was not going as planned. "Oh, so you punch tickets on the bus?"

"Of course I do!" She cast an irritated glance at her son, imploring him to swat Tina away. "Why do you care?"

Irena reminded Tina of her paternal grandmother. Like this old woman, Bubbe's default mode was mocking and defensive. She had a knack for turning compliments into insults. *If I said "delicious kugel, mom,"* her father would recount, *she'd say, 'What, you didn't think I could* cook some noodles?' If I said, "Nice dress," she'd say, 'What, you mean not like the shmatas I usually wear?' "

Was the belligerence of the elderly a product of pain? Tina wondered. Or was it simply, as so clearly in Peter's case, wild impatience with anyone wasting even a second of their time on nonessentials?

She decided not to answer Irena's question. "How did you end up in Australia?" Tina asked instead.

"That's where they sent me from the DP camp after the war."

Tina tried to contain her exasperation. This woman was amazingly literal. "Where were you during the war?"

"In Theresienstadt."

"I've been there!" Tina said with what she knew was foolish-sounding excitement. But she felt a shiver run through her at the knowledge that she might have stood in the same room that housed Irena as a child. It was a long, narrow room, she remembered, a community hall that housed an exhibit of artwork created by the children of the concentration camp. The pictures depicted many ordinary scenes of classrooms, teachers, families, soccer games, dinners. The pastels and watercolors were faded by time and light. Row after row, picture after picture—the sensation wasn't so different from casually looking at the kids' artwork stuck up on a friend's refrigerator door—until she noticed that very occasionally, the word "Survived" appeared next to the name and age of the artist. "Were you there with your family?" she asked.

"With my sister, yes, and my mother. My father was already dead before we went, and my mother died soon after we got there."

"And did your sister survive?

Irena sighed heavily. "Yes, but you never knew her, so why do you care?"

Why did she care? What the hell did she actually want from this woman?

To know. Just to know her story, for a change, not the one Tina had made up for her.

But why? She heard her father's voice in her head, interrogating her. Well, no. "Interrogating" is what she'd called his questioning dialogue when she was sixteen. She understood now that he was simply asking her to think.

To see if the promise in that child's dark dancing eyes was realized, she answered, if Irena was as arresting as her photo. She envisioned Bob now, sitting in the blue club chair, right foot crossed over left knee, cigarette in one hand and coffee cup in the other, looking quizzically at her as she stopped on her way into the kitchen or out of their apartment, always standing, always en route away from him.

And once you know, what will you do with that knowledge?

Why do I have to do anything with it? Sixty years old and inside her head she was whining like a petulant child.

"I think that other people can learn important things from your life story, lessons about survival and thriving through change," Tina answered carefully. Lessons I could sure as hell use. "So I'd like to help you tell it."

Irena waved her hand as if batting away a housefly. "There's plenty of movies and books and shows about the war and the camps. Let them learn from those things. My story is just *my* story, and I did what we all did. You put one foot ahead of the other, you work, you do what you need to do."

Tina could see Irena's son—a man roughly her age—at the edge of the frame, arms folded over his chest, nodding vigorously. She had the feeling that he'd spent a lifetime demonstrating his agreement with his mother. Still, perhaps Irena was right. Why should she have to be emblematic?

"Fair enough," Tina said. "But please, let me ask you just one more question. Do you remember Mr. Vishniac taking that picture of you when you were a child in Mukacevo, that picture that was in the *Australian Jewish News*?"

Irena creased her already creviced brow. "Maybe." She looked over at her son, then said "I think so."

"Do you remember what you were doing, or how he found you?"

"I must have been playing, or maybe collecting the coal or wood that had fallen off of the wagons and trucks. But I do remember a man with pink cheeks and cameras around his neck. He was just walking down the street, taking pictures of stores and of other children, other people walking around on their business."

"I know this is a crazy question, but do you remember what you were thinking when he took your picture?"

She blew a short shot of air out from between pursed lips. "Smile for the camera, that's what I was thinking." Tina couldn't tell if she was disgusted or amused ... or if in Irena's case, the two feelings were always conjoined. "That's what my parents taught me when we posed for that family portrait after my sister was born. It's what I did in every picture they took."

"There are other pictures?" Tina asked.

"Not by him, not by Vishniac. But when the Red Cross came to Theresienstadt just before the end of the war — after the Nazis shipped a bunch of us off to Auschwitz so the barracks would be less crowded, after they gave us supplies to build some bathrooms and that community hall, after they let the musicians get together to play and us kids to sing and color and paint, you know, after the Nazis let us fix up the barracks and plant a garden and paint the buildings to impress the Red Cross — the visitors took lots and lots of pictures. Look at the happy, healthy Jewish children!" Irena sang out scornfully. "This isn't a death camp. It's a community!"

She paused for breath. "So then too, I smiled for the camera."

February 2012

Some days, the mourning dove's dawn coo sounded almost festive, like Tina's grandmother's happy humming as she scrubbed the stove top or ironed her dressing gown, bringing mastery and sparkle to her small domain. But this morning, with an icy wind pushing the temperature to the teens (she still thought in Fahrenheit, even after all those years in Canada), the bird's cry was drowned out by the frantic footfalls of the squirrels and raccoons. They skittered and slid across the icy roof, though Tina didn't know where they were running from or to.

The sound chilled her as much as the Arctic air leaking in through the windows. She wore two shirts and a sweater, and both hands were jammed into her pockets when Peter wheeled into the study later that morning.

"Back to Rothstein?" Tina asked. As Peter's stamina flagged, his sense of urgency mounted. Between congestive heart failure and the toll of his reawakened polio, Melissa had explained to her, Peter's time was running out. So when Jean-Pierre wheeled him into his study each morning, Tina knew to go straight to work

Peter nodded.

"The bleached cow skull?" Tina asked, by now familiar with the more iconic images from Depression-era photography.

"No. 'Fleeing a Dust Storm.' The one where he posed living people, not just dead bones," Peter answered. Even in his increasingly weakened state, he could still do scorn better than anyone she knew.

"He admitted that?" she asked as Jean-Pierre left the room.

"He had to! The real dust storms were so dangerous, and the air so thick with dust, that you couldn't stand out in one and take a legible image."

Tina visualized the 1936 photograph, an original print of which was entombed in a light-resistant sleeve in Peter's archive. A tall, skinny man in a black jacket and wide-brimmed hat leaned into the wind as he approached a low, ramshackle structure made of bleached wood and raggedly patched with tar paper. Running next to him was a boy in an engineer's cap who looked to be about ten years old. Several yards behind them, a small boy in overalls, one hand to his forehead protecting his eyes, struggled to catch up in their race towards the sanctuary of the chicken coop. A few slender, broken tree trunks jutted up from the sand that had once been fertile soil.

"I could have sworn that I read some article by Rothstein where he explicitly said that the picture wasn't posed."

"That's what he claimed in the 1960s," Peter said tiredly. "But in the '40s, he did an interview in which he explained how he'd posed the farmer and his kids to make a more effective picture. He asked the farmer to lean forward. He told the little boy to cover his eyes. And then he put them in front of the shed because he needed to demonstrate the impact of the storms on the farm buildings. And, of course, because he wanted to exhibit their poverty."

"So you're saying that the only way he could illustrate the dust bowl, the destruction of the region, was to shoot it in clear weather?" Tina asked.

"That's what I'm saying. Ironic, isn't it?"

Tina paused, debating with herself whether to revive their running debate. Go for it, she decided. Conflict revives him. "I get why it was misleading to title the picture 'Fleeing a Dust Storm' if that's not what they were actually doing," she said, picking her words carefully. "But how else can you photograph a dust storm?"

"You don't," Peter snapped.

God, she hated his certainty. "So is it also wrong to use a flash when there's not enough ambient light?" she said with adolescent sarcasm. "Or should one never try to take a photograph in a dark room?"

Peter recoiled. "Don't be ridiculous. A flash bulb is merely illuminating what's already there." He looked around fretfully. Did he want Jean-Pierre back in the room for comfort?

Tina was slammed with remorse. And he was right. But he wouldn't be soothed by surrender. "So are reproductions or reenactments always inherently wrong?" She paused, thinking of what she aspired to in her own drawings. "If you are honestly trying to depict what you believe to be the truth of a situation, then isn't it justifiable to pose a scene that couldn't otherwise be captured?"

"Not in a photograph," Peter snapped. "If you're drawing or painting—sure, go wild. Make up whatever scene you can imagine. But if you're using an instrument meant to capture reality, then what you're shooting has to be real."

"But the poverty was real! The dust storms were real! And if we know that—if we know anything about what we're looking at—isn't it inevitable that we're going to inject our beliefs into what we're looking at, regardless of how much the image has or hasn't been constructed?"

"Your point?"

Tina felt her mind casting about for a buoy, feeling that not just her ideas but her integrity, her identity, were somehow at stake. Stalling, she stood to pour Peter a cup of tea from the pot she had steeping on the bookshelf. "My point is that we only imagine that photographs depict truth more than other art forms. My point is that in art just as in life, we project our hopes and our beliefs into whoever and whatever we look at."

"Of course we do." Peter sighed, bone-weary. "But shouldn't we do our best to see people and things for who and what they are, independent of how we want to think about them?"

Silenced, Tina set the cup of tea and a piece of dark chocolate on a napkin in front of him and sat down heavily across the table.

"I know we can never shed our own convictions," Peter said more gently, "but don't we owe it to the people we're freezing in time— don't we owe it to them to at least try? Would Arthur Coble—the dust storm farmer—would he and his boys have mattered any less to the people who knew and loved them, if their farm had prospered? If they hadn't been battered and poor?"

"If they hadn't been battered and poor, would anyone have bothered to tell their story?"

"Listen to yourself, my dear. You know as well as me that those Depression-era photographs are the anomalies. Usually being poor is a cloak of invisibility, a guarantee that your story won't be told."

Tina sighed. "Right as always, oh Wise One."

Peter arced his eyebrows. "Sarcasm. You don't generally do much of that. Rough morning?"

What's rough is the sight of you, pale and laboring, she thought but didn't say. "No, I'm fine. But listen, before we get into Rothstein, we need to talk about another photo. Have you picked out a picture of yourself to go on the dust jacket of the book when it's published?"

"Dust jacket. What a quaint concept."

"People still read print books. And they'll definitely want to read this one in physical form. So, no dodging it. We need a picture of you."

He shuddered. "I hate being in front of a camera. And now, my God, I'd break the lens."

"You were a national news anchor for twenty-five years and you hate being in front of the camera?"

"Always. But video footage didn't bother me as much as still images."

"Why?"

"Video captures motion, the minute changes in facial expression and body language. It doesn't entomb you in a moment that may or may not represent who you really are."

Tread lightly, Tina told herself. "But doesn't every moment represent some aspect of who you really are? Isn't that why you so staunchly defend the pure documentary image?"

Peter wagged his finger at her. "I know where you're going, young lady. You want me to acknowledge that I hold a double-standard, championing the truth of the camera except when it comes to myself." He hung his head in mock chagrin. "Guilty as charged."

"You and everyone else," she said, squelching the impulse to pet his skeletal hand. "We all want some measure of control over the image we present to the world, right?" He nodded. "So, where's your stash of head shots? We could rummage through them and find something that represents how you want to be seen. Peter Bright: Clear-eyed Skeptic ... unless you'd prefer Peter Bright: Dreamboat."

"Don't patronize me, dear," he said, but his reprimand was a happy one. "Look in there." He pointed to a roll-doored cupboard beneath one of the built-in bookshelves. "There ought to be a box labeled 'souvenirs' or 'mementos' or something."

Tina peered into the cupboard, excited to finally have permission to explore what wasn't in plain sight.

The first box she pulled out contained reels of tape in round metal canisters. Each was labeled "Week in Review" — the Sunday talk show Peter had moderated for about a decade — followed by a date. Another, smaller, wooden box held cameras. She passed them to Peter, one by one.

"The Rollei," he said fondly, pulling a twin-lens reflex camera out of its faded and brittle leather case. "This may have been my first camera. I shot lots of pictures of Otto, our schnauzer, with this. Maybe even a few of Evelyn, my date at my senior prom."

"You went to the senior prom?" Tina was astonished.

"Why wouldn't I?"

"I don't know — it's just so juvenile!"

"But I was juvenile. At sixteen — well, that's the definition of juvenile, isn't it? Mid-teens, pimply, eager, perpetually confused. I was no different than any other sixteen-year-old boy. I was just smart enough to know that if I walked around with a camera, I could take the focus off myself ... though of course it probably was never on me in the first place. But such abiding self-consciousness in the agonies of adolescence — well, it gives one delusions of grandeur."

"I can't imagine you as an awkward teen."

"You're just not trying, dear. I was, but made less awkward by the confidence the camera gave me. TLRs like this Rollei, it's what all the portrait photographers used well into the '60s. You've seen those pictures of Diane Arbus, haven't you, her cropped hair and long, boxy face mirroring the camera she held below it. That discomfort you feel when looking at her pictures — are we responding to the face her subjects want to present, or are we responding to their wanting? To create that experience, you need a certain stillness. That's what the TLR gave her."

"Is that what you aspired to?"

He chortled. "I'm no Arbus, thank God. Never wanted to be. I never took pictures of Otto in drag, and there was nothing freakish about Evelyn either. But I did learn from the concentration that the viewfinder required. No snap, snap, snap. You had to frame the shot, be mindful of what you were doing."

"How about this one?" Tina held up an old, battered Leica.

"The M3 Rangefinder! Cartier-Bresson's tool of choice." Peter rubbed his hands. "Now, that camera I did buy in my slavish attempt to emulate a master. Woefully inadequate, of course. The camera's not enough; you still need an eye for composition and I never developed that. But my goodness, I took thousands of muddy, mediocre Toronto street scenes with that thing. Hopefully, none of them have survived."

He fell into silence, still cupping the Rolleiflex on his lap, as Tina continued digging through the contents of the deep cupboard. But she found no boxes of photographs, just more reels of tape.

"Is there somewhere else I should look?" she asked.

Peter shrugged, indifferent to the quest.

"Because if not, we should probably arrange a photo shoot soon."

"Before I look even more mummified than I already do? Before time runs out on shooting me while I'm still alive?"

Tina looked up sharply. But she couldn't muster a denial, and knew that Peter wouldn't appreciate a lie. "You must know some good photographers."

"You're an artist" he said after a long pause. "Sketch a portrait of me. We'll use that."

Tina felt her face flush. "That's ridiculous. I couldn't possibly do you justice."

"But there's nothing intrinsic to the image. Isn't that what you're always telling me — that the image derives its meaning from what the viewer brings to it?"

"You don't think it's a little weird to have a charcoal portrait of you on the back cover of a book about photography?"

Peter gently wagged his finger at her. "You're dodging the question, my dear. No, it's settled. You can either draw me or we'll skip the author picture altogether."

Tina threw up her hands in surrender. "I'll draw you, but no promises. Not that I have anything to worry about. You're going to hate it."

Peter leaned back in his chair, turned his face towards the sun streaming in through the study window, and smiled. "I'm sure I will." Then, after a brief pause, he added, "And while you're at it, draw a picture of yourself too."

Jesus Christ, Tina swore to herself that night as she labored over yet another iteration of her twice-failed portrait of Peter. Am I even capable of drawing a face that's got not just the close-set eyes and thin lips and high cheekbones and bushy eyebrows of this man, but the character I see in him? Or am I reproducing a face as simply degrees of light and shadow, as if I am an autonomous camera with nobody framing the shot?

She was keyed up. Peter's face shrank, seeming to tighten on the page under the tense jabs of her charcoal. All of the looseness, the mental surrender to the impulses of her drawing hand that had taken her years to develop—it had all left her.

Stop wanting it so badly, she told herself. Things will turn out better if you don't.

She'd said something similar to Carl, she remembered, one night early in their romance, when she was still approaching their relationship with apprehension and excitement, as if it were a blank sketchpad.

They'd gone stargazing at midnight, at some astronomy-club shed atop a hill about fifty kilometers outside the city. To escape light pollution, drivers were instructed to turn off their headlights for the long drive up the dirt road to the shed.

"Of course, my little telescope is to real observing what a box of Ripple is to ... some fancy French wine," Carl had nervously told her, "so don't get too excited."

I'm not, she refrained from saying. She was puzzled and a little amused by how anxious he was. She knew Carl had nervous habits.

He jiggled his knee at meals or sitting on the couch watching television. He rubbed the sides of his feet together in bed as she was trying to drift off to sleep. He stroked his mustache, flattening it, creating grooves outside the snaking line the hair made from lip to chin.

But tonight, far from the city light, on this dark hillside studded with other men and some women standing at least fifty yards apart, he was more than nervous. He was possessed.

"Come on, just a little bit, just a tiny …" he babbled sweetly to the telescope as he adjusted its lens. "Now I know you can …. Yup, you see Alpha Centauri now, don't you?"

Was this how he would have talked to their baby if they'd had one?

"Yes, you do," he murmured inanely. If the telescope lens had had a chin, he'd be tickling it. "And Cassiopeia. Now come on, just a little more focus, just another degree or two and we can—goddamnit." He looked up, and Tina followed his gaze. A wispy trail of cloud seemed to pass over the general vicinity in which he was looking. "Goddamn low-pressure front!"

"Goddamn low-pressure front?" she repeated. "You're berating the weather?"

"I thought tonight was going to be so great," he said, now pounding the side of his thigh with his fist. "Just five minutes ago it was clear, so clear …"

"But isn't this what you love about the natural world?" she asked, now gently, alarmed by his obvious distress. "Its changeability?" His obsessiveness, normally so endearing, seemed to have crossed some line.

"On a quantum scale! On a universal scale! Not on a fuck-up-the-one-good-night-of-stargazing-in-a-month scale!"

"You can stop wanting a clear sky so badly. I'm just happy to be out here with you," Tina said, stroking his back, "even if it is a little cloudy."

"I don't need to be comforted," he hissed.

She let her arm drop, stung.

"I'm sorry," Carl hastily whispered. "I'm just frustrated. I wanted you to be able to see what I see."

Why is that so important? Tina wondered. Why do we need others to see what we see? To stave off loneliness? "Well, tonight we're both seeing wispy clouds, so mission accomplished," she answered lightly.

That had been enough to calm him, and though the details were now dim in her memory, it seemed to her that they'd ended up staying almost until dawn, looking at endless tiny clouds and blobs that were, Carl had told her, entire galaxies and galaxy clusters. And though she knew they were supposed to be awesome, supposed to make her muse about the vastness of the cosmos, they failed to move her in the way that the scarred moon had, giant and so suddenly unfamiliar through the telescope's lens.

"Do you remember that time you took me stargazing," she asked Carl on their Skype call later that night. "Somewhere up around Bracebridge?"

"Vaguely. What made you think of that?"

"Oh, just because I'm making a hash of things, you know, trying too hard."

Carl laughed. "Is that what you did that night?"

"No, it's what you did." Tina forced a smile, needing to signal that she wasn't picking a fight.

"And you're bringing this up now because …"

"Because, I don't know, because I'm thinking about how difficult it is to know if two people are ever seeing the same thing."

"That's why we have math and cartography. It's why we have measurement, so that we can agree on truth."

"You answered that so easily," Tina marveled.

Carl shrugged. "That strikes me as an easy question. The hard question is how we can learn the truth about what we can't see."

"Like dark matter?"

"Exactly. The truths we think we know about dark matter are just explanations we've constructed for visible phenomena. They're not really truths, just inferences."

"But I thought you liked that ambiguity. I thought you liked having room to create new theories."

"Oh, I do." He nodded. "Almost as much as I like you and Cheerios. But a little unarguable clarity every now and then can be quite nice."

Tina held up her most recent portrait of Peter to the tablet. "So what do you see?"

"It's kind of hard to answer at 1920 by 1080 resolution, but what I think I see is a distinguished old man, a bit haughty, a bit amused."

"What about pain?" she asked. "Do you see any pain in his face?"

Carl squinted. "Not so much pain," he answered slowly, as ... I don't know ... fatigue, I guess."

"That'll do."

Carl looked anxious, as though he'd flunked the test. "It's good! I mean, it's a good picture. It looks like an older version of the Peter Bright I remember from the nightly news."

Tina was silent.

"Really, it's fine." Carl now sounded almost beseeching. "Excellent."

"Where do you think he is?" Tina abruptly asked.

"I don't know. At his desk? Does it matter?"

"Would you read the picture the same way if he was on a motorboat or in the doctor's office or sitting on the toilet?"

"I don't know."

"Or watching a cartoon? Or a pole dancer?"

Carl sighed. "What's this about?"

Tina carefully put the drawing back down on her desk. "I'm sorry. Peter wants me to draw his portrait for the back of the book. It's about me feeling inadequate, you know? How do you depict who someone is independent of the context? I don't think I'm up to the task."

"Well, obviously he thinks you are."

Tina rubbed her eyes, suddenly exhausted. "Yeah, but what does he know?"

"You," Carl said urgently. "He knows you, and he trusts you with his legacy."

"But if this picture goes on the book jacket, it'll be *my* legacy. And I don't want that."

"Why?"

"Because it's not good enough! And it doesn't really say who I am, or what I've done with my puny life."

"Whoa. Take a deep breath. Puny?" Carl was trying to comfort, but Tina could hear the impatience he was trying to suppress. And who could blame him? She couldn't stand herself either in these wailing, self-pitying moments.

"I know. I'm sorry. It's just that it gets worse. He wants me to do a self-portrait too."

"For the book jacket?"

Tina felt her breath suddenly lodge in her chest. "I don't know. I mean I assumed … but I don't actually know."

"Do you deserve to be shown as his co-author?"

"Deserve? That's kind of a loaded term …"

Carl rolled his eyes, releasing his frustration. "Come on. Don't get all semantic on me. You know what I mean. Are you as much the author as he is? Are your words on the pages?"

She knew they were. Not only had she significantly revised the early chapters that he'd begun before she started working for him, but she had largely written the latter ones based on their increasingly rambling conversations. So why was it so hard to say yes? Because the words were just instantiations of the ideas, many of which were his. "It's a collaboration," she answered.

"Well, that makes sense," Carl said instantly. "That's who you are — a collaborator, a …" He waved his arm as if beckoning her to step in front of him. "A helper — not in an obsequious way. I mean you're a person who works with other people to make things happen, whatever you call that. And that's great. There's nothing wrong with that. Too few people know how to do that." He slumped, exhausted by the effort of trying to describe a quality that didn't involve mass, speed, or light.

Tina felt her face soften. "That's okay?" she asked quietly. "I spent so much of my adulthood arguing with my father about whether that was good enough."

"We parents," Carl said — one of the rare occasions when he placed himself in the group to which she'd never belong — "we want our kids to shine." He fiercely rubbed his new beard. "We're trained to think that being a good parent means making sure our kid stands out from the pack. It's stupid."

"Did you do that to Keenan?"

Carl looked down, silent. Then, "No. I don't think I was present enough to screw him up in that way." He smiled sadly. "I probably found other ways."

"I doubt that."

"You didn't know me when I was young ..." He offered a crooked smile. "But enough of this! We were talking about you and your self-portrait. Have you drawn one?"

"Not yet. It's been decades since I've tried to do that."

Carl sat up straight and spoke with a false heartiness that disconcerted her. "Decades are a millisecond on the grand scale of things," he said. "Get to it. Try it. You don't have to use the picture if it turns out badly."

When it turns out badly, she almost said, but restrained herself. "You're right," she said instead.

"Okay, then. You get to work, I'll get to bed, and we'll talk again soon, all right?"

Tina remembered how much Carl hated to see her vulnerable, how twitchy it made him. "All right, love. Sleep tight."

Her irritation with him passed the moment they said goodbye. He was such a good man. Richard, and Sean after him—those men had been what her father would have called the two strikes before Carl, the home run. He'd been worth the wait. Still, on this dreary night, she had to admit to herself—perhaps for the first time?—that she regretted the stuck years, the servant years, the years she'd orbited Richard.

• • •

August, 1971, San Francisco

Richard had moved into her house in Haight Ashbury on the day of the Vietnam draft lottery, and they had all huddled around the grainy black-and-white TV to watch it. ("It's like football," her roommate John had said, "only more boring and more dangerous at the same time.") Richard watched it from the doorway to the living room, frozen, his arms wrapped around his chest in a lonely hug.

Richard's birthday was September 6, and when that date was drawn, Tina looked at him, expecting an explosive reaction. But he just linked his fingers, brought his hands to his mouth, and started blowing on his palms. Beneath his waves of coppery hair, he looked very pale.

Tina stood and walked over to him. "110," she murmured. "That's not too bad, is it?"

"Right on the cusp," he answered tersely. "They say the top-third is sure to be drafted, and the next third has a fifty-fifty chance." He turned abruptly and headed up the stairs to his room.

As the lottery slogged on, Tina, her housemates, and a steady stream of friends wandered in and out of the living room. She watched their comings and goings, and drifted in and out of conversations about tarot, *Trout Fishing in America*, and medical conditions that could get you a draft deferment. It was all nice, all friendly — but she needed to get out of this dim, somewhat rancid-smelling living room. She wanted to get away from her roommates, who in this moment struck her as sluggish and kind of dumb.

This experiment in group living isn't exactly forging any fabulous new trails, she thought as she rummaged through her closet in search of a jacket. They called themselves a commune, but other than taking turns cooking and giving the kitchen counter a desultory wipe now and then, was there anything really bold or even collaborative in how they were living? If they'd been eating pot roast instead of vegetarian chili, this evening would have been indistinguishable from any summer night on her family's annual vacation in the Catskills.

Am I intolerant? Tina wondered. Am I just a spoiled only child? And was this experiment in communal living not an idealistic expression of a new culture, but just the realization of her wish to have had siblings?

Her parents had always been vague when she'd asked for a brother or sister, answering "We'll see" when she was young, and "It's too late" when she was older. She'd pressed her mother on the issue a couple of years ago, no longer asking for a sibling, but demanding to know why she didn't have one.

"We had enough trouble conceiving you," Joan had answered. "I had endometriosis, and it's frankly a miracle not just that I got pregnant, but that I actually carried you to term." Then, turning things around as she always did, "But don't assume that you'll have the same fertility challenges that I did. In fact, assume the opposite. Assume that unless you are very, very diligent about contraception, you'll get pregnant every time you have sex."

That they were having this conversation about her own still largely theoretical sex life was bad enough. That they were having it on the C Line on the way to see the New York City Ballet's performance of The Nutcracker was excruciating.

"Mom," she'd whined. "Please. Can we please just not talk about this now?"

"Of course," Joan answered with gracious equanimity. "We can talk about it later."

Now, two years later and decades older, Tina could smile at her mother's craftiness. And the fact was that her warning had worked. If and when Tina ever had kids, they wouldn't be accidents.

Out on Haight Street, the sidewalks were clogged with hippies and the tourists who'd come to look at them. She walked as quickly as she could up to Page, then headed west towards the park. Despite the bright clothing and the downy bearded faces around her, despite the boisterous Hare Krishnas chanting and shaking their tambourines and proffering cool little vials of patchouli oil for sale, through her suddenly critical eyes, the scene looked neither exotic nor charming. The small bands of people Tina's age sitting cross-legged on the park grass strumming guitars looked just as pretentious as the kids back home. They were all wearing the same clothes, singing the same songs, and now, watching the same shows, hoping and believing that they all saw the world in the same way.

Until yesterday this unity of vision had felt intoxicating, but today, it felt dull.

Was it the letter from her cousin Elaine that was making her feel so restless? *I can't wait to get back to Binghamton,* her cousin had written, her spacious, lopey handwriting as breathless as her voice. *If I want to do pre-med, I'm going to have to declare my major this year. But I don't know if I want to sign up for SOOO MUCH WORK! My mother thinks I should do psychology or math, but those mean graduate school too, and I sort of feel like if I'm going to be in school forever, I want a job with some status when I get out.*

Tina appreciated her cousin's candor, and she had to admit that she did not want to wait tables for the rest of her life. Guileless and well-informed, Elaine was on a perfectly reasonable path, one that sometimes looked more appealing than the muddy trail Tina was blazing. This life, unconventional only in trivial ways, wasn't shaping up to be what she was looking for when she moved out here. After all, what were they actually building together, she and her roommates and these supposedly kindred spirits? The counter-culture had to be something more than an agreement to look in the same mirror. It had to be a collaboration, a joining of hearts and skills to create … what? She didn't know. But as happened so often, one of her father's pet phrases popped into her mind and stayed there, forming the backbeat to her footsteps through the circus that was the Haight: The whole must be greater than the sum of its parts.

Richard seemed to share her restlessness, and despite what Tina chose to call Richard's gruffness, they quickly became a couple. She admired his intellect and the nakedness of his passions. And like Tina, Richard had tired of the druggy squalor of their home in San Francisco. When he found Organic Agricultural Theatre Soviet (OATS) in Enosburg Falls, Vermont, an agricultural commune that was looking for new recruits, Tina instantly agreed to move there with him.

The relationship between her parents and boyfriend should have been promising. Bob and Joan were thrilled to have their daughter back on the proper coast, and when Tina and Richard first arrived in New York en route to Vermont, they thanked him for being such a good influence.

"I'd say you're welcome, but I wasn't doing it for you," he said sourly as they sat eating cheese and crackers in the living room on West End Avenue.

"Richard's not sold on the social graces," Tina quickly said to her stunned parents and simultaneously reached over to rub her boyfriend's shoulder, trying to take the sting out of her words. "But he's a big fan of honesty, so you guys have that in common."

Bob took a deep breath. Tina recognized his ostentatious effort at self-control. "So, what else are you a fan of, Rich?"

"It's Richard."

"Gevalt," Bob muttered. Then, "What else are you a fan of, Richard? Besides my daughter, I mean."

Tina glanced quickly at Richard, who offered a tight smile. "Lots of things. The writings of Paolo Friere, Frederick Engels, Buckminster Fuller..."

"I was thinking more along the lines of Yankees versus Mets, but okay," Bob trailed off.

Richard looked upward, rifling through his mental index cards. "Oh, and vanilla ice cream, The Whole Earth Catalogue, and motorcycles."

"That's the complete list?" Joan asked drily. "If there's more, we can wait. I wouldn't want to miss anything."

"That's it for now." He popped a slice of cheddar into his mouth, then ruffled Tina's hair with his cheesy hand. "Oh, and yes, your daughter, of course. She's great."

Tina looked at him with gratitude. He was a bit of an oaf, Richard, but fundamentally good-hearted, and so smart. And he wasn't just a talker, either, she told her mother the next morning when the two of them tiptoed past Richard, who lay gently snoring on the couch, and into the kitchen. He acted on his convictions.

"So, speaking of acting, what is 'organic agricultural theatre?' " Joan asked. "I didn't know you were even interested in drama, except to watch it."

Tina felt herself blush. "I have no idea. To be honest, I think the founders of the commune were just looking for an acronym, because as far as I know, they don't put on plays."

After about a year, she knew for sure that the only drama in the OATS collective lay in the occasional spats that broke out between the twelve members about where to sell their surplus produce besides the farm stand, what to charge for it, and whether they should hire the kid down the road to kill the occasional chicken for them, or if it was simply unethical to eat what they couldn't bring themselves to kill with their own hands.

When the government started drafting men whose number was 100, Richard decided it was time to go to Canada. And once again, bored and dissatisfied with the gap between the mundane reality of her life and what she'd envisioned, Tina didn't hesitate to go with him. Montreal was a cosmopolitan city, with museums and galleries to feed her soul, and an expatriate network of draft evaders to provide them with an immediate community.

Of course, her parents hadn't seen in it that way. On every visit home she could count on an argument about the choices she'd made. Joan tried to give her the benefit of the doubt and, after one wrenching blow-out between Tina and Bob, had mustered the grace to say, "I get that there's more to your relationship with Richard than meets our eyes."

At the time — what time was it? — Tina had hoped her mother was right. But even back then, she now realized, she knew otherwise.

God, how I dug my heels in, she thought. My only expectation of myself was to defy other people's expectations of me. Way to go, Gabler.

The next night, needing a break from her attempts to make a satisfactory sketch of herself, Tina reached for the photo albums she'd brought along with the shoebox of pictures. If she was going to draw a self-portrait, it wasn't going to be by studying her face in a mirror.

The smaller of the two, now balding as its black fabric cover shredded and thinned, held photos of her life after leaving her parents' home. On the first page was a black-and-white photo, clearly developed and printed in someone's amateur darkroom. She stood in front of a Greyhound bus, hands on hips, looking more defiant than she remembered ever feeling. She wore sandals, bell-bottom jeans, a white peasant blouse — God, she'd loved that blouse with its blue embroidery around the neck and puffy half-length sleeves—and an Army jacket adorned with anti-war buttons. *Give Peace a Chance. Free the Chicago Eight! Make Love, Not War. Out Now!!*

Of course the picture was undated. When you're young, she realized, it doesn't occur to you that you won't remember everything. But she was pretty sure it had been taken sometime in the fall of 1969, while she was still living in San Francisco, on the way home from a weekend trip to Los Angeles. She could no longer recall why she went or who she stayed with. But she remembered these clothes, these buttons, because when she made her way to the back of the bus looking for an empty seat, she walked past rows and rows of soldiers on their way to the Oakland Army Base. They had the shining complexions and half-childlike faces of the boys she'd left behind after high school only a few years earlier. They had had loud voices, some of them, and pimples and peach fuzz clouding their upper lips. A few bayed more than laughed. Their temples and necks were painfully bare where the automatic razor had shorn them. Such tender skin, she thought.

She remembered their vulnerability and was now shocked by her own ... what? Her own casual appropriation of their jackets as a backdrop for her sloganeering.

But as she leafed through the album's pages, it seemed to her that she was perpetually costumed. There was another shot from the San Francisco years—this one in color—of herself and five other people seated cross-legged on the ground. One of them she recognized—it was one of her roommates in the Haight. John? The house painter, whatever his name was. The others were unfamiliar; she'd probably just met them, wherever this was. But in this photo, she was wearing a beaded cuff around her forehead and an elaborate necklace made from leather and bone-colored beads. Her skirt was long and adorned with vertical ribbons. All she needed was an eagle feather in her hair for the Indian Souvenir Store fashion statement to be complete.

The progression of acquired personas continued: Tina in overalls, on her knees digging potatoes at the commune in Vermont, grinning up at the camera with the affect of a TV hillbilly drunk on moonshine; Tina in a mini-shirtdress, shiny patent-leather heels, and enormous leather shoulder bag, trying to look respectable and almost succeeding, on her way into the Office of Immigration in Montreal to lobby for the rights of draft-evaders; Tina with Richard's arm around her outside their three-story walk-up on Durocher, both of them in Navy pea coats, their faces pinched and grim in the cold beneath their green, red, yellow, and blue striped Hudson's Bay blanket-woolen watch caps.

The older she got, the fewer pictures there were, and the less they told her about how she felt when they were taken. Her hairstyles—the 1980s poofiness, the '90s simplicity, the severity of the early 2000s— signaled more about the era than about herself. And her clothes settled into a certain uniformity. If it weren't for the changing cast of people whose arms encircled her shoulder—Eric, her then-new friend Marnie, Richard, Kris, and just one of Carl when they got off the boat in British Columbia—she would have had no way to place herself in time, let alone in emotional space. This woman on the page was as inscrutable as her adult clothing.

She reached for the older, more fragile photo album, its cacophonous Jackson Pollack-inspired cover now faded and muddy.

The first page held a large picture of her parents taken at their 25th wedding anniversary party. How strange it had been to sneak into their apartment earlier that day to prepare the surprise. She'd been gone for long enough to see her childhood home as if it was someone else's. And it was. It was her parents' home, remarkably unchanged through the years. But now there were shiny patches on the couch cushions where the nub had worn away. Her bedroom, she realized, was tiny, and Bob and Joan's, dominated by an ornate oak dresser that Joan's father had made them as a wedding gift, wasn't much bigger. Their stove lacked the gleaming right angles of her stove; their porcelain sink and counter, noticed for the first time, were a single, molded cast, its porcelain coating starting to chip. Unlike her charmless but functional Montreal kitchen, built less than a decade ago, everything in her parents' kitchen was rounded.

Sitting now on the edge of her gleaming sleigh bed in this dark and silent house, the snow-reflected moonlight slanting through her window like a razor blade, she studied a photo taken that night. A skittering tom-tom, a wailing clarinet, a roomful of flushed and tipsy people, each moving uniquely, all moving together, individual but coalesced. And in the middle of it, beaming, gleaming with sweat, right hands clasped, right feet planted, left arms flung out to the side, her parents formed a joyful chain, linked and unbreakable. Those bodies, one doughy, one taut; those faces, hilarious and keen, were more familiar than her own.

April, 1975, New York City

Her Aunt Carol and Uncle Barry took Bob and Joan out for dinner that night, allowing Tina time to ready the apartment and assemble the guests—then insisted that they accompany her parents up to their apartment so that they could give them their anniversary present within their own four walls. Bob was yawning loudly when he unlocked the door to 4F, and his mouth was still open as he flicked on the lights and was barraged by cries of "Surprise!"

The hall and living room were packed with people—their neighbors, her father's friend Charlie and his wife, Judy, Roger and Eddie and Sally from Bob's office, some of Joan's sorority sisters and lifelong friends, and, at the head of the pack, wearing a ridiculous conical party hat, Tina.

"Happy anniversary, Daddy."

"I don't believe it!" he said as she released him to hug Joan. "I can't believe—how did you get here? When did you get here?"

"By bus, last night."

"From Montreal?"

"It's not exactly Mars, Dad. They have honest-to-God Greyhounds that go from Montreal to New York."

"She stayed with us!" her Aunt Carol announced, triumphant that the surprise had come off so flawlessly. She began recounting the details of their party conspiracy. "Tina and I hatched this plan a couple of months ago—"

"I wish I could take credit, but really, it was all Aunt Carol's idea," Tina interrupted.

"It was a joint effort. I arranged for the catering—"

"There are piggies-in-blankets, Dad! And egg creams!"

"—and then Tina went out and got the decorations today. Then while we were out to dinner—"

"I was casing the joint," Tina burbled to her parents. "I sat at the counter at West Side Diner across the street until I saw you guys leave, and then I swooped in with supplies and mementos." She pointed to an array of dollhouse furniture carefully arranged on the coffee table in the packed living room. "I spent the day on Canal Street and came back with this stuff. It's your life history in miniature."

Sitting atop the bamboo placemat with the watercolor of a giant wave was a miniature television set to symbolize Bob's job. Facing it was a tiny, immaculately embroidered couch. At one end it held a little wedding cake man sitting stiffly in his tails, knees bent at a perfect ninety-degree angle, and a bride, her veiled plastic head lying on the other end of the couch, her legs outstretched, with her white stilettoed feet resting in the groom's lap.

Tina led her parents to their crowded bookshelf, pointing out an armchair and another tiny couch, this one holding a priest lying with his arms folded on his chest. "It's your office, Mom," she said, "with your shrink couch." Then, before her mother could protest, "I know, I know, you're not a Freudian Analyst, thankyouverymuch."

Joan stood, her hand over her mouth, in delighted amazement. "A priest?"

Tina laughed. "Yeah, that's great, eh? All they had were grooms, brides, and priests. If they'd had a rabbi, I would have made him your patient. But I'm happy with the priest. I think the idea of Father Francis lying there telling you his dreams is rich with possibilities."

She put a hand on each parent's shoulder and steered them toward the kitchen. "In here is the final diorama, the piece de resistance."

"Ray-zee-STANS!" Bob and Joan shouted happily in the faux French accents they normally used only with each other, more delighted still to realize that they'd done it in unison.

Atop the small pine table, its leaf down ever since Tina had moved out, was an intricate tableau. A miniature stove, countertop, and refrigerator—all made of pastel plastic—sat at right angles to each other. Atop one burner of the stove was a brown skillet holding a yellow plastic omelet that looked to Bob like a shrink-wrapped life jacket. A Barbie doll in a stewardess suit towered over the counter, a tiny knife protruding from one hand, her forearm raised in mid-chop over a plastic carrot on a petite cutting board. Ken stood next to Barbie, holding a telephone receiver at the end of one unnaturally bent arm.

"Welcome to Joanie's Dream House. This is where your domestic life plays out," Tina announced. "And yes, I know the stewardess outfit is a little weird, but the clothing selection was very limited. My alternatives were to have you dicing vegetables in a bridal gown, a bikini, or in the nude."

"I appreciate your choice," Joan said.

Bob stood, a glass of champagne in one hand, drinking in the sight of his wife and daughter. "I am a lucky, lucky man," he said, kissing Tina on her forehead, then briefly holding Joan's cheeks between his palms.

"There you are," Charlie bellowed as he entered the kitchen. "Get your asses back into the living room! We have songs to sing and toasts to make!"

Joan sighed theatrically. "Dear God, please make it end quickly," she muttered to Tina.

Charlie thumped the bookcase several times, making A through M/N of the World Book Encyclopedias jump up from their perch. "May I have your attention please," he shouted to the noisy room. "I'd like to make a toast to the lovely couple." He ostentatiously pulled a creased sheet of paper from his breast pocket. "Because this marriage represents the union of classy—" he bowed to Joan—"and, shall we say, earthy"—he jabbed a thumb in Bob's direction—"I thought, what better way to honor the anniversary couple than with a poem, or rather, a poym. Specifically, with the highest form of poetry, a limerick."

Bob laughed and Joan, encircled in his arm, hid her face in her hand.

Charlie loudly cleared his throat. "I begin. There once was a man from Nantucket—"

The room groaned. "Careful, buddy, there are ladies here," Barry shouted.

"There once was a man from Nantucket," Charlie repeated, "with a heart string so long you could pluck it." He smiled broadly and a few people broke into relieved applause. "Wise Joan saw his need; The two did the deed; And this pair has become a great fit."

The crowd broke into raucous applause as Charlie gave a deep, flourishing bow.

Tina stepped up beside him and silenced the room. "I lack Charlie's literary talent," she declared. "But I do know a bit about yin and yang."

"The Siamese Twins?" Eddie shouted drunkenly.

"No, the unity of opposites," Tina answered. "You know, fire and ice. Bob's always hot, Joan's always cold. Bob likes milk with his chocolate; Joan likes Seltzer with her lime. Bob thinks Groucho, Harpo, and Chico are the consummate comics; Joan confuses them with Moe, Larry, and Curly. Bob likes chopped liver, Joan pate. Bob roots for the Yankees, Joan for the Bolshoi. Bob thinks that engineers will save the world; Joan doesn't believe anyone will. But as an insider, I can tell you that they are the perfect pair. Fire and ice, sun and rain, peanut butter and jelly, brisket and horseradish. They are the best parents anyone could hope for, and my role model for what a marriage should be." She held up her glass. "To Bob and Joan, Mom and Dad."

"To Bob and Joan," everyone in the room roared.

Someone—the guy from 4C?—handed her father a bottle of champagne. He peeled back its metal seal and began twisting the cork. Suddenly it gave, rocketing out of the bottle, out of his hand, and into a brandy snifter someone had left on the bookshelf. But Joan—strong, unflappable Joan—was unfazed by the shattering glass.

Someone put "Sing Sing Sing" on the record player, and her father grabbed her mother's hand. "You lead," he yelled into Joan's ear, and she did, calling out jitterbug instructions to him. *Step, back, step back, step back*, her crimson lips mouthed. *Left, right.* Soon, practically the whole room was dancing—Barry on unbendable legs, like

Frankenstein's monster; Roger surprisingly smooth with Sally attached to his right hand; Eddie madly swinging Tina away, then towards him, then down in a floor-grazing dip.

The next morning, Tina was the first one up. Still wearing the knee-length camouflage tee shirt she used as a nightgown and ludicrously fluffy pink slippers, she padded into the kitchen. She scraped the remains of cake and knishes and baked brie from the plates on every kitchen surface, filled the sink with hot, sudsy water, and started to wash them.

"I'll dry."

She startled, then turned to see her father. His hair, dry in the overheated apartment and diaphanous in the thin morning light, shot up like flares around his pudgy face.

"It's a deal," she said.

They worked together in a companionable silence. When the dishes were dried and put away, Bob scrubbed the table with a sponge, then pulled out a loaf of rye from the bread box.

"I don't suppose you have any yogurt," Tina said.

"You don't suppose right. But we just might have some cottage cheese. Will that do?"

"Yeah, that would be great."

Bob took a container out of the refrigerator and scooped some into a bowl for Tina, while she put two slices of bread into the toaster oven for Bob. She poured two cups of coffee, he topped each with cream, and then the two of them sat down.

After a loud, lip-smacking slurp of coffee, Bob asked, "How's Richard the Red?"

"You can really stop calling him that, Dad," Tina sighed. "He's a draft evader, not a Communist."

"I wouldn't mind if he was a Communist," Bob retorted. "I just mind that he's got you chasing after him to a new country, waitressing yet again when you should be in college, and squandering your potential."

Tina rolled her eyes. "I'm a self-directed learner, Dad. Don't you remember telling Mrs. Spasky that when I was in second grade and spacing out at school? You were right then, and it's still true. I don't need to be in college to learn. Life is teaching me a lot."

"What?" Bob asked, not looking up as he vigorously applied butter to his toast, then spread raspberry jam on top of it. "What is life teaching you?"

"How to get to know new people, learn a new language," she sputtered. "It's teaching me that I can be strong and self-supporting and of use to others."

"How are you helping others?" He took a big, deliberate bite of toast.

"I'm volunteering at the Resettlement Center for other guys like Richard who are fleeing the draft."

"How about Richard? Is he being strong and self-supporting and of use to others? Is he pulling his weight?"

Tina pushed back her chair, stood, and opened the cabinet over the sink. "Where are the napkins?" she demanded. "They used to be up here."

Bob pointed to a door under the sink. "You were saying?"

"He's applying to graduate school in Political Science and writing a handbook for draft resisters," she said, rushing to protect her boyfriend from her father's judgment. "That's his real work right now, and it's important work."

"And unpaid work," Bob answered flatly.

Tina sighed heavily and poured them both more coffee, then sank back into the chair opposite Bob. "We had such a great time last night, Dad. Can we not ... can we just ..."

"I'm not trying to start an argument," Bob said with sudden urgency. He dropped the toast onto his plate and leaned towards her. "I'm just trying to get you to take a look at yourself, to value yourself. You should be finding your own strengths, following your own path, not chasing some guy to Canada and supporting him while he sits there with his thumb up his ass, feeling virtuous."

"Dad!"

"Oh, come on!" Bob smacked the table. "Don't tell me you're shocked by my language."

"Not by your language, by your attitude! You know the war is wrong. You've opposed it for as long as I have! So why are you trashing Richard for not wanting to fight in it?"

"Oh sweetie, sweetie, listen to me," he implored. "This isn't about Richard. I don't give a damn what he does. It's about you. First you're living in a commune in San Francisco, donating your paltry income to the collective, but you leave that when it gets too druggy. Then you go to a commune in Vermont, but you leave that when you discover just how goddamn boring farming really is. Now you're living in a commune in Canada, waiting tables and harboring draft dodgers. Is that really what you want for yourself — to be serving others at the cost of your own ..."

"My own what? My own advancement? My own ego? What?!"

"Your own development. And yes, your own advancement. What's wrong with that?" Bob's eyes darted frantically around the kitchen, as if expecting Joan to charge in to rescue him.

"This is my own development! Jesus, Dad, I don't have to be the star of my own life!"

Bob stared at her, stunned. "What happened to you? We tried to raise you to have your own mind and follow your own passions. Why are you so self-effacing?"

Those words hurt to the quick, confirming as they did her own worst fears about herself. But of course they did. He'd raised her, imbued her with his own views, exactly the outlook that she was trying so hard to break away from. "That's not how I feel, Dad. I'm not diminished by casting my lot with others. I'm just ... I don't know ... connected." She studied his face. Her father looked more hurt than angry, and Tina crumbled inside.

"It's a good thing," she said gently.

"What's a good thing?" Joan appeared at the entrance to the kitchen, her black hair brushed and glossy, her eyes clear but narrowed, her voice too alert.

"My life in Montreal." "Her lack of ambition."

Joan glared at Bob. Then she turned pointedly towards Tina. "Are you happy, dear?" she asked.

"Mostly."

Joan raised an eyebrow.

"I mean, I love Montreal and the friends and colleagues I've found there. And Richard—well, he's brilliant and witty and ..."

"And?"

"And difficult." Tina took a breath, reanimated, and addressed herself to Bob. "I never said he wasn't difficult. He's self-righteous and self-involved, okay?"

Bob nodded graciously, recognizing Tina's concession, her unspoken *Are you happy now?*

Tina started sketching on her napkin. Looking down as she drew, she said, "I don't know if this relationship is going to last forever. But even if it doesn't, I don't feel—I won't feel like I've made a terrible mistake or like I'm wasting my time doing what I'm doing."

"You feel proud of your work," Joan quietly stated.

Tina, still drawing, didn't look up. "I don't know, not proud exactly, but satisfied."

"You feel fulfilled," her mother restated.

"Honestly, Mom, I'm not a patient. You don't have to echo back everything I'm saying." Her exasperation was now directed at Joan.

"Your mother's just trying to make sure she understands what you're saying," Bob said gallantly.

"I don't need you to translate for my mother, Dad! We're all speaking English here."

Joan looked wounded. "Your father's just trying to de-escalate things. I, for one, think that's a good idea."

Tina sighed, tossed her pencil aside, and tamped down the suddenly heated air with two level palms. "You're right," she said with forced calm. "That is a good idea. I'm only here until this evening, and I don't want to spend our time together fighting."

"If we did, I'd put my money on you," Bob said with forced jocularity.

Tina and Joan both cast him weary glances. "So let me just reassure you guys that I'm fine, I'm happy, I'm healthy, and I'm not wasting my life. It's true that I don't have a career all mapped out for myself and I'm not likely to get married any time soon. But I'm fed and housed and fulfilled." She picked up her pencil and resumed sketching. "I'm doing work that matters — maybe not serving up Greek omelets to the beat cops —" She smiled ruefully down at the table. "But *some* work that matters."

"So, what I hear you saying," Bob said, gently mocking his wife and earning a faint, desperately needed smile from his daughter, "What I hear you saying is that you don't want to move back to New York and go to law school."

Tina grinned broadly.

"You don't even want to audition to be the best, most politically committed weather girl on public television, is that what I'm hearing?"

Now Tina laughed outright.

"Weather woman, Bob," Joan corrected.

She is one tough cookie, my mother, Tina thought for the millionth time. If they'd hurt her feelings, she wasn't going to let it show.

Still, when Bob left the kitchen to take a shower, Tina enfolded her mother — so tiny, she realized with a start — in a hug. "Sorry if we ganged up on you there," she murmured into her hair.

Joan pulled back and shrugged. "Sometimes that's the only way to resolve a conflict," she answered, then after a pause, "But thank you. And listen, I get that there's more to your relationship with Richard than meets our eyes."

Tina had hoped her mother was right. But even then, she now realized, she knew otherwise.

Many years later, as she sorted through her dead parents' belongings, Tina found her napkin drawing from that day. On it, in pebbly but bold strokes, Tina had sketched two moose, antlers locked. The smaller of the two had a floral skirt ludicrously wrapped around its midsection and rear legs. The larger one was unadorned. But perched in front of its wideset, mournful eyes was a pair of reading glasses shaped just like Bob's.

• • •

Now Tina turned the page in her photo album to see, faded under the brittle plastic sheet, a picture of her father and herself at the kitchen table, a set of arithmetic rods spread out in front of them. The gleaming wooden blocks of different lengths were intended to help kids understand fractions and division. Ten blue rods laid end to end were the same length as one red one; two greens also equaled a red. Tina had grasped the concepts quickly, and Sunday evening math time with Bob quickly became Sunday evening building time, as the two of them erected houses with horizontally stacked rods and skylines with vertically arrayed ones. The camera had caught Tina with her arm outstretched, reaching for a distant one. Bob, his head lowered to be parallel with hers, had his face tipped towards her. The crows' feet radiating out from his left eye and the corner of his smiling mouth almost brought her to tears. Had she ever received that kind of delighted attention since?

Slowly advancing the stiff, sticky pages, she saw pictures of her young self with Joan—outside their building, hamming it up in front of the monkey cage at the zoo, making flour-coated hand prints on each other's cheeks. There were a few of Tina alone, one sitting on a merry-go-round horse and clinging to the attached pole for dear life, one standing glumly at the entrance to Leonard's Function Hall on Long Island wearing patent-leather Mary Janes, a floral dress, and, beneath it, a crinoline slip that flared the dress's hemline and made her so itchy that she was ready to jump into the ornate Peeing Boy fountain in the lobby.

And then abruptly, color photographs starting when Tina was in high school. In these her hair was long and straightened, her clothes were flowing and made from Indian cotton prints, and she and the occasional friend or cousin invariably looked serious, self-conscious, and unbelievably skinny as they leaned over the record player or sat cross-legged in a circle on some grassy slope in Central Park.

These photographs—they were moments turned into monuments. Tina could still remember, almost even inhabit the general time frame in which they were taken. Yes, I loved the zoo, she thought, yes, I remember that it was fun to build stuff with my math rods. But did she remember the specific instances in which the camera's shutter was opened? No. These snapshots were Bob and Joan's chronicle of her life, taken to remind their future selves of how they felt on that day, capturing their child before she changed yet again. And flipping back to the front of the album, looking again at her wildly dancing parents, Tina realized that she knew even then that this was how she would want to remember them.

Not that she chose to paper over the blemishes in their relationship—Bob's worshipful acceptance of Joan's sense of entitlement as the cost of her sophistication, Joan's circumvention, even manipulation, as a substitute for open conflict. But at least they'd really seen each other. Their love was informed, their commitment unwavering. They both knew how to bend and meld and diverge, how to be in multiple places at once, like those dancing quantum particles Carl would describe to her in bedtime stories.

Bob made it his life's work to be a cog in larger living machines— his Army battalion, his marriage, his television productions, even his poker club. And yet he'd been so frustrated with her for failing to shine brightly enough, for her unwillingness to be the star around which others orbited. If only he'd lived long enough to recognize himself— his best self—in her.

It seemed to her that they had repeated this same argument on almost every subsequent visit up until her father died six years after that party. And more astonishingly, though he was long gone, she was still having the argument with herself.

No more. This had gone on long enough.

March 2012

Feeble, failing, sleepless by night and groggy by day, Peter rarely woke before noon now, and Tina had taken to going to the gym in town for a swim most mornings. She walked down the still-icy path to the driveway and into her Corolla. Traffic permitting, she might actually get there in time to nab an empty lane in the pool.

On the news they were talking about heart attacks. As she drove down Oxford, left on Garfield, right on Strathcona, left on Linnean, right on Mt. Pleasant, past the Tim Horton's — *no, no Tim Bits for you* — past the hospital, checking for bicyclists riding up into her blind spot at the corner of Lowell, she heard how crucial it was to get fast action. Some aspirin or stronger blood thinner, promptly administered, could minimize the risk of any serious damage to the heart. But wait too long, and — damn, the left arrow at the corner of Auburn Street turned red. As usual. There was no oncoming traffic. Make the turn anyhow? Why did she ask herself that every day? She should set a policy. She should be like that physicist who just decided one day that he would only ever have chocolate pudding for dessert, just to save himself the five seconds it would take to consider other options. Chocolate pudding or nothing. Done.

She waited — there could be a cop lurking nearby — staring at the empty lanes stretching out in front of her. Despite the fact that more men had heart attacks, they tended to be more lethal in women. Apparently, women didn't necessarily have the searing pain in their chest or left arm; they might just feel nauseated, or breathless, or think they had a toothache.

A big black SUV approached. Was there such a thing as a land shark, a monstrous, malevolent vehicle that dwarfed ordinary cars and sent them scurrying? It veered into her lane as it prepared to turn right—the usual wide-angled turn that these road hogs—that's it, hogs—always seemed to take. A thin woman in a polka-dotted hijab, holding the hand of a small, restless child, waited patiently at the curb for the fat-assed Esplanade or Explorer or Odyssey or whatever the hell it was to maneuver itself onto Auburn. This wasn't the immigrant part of town. Were they going to the private school, Shady something, down the street? Wasn't it a Waldorf school? Would a woman in a hijab be okay with her daughter getting a hippie Waldorf education? Was this a racist stereotype, or an honest question?

And of course, the red arrow had once again turned green, and here she still sat, waiting for the SUV to complete its lumbering turn.

If time was of the essence in treating heart attacks, should people over a certain age ever lock their doors? How would the EMTs get into the house if your door was locked? What if you were at an observatory at the top of a mountain in the Canary Islands? What if the medics' frantic doorbell rings at the door to your mansion sounded like braying donkeys or laughing babies?

And here she was—having arrived with little consciousness of getting there—but unmistakably pulling up at the handsomely renovated old school building that now housed a coffee shop, some sort of crystals-and-aromatic-oils place, a warren of lawyer and therapist offices, and a gym.

Parking, parking. If it was this hard to find a space in the parking lot, dappled with wind-blown fast-food bags and the odd patch of muddy snow, what were the odds of her finding a swimming lane? Bleak.

A quick look through the window into the pool confirmed that this was probably a wasted trip, or at least a case of deferred gratification. Frantic but logy at the same time, she bought herself a cup of lukewarm coffee at the snack bar, sank into one of the cracked yellow-vinyl chairs, and pulled out her phone.

A month or two after Jean-Pierre had introduced her to The Traveler (now followed by more than a million people), Tina had stumbled across footage taken in some Arctic locale. She could see nothing but a flat, blazingly bright vista of snowy tundra and ferociously blue sky, occasionally fogged by The Traveler's steamy breath. The silence, broken only by the sound of feet crunching on icy ground and the occasional flare of wind buffeting the camera, was astonishing. It seemed to have hushed even the chattiest of her devoted followers, with only the occasional *Wow* or *Brr* floating up over the landscape.

Since then, The Traveler had guided their gazes in duller locales with far more muted palettes—a snow plow rumbling down a dark residential street, a gray squirrel skittering up a brown phone pole, then dashing across a power line like a demented Wallenda, ocean waves against a granite sky pummeling a rocky shoreline.

But today the scene on Tina's screen had different hues. It looked like Mars, dotted with orange hoodoos jutting skyward amid wisps of reddish dust. The Traveler approached a narrow path—maybe a dry riverbed?—cutting into what appeared to have once been a mountain. As she followed the narrow trail, the sun's rays seemed to slice through the porous rock, lighting up the multi-colored stipples of canyon wall from within.

American Southwest? Tina typed, having long since surrendered her observer status for that of active participant in this endless, unresolved guessing game. *Canyon de Chelly*, another follower suggested. *Drumheller!* insisted someone else. *Badlands and fossils. I know it well.*

A small cluster of houses appeared as the Traveler left the canyon and emerged onto a flat mesa. They seemed to be arrayed in a large, loose circle. She seemed to pick up her pace as she approached the settlement, and Tina could hear The Traveler's breathing become a bit more ragged. She walked right up to a mud-colored stucco house and stopped. The camera gazed into a tall, narrow, vinyl-framed window and inside the dim room that lay on the other side, Tina could see silhouettes of a straight-backed chair, a twin bed with a half-moon-shaped wrought-iron headboard, and what seemed to be a framed rectangular picture on the wall. The camera stayed fixed on this motif for a moment, zooming in and out as if struggling to find the right depth of field, the distance that would clarify what lay within.

But the dominant image on Tina's phone screen was not the room's interior, but the reflection of The Traveler in the window — a hand with elegant fingernails holding the phone, half of a woman's broad face behind it, an ornate earring, silvery and feathered, dangling from her one visible ear. Tina heard a gasp as The Traveler seemed to realize that she was being seen. She dropped her hand, the exterior wall blurring by before the camera focused on the pebbles on the ground. Then, regaining control of the image, The Traveler stepped back, focused the camera once more on the backside of this house, which had, Tina now noticed, a thick red stripe painted below the window and running the full width of the building. She stepped back again, panning the village in one long, medium shot. Then, before more guesses as to location could come streaming in, the screen went to black. Today's broadcast was over.

Tina dragged the tiny video controller back to the beginning and watched it again. She strained to concentrate against the ambient noise in the gym — squeaking sneakers on the basketball court, the loud white noise of the espresso machine at the lobby snack bar, a woman in a chair next to her on the phone correcting someone on the other end with exaggerated patience, saying "No, not the brown shoes, the tan ones."

There was something familiar in this house, this strangely shaped window, and the red band belting the muddy stucco, lending a handsomeness to this scrubby scene. She'd seen it before, and as she reluctantly clambered onto the elliptical trainer, she tried to remember where. *Think, 2, 3, 4, Think 2, 3, 4.* When she first started working out decades before, she'd found that little improvised mantras helped her get into a groove and stay there. But these days, jangled and anxious, she found it impossible to stick with any mental activity, let alone her own thoughts, for more than a few minutes at a time. That's why she so needed to swim, she realized. She couldn't check her phone in the pool.

She knew she was out of sorts, to put it charitably, and she knew why, despite having asked the voice assistant on her phone that very morning, "Hey, Siri, what the hell is going on with me?"

"I'm sorry. I don't know how to help you with that," the unfailingly courteous machine had answered, "but I'm working on it."

"Yeah, keep working on it," she'd muttered, but Siri had gone back to sleep and blessedly didn't respond.

Tina was stranded in rural Ontario (okay, rural-ish, she corrected herself), trying to realize the dream of a dying man who was more irascible and less coherent by the day. Though he wasn't her father, he could have been. He was the right age, and had her own father's familiar meld of passion, wit, and moral superiority. She admired Peter, she cared about him despite his subjective and intractable vision of her—of who she could and should be—just like Bob had. Though she was now older than Bob had been when he died, she still resented being cast in her father's, or father figure's, drama. Just like any daughter, she thought.

Daughter. That was it. She'd seen that striped stucco house, that window, in the picture of Sandy that Peter had angrily proffered a few months earlier. Without breaking stride, she jabbed her phone screen and went back to The Traveler's video one more time. The image of that reflected face in the window was too diffuse to be recognizable, but what few features she could make out seemed to fit. Sandy was Cree, and this woman looked aboriginal. Sandy would be in her early fifties, and The Traveler had the broad and settled-bordering-on-sagging face of a post-menopausal woman.

Come on, Tina chastised herself, talk about an over-active imagination. What are the odds that it's the same house? That the stripe would have endured for all these years?

But her own skepticism didn't stop her from searching on *Cree reservations Alberta* and *Cree architecture Canada* and *stucco and red stripe* when she got home. Her queries retrieved maps and government documents, sepia-toned photos of Indians from the late nineteenth century, signage of Administration and Management offices—crisp ranch-style structures that resembled highway service centers—

dazzling images of hoop dancers, and dripping cold cans of Jamaican beer. But no pictures of this house. It was not typical.

"Hey, Siri," she quietly demanded behind her bedroom door, "Find Sandy Bright."

"There are eighty-plus profiles of Sandy Bright on LinkedIn," the machine responded after a brief pause. "Would you like to hear them?"

"No," Tina sighed. "Find Sandy Bright Ontario."

"Would you like to know about Sandy Beach, Lake Ontario?" Tina thought Siri sounded a bit exasperated, kind of like that woman next to her at the gym.

"No," she snapped. "Find Sandy Bright Alberta."

"Would you like to know about Sandy Beach, Onion Lake, Alberta?"

"No. I surrender."

"I'm sorry but I didn't understand."

"Hey, Siri, stop." That, it understood.

Tina turned on her computer and desultorily started pecking through the eighty-something Sandy Brights on LinkedIn. It was amazing how many Realtors and CPAs and retail professionals there were named Sandy. And so many of them—a disproportionate number, she thought—lived in Alabama. But most were just names, with Canada or United States as their homes, no bios and no pictures. Had a single Sandy Bright just kept recreating the outlines of her profile over and over again, at a loss for how to actually fill it in?

Did she actually want to think about that for one more second?

Tina stood up, stiff from her activity and then inactivity, sore from the weather, bored with her new, anxious, obsessive self, and decided to get to work. She went to the study and opened the file she and Peter had been working on yesterday. Cindy Sherman, the New Jersey-born photographer who was Tina's age, was the subject of what would be the book's penultimate chapter … if she and Peter could muster and maintain enough interest in her.

"Conceptual art, my ass," Peter had muttered as he leafed through a series of black-and-white self-portraits of Sherman, dressed up like the real and imagined heroines—the waitresses and salesgirls and mistresses—who populated the film-noir movies from the mid-twentieth century. "She's an actress playing actresses in imaginary films, and using a documentary medium to do it. Just shoot me now."

They're art, Tina thought, not photojournalism, and while Sherman's work didn't particularly excite her, she liked the fact that the women in these stills rarely looked at the camera. They were looking away, towards some action or promise of one that always lay outside the frame. That felt true.

But Peter, who even a few months earlier would have relished this kind of debate, now had no patience or stamina for it. Dissent made him querulous, and that in turn made her feel ashamed.

She picked up the phone lying mute on the desk, went back to The Traveler's Twitter stream one more time, and sent her a direct message: *Are you Sandy Bright?*

• • •

When her phone dinged at midnight—sadly, not awakening her, just alarming her—she assumed it was Carl, up uncharacteristically early.

Who are you? The message was from The Traveler, whose profile picture showed only the darkened outline of an unreadable face.

My name is Tina. No need to offer a last name, which was absent from her social media handle of T_Futzer, the exasperated nickname that Bob had assigned her as a child for her fascination with small tasks and her chronic tardiness. She paused. *I work for a man called Peter Bright.*

And?

I am trying to locate his daughter Sandy.

Why?

How much should she reveal? Peter still guarded his privacy, even though he was no longer a household name, and this person could be anyone. *Are you Sandy Bright?*

Why do you care?

I have news to share with his daughter.

Why do YOU care, Tina?

Because I care about Peter.

179

There was a pause. Should she have been more explicit about her motives? Just told her that Peter was dying?

Good for you.

Now what the hell was she supposed to do with that juvenile response? *Are you Peter's daughter?*

I am the daughter of Kimi LaFountain and Russell DesJardins.

Were you adopted by Peter and Grace?

I was taken by Peter and Grace.

Whoa. Now what? Don't challenge her, Tina thought. Keep her talking. *That was a long time ago.*

History isn't a snapshot. Tina watched the small screen. Nothing. Then three bouncing dots, indicating that Sandy had resumed typing. *It doesn't stop.*

That's true, Tina wrote after some hesitation. *We can't change the past, but we can the present.* Jesus, she was sounding like some sort of Hallmark card. No, like the Magic Eightball that she and her neighbor Marcie interrogated in fourth grade when they wanted to know if Michael Miller down the hall liked Marcie or whether Tina would get her own Princess phone for her birthday. She wouldn't blame Sandy if she responded with "Duh."

But she didn't. *Peter has nothing to do with my present. I intend to keep it that way.*

Why? Stupid question. That was impossible to answer in a text message. *Can we talk? I would love to hear your story – from you.*

No need. Sandy's response was immediate. *Ehachimisochik.*

Tina waited for Sandy to correct that last nonsense word, but when the screen stayed silent, she typed *????*

No response. *Are you there?* Tina asked, willing the words on the screen not to look too desperate.

She wasn't.

Tina plugged in the phone to charge it and burrowed under her blanket, but sleep was more elusive than ever. She got back up, pulled on a pair of sagging black sweatpants under her oversized t-shirt (*Sleep Natural!* it exhorted), and opened her computer. Carl would be finishing his shift at the observatory around now and making his way back to his austere-looking room in the astronomers' quarters. Above his Skype handle, Dr. DarkMatter, was a goofy photo of him in a Vancouver Canucks hat and a ratty scarf printed with Van Gogh's "Starry Night." She gazed at it, both wistful and warmed, but her call to him went unanswered.

She closed Skype and typed Sandy's last message — *Ehachimisochik* — into Google. For the first time in her experience, only one search result was returned, from an online Cree dictionary.

"ehachimisochik VP 1. They tell a story about themselves. 2. They do penance (in most religions). (MD); e ikatehtahiht VP He is brought somewhere else. (MD)

She had no idea of what the VPs or MDs meant, and still didn't know how to pronounce the word. But she was intrigued by three such seemingly unrelated definitions.

This time she searched for *Ehachimisochik Sandy Bright*.

"Did you mean *Ehachimisochik **Sunday** Bright*?" Google queried.

"I'll probably get the weekend weather forecast," Tina was startled to hear herself say aloud as she clicked on the link.

Centered in a reddish-gold banner at the top of the page were characters unlike any Tina had ever seen: ∇"◁ΓΓ ⁄ᒋ` .

Below them was written: ehachimisochik

We tell stories about ourselves

A woman in her 50s, her hair pulled tightly back into a bun, stared out from the screen. Her plain face was dwarfed by two large silver butterfly earrings; they looked as if they'd been caught by a flashbulb as they flitted from her earlobes across her cheeks. To the right of the image were the woman's name and a brief bio:

Originally and Again … Sunday LaFountain DesJardins
Silversmith, Blogger, Aide Worker, Self-Taught Historian.

And below it, in a wide, airy font:

This is my blog, but a place for OUR stories, a place to name them and reclaim them. A place to broadcast them to a world that's always on, but too often attentive to the distractions and blind to the essentials.

Not here. Here you and I, writers and readers, form our own band of truth tellers. We are history hunters and story gatherers, wounded warriors and cultural amputees.

Sixty years ago we were silenced, scooped from our homes and forcefully immersed in someone else's murky brew. But what was suppressed cannot stay submerged forever. Minutes, hours, days, months, years, decades pass, and slowly we rise.

That passage was pinned to the top of the page. Below it was a series of posts, all by Sunday, but some with comments lengthier than the post itself. Tina began reading some of the comments at random.

"In 1964 Child welfare took me from my grandparents' home when I was 5 and I ONLY SAW THEM ONCE EVER AGAIN," wrote someone named Hannah S.

"They said I'd be better off in a 'nice home' by which they meant a white home and so they shipped me off to Chilliwack where I didn't know nobody to be a foster child for a family who believe me, just wanted a cinderella and believe me it wasn't nice at all."

Below that, Sunday had written,

"From your mention of Chilliwack, Hannah, I assume that you were born in British Columbia. There, according to Patrick Johnson, the number of Aboriginal children in provincial care increased by more than 30% in a single decade. Perhaps you were one of the 1,466 who were kidnapped by the Child "Welfare" system?"

"I was, tho I didn't figure that out until about ten years ago," Hannah replied. *"My foster parents, they told me I was an Italian orphan. Can you fucking believe that?!"*

Tina kept scrolling, past essays that Sunday wrote about the Truth and Reconciliation Commission, about the federal government's proposed settlement to compensate all First Nations and Inuit children who were removed from their homes, about the establishment of the *Aboriginal Peoples Television Network National News*. Finally, she got to the first posting on the site, titled "My Story."

My Blackfoot mother, Kimi LaFountain, died shortly after giving birth to me in an Edmonton hospital. My Cree father, Russell DesJardins, took me to Enoch, Alberta, to live with his parents. He was a construction worker, gone for months at a time on jobs, so he wanted me to have a stable home. And I did. We were poor – everyone on the Reserve was – but I wasn't starving. I had a cot and a blanket and a dress and a jacket and a plate and a cup. I had porridge for breakfast and carrots and jerky for lunch and soup and bread for dinner. We had an outhouse that my grandfather cleaned and a gravity shower, and I had chores to do. I swept our house every day with a broom made by my grandmother from a birch branch and porcupine quills. I helped her weed in the garden. At least I assume that's what I did when my hands dug in the dirt, rummaging through dry soil and pebbles to find the bulb, the root, the nub of whatever was growing where it shouldn't.

Some of this I remember; some was told to me later in life by my grandmother. She was blind when I found her 18 years after they'd taken me from her. "I thought I'd never see you again," she told me, "and I was right. But here you are, and I can squeeze your hand."

I was taken by two policemen and a social worker from Child Welfare. That I do remember. It was a very hot day and the policemen had no jackets. They wore short-sleeved white shirts and one of them had big yellow stains under his arms and stank of sweat and onions. The social worker wore a batik skirt and sat with me in the back seat of the cop car quietly saying, "You're going to be fine," over and over, as if by repeating this idiotic phrase she could make it true. "You're going to a beautiful new home where you'll have lovely things, everything you need," she promised.

And she wasn't lying. In my new home in Toronto I had a soft yellow velour rug in my bedroom, and a ruffled skirt for my bed. I had Barbie dolls and different clothes for every season. In the winter, I got taken to ski resorts, and in summers, stayed in the family's four-bedroom "cottage" in the

Thousand Islands where we swam by day and cooked steak on the barbecue at night. The woman who took me – my adoptive mother – died when I was six. The man who raised me for the next twelve years was Peter, but his name could have been Pygmalion. Mine was the face that he thought he'd sculpted, then loved; the canvas that he tried to turn into a mirror. But my face is broad and brown; it will never reflect his.

I would have written all this in Cree, but am only now learning to speak my own language.

Tina pushed back her chair, wrapped a blanket around herself, and walked through the dark living room and kitchen—muscle-memory now guiding her—and out to the deck. The air was damp, and under the dimly starlit sky, a fine mist was rising from the river.

Ehachimisochik. She whispered it over a few times, trying to speak this one Cree word more fluidly. Sandy, or Sunday, had told a story about herself. She had indeed been brought somewhere else. But nobody seemed to be doing penance—certainly not Peter. He was, however, grieving. Would Sandy find that an acceptable substitute for contrition?

April 2012

She heard Jean-Pierre and Peter in the sun porch, though these days Peter's physiotherapy was limited to a few cycles on the hand pedals and some half-hearted swats at Jean-Pierre's vertical palms.

"Can you turn up the heat a little?" Peter asked peevishly. "It's like a goddamn morgue in here."

Don't let him die yet. I'm not ready, Tina thought, and just as quickly, Don't let him suffer.

When Jean-Pierre wheeled Peter into the kitchen an hour later, he was slumped in his chair, his face stubbly and gray. He stared out the window and waved away his customary soft-boiled egg.

"You've got to eat something, Peter," Tina said, straining for firm kindness but feeling like Nurse Ratched.

"I don't, actually," Peter answered, giving her only a passing glance before returning his gaze to the slate-colored river outside the window. Then, after a moment, he said, "Toast. I'll have toast."

When the browned bread popped up, Tina repressed the impulse to adorn it with a smiley face made out of sprinkled cinnamon and sugar. That was what her mother had made her when she was home sick. But Peter did not have chickenpox.

"Ready to finish the book?" she asked him with false brightness.

"I'm not in the mood," he answered. "I'm too .... too ..." He'd taken to stammering, especially when he'd first woken up and after the sun went down. "Too .... tired, goddamnit! Too tired to read. Too tired to write."

"We're so close to the finish line," Tina urged.

A sour smile flickered over Peter's face. "I am. Not you."

"I mean the book."

Chin sinking to his chest, Peter shook his head. "Not close enough."

Tina set the plate of toast and a steaming cup of tea in front of him. "Just the moon-landing chapter and the conclusion—the what-it-all-means—and we're done." She heard how ridiculous her own words sounded as she said them.

He raised his head and darted a quick glance at her, his eyes briefly lit with the essence of the old Peter. "That's all?"

She smiled ruefully. "Okay, point taken." They fell silent, each sipping from their cup. "So how about this? How about if we just kill the moon-landing chapter? After all, after nine chapters about how images actually were manipulated, to close with a chapter about how right-wing conspiracy theorists don't believe the truth of images that weren't—well, it could send the whole thing off the rails, right?

"Maybe."

"So the hell with it. Let's not write that chapter and go straight to the conclusion."

"I hate conclusions," Peter muttered. "On the news we didn't have conclusions. We just stopped." He shifted in his chair, suddenly energized. "Why finish? Why not just stop?"

"You mean stop writing?"

"Yes, that's what I mean. We did what I set out to do …" He waved his hand in circles in below his chin, as if trying to churn the words up and out of him. "We exposed lies, told truths. Stopping now is as good as stopping later. The lies will keep coming, no matter what we do. And people have stopped believing the truth even when it's there in black and white, right in front of them."

He wheezed heavily; Tina couldn't tell if this was laughter or a new struggle for breath. "Are you okay?" she asked.

"No, my dear. I'm ancient and miserable and utterly useless. But other than that—" He touched thumb and index finger together in a small, perfect loop—"A-okay."

This defeated, resigned Peter saddened her too much. She wanted to get a rise out of him. "I found your daughter," Tina said abruptly, regretting the words the moment they escaped her mouth.

Peter's eyes blazed. "What?!"

"I wasn't looking for her, but I found Sandy accidentally."

"How do you find someone accidentally?" He jolted upright, rigid, head jutting forward from his reed-like neck.

"She broadcasts videos on Twitter. I didn't know it was her." Tina found herself speaking imploringly, recoiling from Peter's anger. "Jean-Pierre introduced me to her. Not that he knew either. Nobody knows. She calls herself The Traveler and keeps her identity secret."

"I know that my mind is a bit ..." He slapped the air impatiently, searching for the word "... not working right. Broken! Impaired — that's the goddamn word — impaired, but as best as I can tell, you are making no sense." Dots of color appeared on his cheeks, like amateurishly applied rouge.

"Your daughter Sandy —"

"Yes, I know my daughter's name."

"Sandy is a social media star. She streams videos from unnamed locations all around the world, mostly silent movies with nothing but ambient sound. Her videos are ... I don't know, they're compelling. They leave it up to us to provide the story, to project it onto whatever she's showing us. And there's a lot of us. She's followed by a million people."

"You're saying she shoots little silent movies on her phone and people watch them?"

"They watch them, they guess her location, they comment on them."

"Why?"

"Why." Tina emptied her lungs, a little puff that hung in the air. "I don't know why. I guess perhaps because it's a kind of active entertainment that she offers. We get to watch — because that's what modern people do, we watch — but we get to do more. We get to project our own stories onto her locations."

"Show me."

Tina pulled her phone out of her apron pocket, went to Sandy's Twitter page, and scrolled down. "This is one of my favorites," she said, and tapped on a short video of a shrunken, wrinkled, metallic yellow balloon emblazoned with the words Hank's Hamburger Haven spelled out in dripping red ketchup letters. It skittered down a boardwalk, sometimes gently colliding with the shins of oncoming pedestrians, sometimes lifting slightly in the breeze and zooming past their knees. Lining its path were sounds emanating from the water on the left, the commercial establishments on the right—the steady white noise of the surf punctuated by the din of videogame car crashes, thumping disco bass, the jingly bells of an ice cream truck, and some cracking adolescent male voice calling, "Sully, you retard!"

"Again," Peter commanded when the 30-second clip ended.

Tina studied him as he squinted at the phone, his brow furrowed as if willing himself to concentrate on the tiny moving image.

When the replay ended, he sank back into his chair. "That's it? That's what tens of thousands of people are spending their time watching?"

Tina smiled brightly and shrugged. "Go figure."

"No," he said tightly, "you go figure. You watch this—" he raised two empty palms in front of him—"this ... vacuous crap. Tell me why."

She let the smile drop. "It makes me notice—Sandy makes me notice—things I otherwise wouldn't."

"Great. Did it occur to you that perhaps you never noticed a— what's the word ... sagging? No—" He raised his hands as if holding an invisible ball, then pushed them together while making a flatulent sound through pursed lips—

"Deflated?" Tina supplied.

"—deflated balloon flying around before because it's not worthy of your goddamn attention?"

Tina took a deep breath. "Peter, I think your anger at me right now is a bit ... misplaced. I don't blame you for being hurt by Sandy, but maybe you should—" He should what? Acknowledge it? Relinquish it? Transform it into some sort of Christian love she'd heard about but never really understood? Tina realized that she had no idea what Peter should do with that pain.

Peter slumped in his chair, the anger that had animated him gone, spent, as quickly as it had come. "There's nothing I can do," he muttered, shaking his head. "What can I do?"

"Do you want to see her?"

He tipped his head towards his right shoulder, which he raised in a hint of a shrug.

"Then tell her," Tina said with a calm certainty she didn't feel. "We know how to reach her now."

"You mean on this ridiculous thing?" Peter pointed one bony finger at Tina's phone. "Hashtag ForgiveMe? Even though I've done nothing wrong?"

"You can say whatever you want to her," Tina answered. "You can say it in a video that I can push to her."

"I'm quite ... I can ..." Peter's fingers began to dance in a pantomime of typing. "Goddamnit! The word, I can't find —"

"I know you can type it," Tina rushed in, desperate to save Peter from more shame and frustration. "But it might have more impact if Sandy saw your face and heard your voice."

"You mean saw how old and frail and pathetic I am, don't you."

Tina held his gaze, not responding.

"Forget it. There will be no plucking of her ... chords" — he tapped his heart — "no pleas for her sympathy."

"I'm not suggesting that," Tina said calmly. "Just tell her whatever you want her to know about your motivations, your feelings, your reflections at ..." She trailed off.

"At the end of my life?" Peter smiled weakly, seeming to savor the irony of for once being the one to provide the missing words.

"Yes."

"All right," he said mildly. "Make up?"

"We didn't fight," Tina reassured him.

Peter laughed, startling her. "No, I mean do I need make-up for this broadcast?"

She looked at him, aghast. Had he never seen a selfie? "No, I don't think so," she said with forced gentleness. "We'll send it to her privately, so it will be visible only to her."

"I don't want her seeing me like this."

Was this protectiveness or pride? Tina wondered. "Let's not worry about that. Like you said, the image is awfully small."

"All right," Peter muttered. "Let's get this goddamn business over with. Let me just ..." He licked the fingers of his right hand and drew them over his pink scalp, trying in vain to tamp down his wispy white hair.

"Okay, ready?" Tina pointed her phone at Peter.

Peter rubbed his face with his hands, as if to revive himself. "Jesus, I haven't shaved!" He shot Tina a baleful look. "You were going to let me go on air like this?"

"Well, it's not exactly on air," she mumbled.

"What?"

"Never mind." Tina beat a hasty retreat. "Do you want to shave before we start? That's fine."

Jean-Pierre magically appeared, and Tina wondered if he'd been sitting in the dining room listening to their conversation. "Come on, man, let's get you cleaned up," he said soothingly, and wheeled Peter off to the bathroom.

Tina resisted her impulse to follow them. As a child, she'd loved to watch her father shave. He had let her apply the airy shaving cream—like Cool Whip, only better smelling—to her own face, and as he pulled his razor through the white lather on his cheeks, she'd create a similar path on hers with her index finger. Years of shaving her legs and underarms had cured her of this fascination, but the comfort of the memory—the steamy bathroom, her father's keen regard of his own face while avidly listening to her chatter on—had endured.

On her last camping trip with Carl, in Maine, when their relationship was still pretty new, she'd told him about those bathroom tete-a-tetes as she watched him shave. In the sandy clearing surrounded by scrubby pines, he'd sat on a log, squinting into the flat bottom of an aluminum frying pan that he was using as a mirror. The air smelled like salt marsh and bacon, rich and tangy, and the sun wasn't yet high enough to burn off the morning mist. Shirtless, his clothes-hanger shoulders protruded more than ever, but she'd loved the look, and the muscled feel, of them under her palms. She'd sketched as they talked, and though she failed to capture the awkward strength of his upper body, she got his smile, crooked and curious, as he listened to her.

"I get why you liked it so much as a kid," he'd said between swipes of the razor. "Covering your face in shaving cream is a great way to make a mess, then painlessly, systematically clean it up."

"Or hide," she realized as she said the words. "Hide, then reveal yourself."

And there it was—Carl's delighted grin that leapt out whenever he heard something he'd never thought of before. God, she missed him, especially now, in these grim, anxious weeks. After nine months apart, she couldn't remember why she'd felt that a separation would be a good idea. But whatever had been gestating—maybe it was as simple as self-acceptance?—it was now done. Baked. She was ready to be with him again.

Jean-Pierre and Peter returned to the kitchen.

"Here," Peter said, "use this." He placed a small tabletop tripod in front of her. As she screwed her phone to the stand, Jean-Pierre wheeled Peter around to face her. "No," Peter said angrily. "If you put me in front of the window, I'll be backlit. I should be where she is—" he pointed at Tina—"and she should sit here, where I am."

"That way you'll be staring into the sun," Jean-Pierre pointed out.

"You think I'm not used to staring into bright lights? What the hell do you think I did as an anchor for twenty-something years?"

Jean-Pierre and Tina silently exchanged looks and shifted positions.

"Okay, ready?" Tina asked, zooming in so that Peter's shoulders and head filled the frame.

Peter nodded. "Hi, Sandy," he began, his voice dry and crackly. He shook his head and took a sip of tea. "Start over," he commanded. "Hello, Sandy. I'm glad to talk to you after all these years, and I suppose I'm hoping that you ... that some little piece of your innards—

no, damnit, some inner piece of you—" He lifted his eyes to meet Tina's. "Cut." He took a sip of tea. "Again."

Tina once again pressed Record.

"I hope that you are open to hearing from me," Peter continued. "After all, you didn't always hate me, of that I'm sure."

He paused and cleared his throat, looking inquiringly at Tina. She gave him a thumbs-up.

"I don't know what the hell you've been told or what you believe anymore. We raised you to be an independent thinker, your mother and I."

Tina cringed. Peter saw her knotted face. "Excuse me, Grace and I," he continued. "We raised you to think critically, to think for yourself, and I hope that by now you do. I know that aboriginal children were taken into foster care or transferred to new homes without ... without ... what do you call it?"

"Due process?" Tina asked softly.

"Without due process, and things shouldn't have been done that way. I concede: that was wrong. But I am not a scofflaw, Sandy. I didn't bribe anyone, and we certainly didn't steal away with you in the middle of a moonless night."

Even now, he hasn't lost his aptitude for withering sarcasm, Tina thought. It's a shame that so many other faculties went first.

"Here is what I know. Here is the truth. I studied that picture of you, shirtless and not quite clean, looking out your window, and what I saw was a little girl longing for a better life. The eyes don't lie, and yours were despairing. I saw a child full of promise that would never be realized without our help. So we acted. We brought you to our house and we raised you like you were our own. And you were a happy child under our roof, at least until you became a teenager, when all children are unhappy. Then you went to college where instead of facts, they taught you ideology. Suddenly ordinary human decency was mis- ... mal- ... what the Christ is it? Was bad—decency was bad, and generosity was recast as cultural appropriation."

Peter's hands trembled and he was getting breathless. Tina drew a flattened hand to her throat. "Do you want to take a break?" she asked.

"No. I want to say what I want to say." He took another sip of tea, staring down at his blanketed lap for a moment. Then he raised his head and gave Tina a curt nod. She turned the camera back on. "Sandy, I believe in facts. You were a poor, prospectless child with big dreams, even at the age of four. I saw that in your eyes, and that's a fact. I regret that this has become a grievance for you, but I don't regret what I did. And here's one more fact. I will not be alive much longer." He raised his eyes to meet Tina's. "That's a wrap. I'm done."

"Are you sure? There's nothing else you want to say?"

He gestured towards the camera, instructing Tina to turn it back on. "And that's *today's* story," he added. "Goodnight, Canada."

Then he shot a grim, tight-lipped grin at Tina. "Now I'm really done. Sorry you didn't get the remorseful plea, the *mea culpa* you were looking for."

Screw you, she thought. No wonder Sandy had taken off. "Should I go ahead and send it?"

He waved his hand dismissively. "This was your idea. You do what you want."

What Tina wanted was to call Peter on his hypocrisy, to point out how eager he'd been to invest a childhood snapshot of a little girl with his interpretation and call it "truth." His belief in what he chose to see had made him complicit in a state-sponsored child abduction. And even now, at the end of his life, he couldn't or wouldn't acknowledge that his longing and sense of entitlement had profoundly and in some ways cruelly altered the lives of Sandy and her family of origin. He would take his self-justification to his grave.

Of course he would. The alternative—acknowledging that he'd been as blinded by the desire for some deep human connection—would be even more emotionally devastating than his sorrow at having been rejected by the child he sought to save. Like turning straw into gold, at least he could transform grief into anger.

But how much longer could that fuel him?

Peter spent the day after recording his message to Sandy obsessively checking his tablet for a response. He went back to bed that night and was too weak to get up the next morning. He refused food and struggled to suck any Ensure through a neon-orange plastic straw. The visiting nurse, after spending fifteen minutes alone with him, took Jean-Pierre aside and told him that Peter was ready for hospice care.

"What will that mean?" he asked, as Tina hovered on the outskirts of the conversation.

"We'll stop his heart failure medication and keep him comfortable with higher doses of morphine and Ativan."

"You've discussed this with him?

"I have, and this is what he wants. We'll be sending in a hospice nurse three times a day, but you may want to consider getting a 24-hour nurse to be with him."

"I'll ask his daughter about that," Jean-Pierre answered. "Will you be talking to her as well?"

"I already did. Mr. Bright and I called her together to discuss his wishes."

This nurse—Tina didn't remember her name—was nothing like the woman who had taken care of Joan in her last days. Lola had been warm and affectionate, and her lilting speech had lent a lyricism to even the grimmest moments. But this woman—compact as a fire-hydrant, plain-spoken, and unemotional—could have been advising them on how to unblock a sink. No wonder Peter liked her.

Tina showed her out, then knocked softly on Peter's bedroom door.

"Come on in," Jean-Pierre said. "Peter was just asking about you."

As she approached his bed, Peter opened his eyes wide and flashed a smile. "Pictures," he said, pointing to Jean-Pierre's phone. "He's been showing me pictures."

"Just some photos I shot of the two of you working together over the past few months," Jean-Pierre explained. He stretched out his arm over Peter's shrunken and inert body and handed her his phone.

Tina began scrolling through the images. There were a few close-ups of her poring over prints or typing at the keyboard. A surprisingly flattering one showed her dunking a tea bag while looking back over her shoulder, saying something to Peter. That must have been taken last fall, she thought. Peter still had some flesh on his bones and his eyes still reflected light. There were close-ups of Peter jabbing the air with his index finger, pointing to something in a photograph on his desk, marking up manuscript pages with one pencil in his hand and another held horizontally between his teeth.

But the best pictures — some in color but more of them in black-and-white — were medium shots of the two of them. In one, Peter snapped his fingers, as he was prone to do when concluding a story, and Tina had the startled eyes and open mouth of Betty Boop. What could he have told her that was so astonishing? Was it a well-kept secret about some politician's indiscretions? An anecdote about some photographer's unseemly behavior (as he never had tales about their virtues)? Or the passing reference to the "Now and There" broadcast that made her realize that he and her father had crossed paths, however indirectly?

"Do you remember what you were telling me in this picture?" she asked, holding the phone up to Peter's dull eyes. But he seemed baffled by the question.

She swiped through several more pictures of the two of them, heads close together and bowed over a print. Then she stopped and turned the phone to study a black-and-white landscape image. Peter was behind his desk, his white shirtsleeves rolled up to his elbows, his knit vest uncharacteristically askew. He was clearly saying something to her with great animation as he leaned over, left arm extended, to hand her a sheet of paper. Sitting to his left, her eyes wide and her mouth half-smiling, she reached out to receive it. Their hands met over the middle of the wide, mahogany desk, bridging the space between them.

"This is lovely," she said softly, once again holding the phone in front of Peter's face.

"That's the one," he said through dry lips. "For our book. Our cover, the back. That's the one."

• • •

The first *ping* on her phone — an email notification — awakened Tina at about six in the morning.

"My father told me that when the first contraction came, my mother Kimi was on the bus from Drumheller to Edmonton," Sandy's email began with no preamble.

It felt like someone had grabbed the elastic waistband of her one pair of maternity pants and yanked it tight. She even turned around in her scratchy blue seat to make sure her clothes weren't caught in something. But five or ten minutes later, when the next one came, the sudden tightening came from the inside, like her belly was a splayed hand that suddenly turned into a fist.

Where the hell is she? Tina wondered. And why is she emailing me at this ungodly hour?

My mother must have gasped, because the white lady across the aisle from her asked if she was all right. "How many contractions have you had?" she asked.

"Just one or two, I think. But it's soon," my mother answered, trying to tamp down the fear she felt rising in her chest. "It's too soon."

It was late June and I wasn't supposed to be born until the middle of July.

She introduced herself, this tiny lady in her flowered shirtdress and straw hat.

"Pleased to meet you," my mother said automatically. This was the one lesson from the Residential School that had stuck. When you meet someone new, say, 'Pleased to meet you.'

Is Sandy writing this on the fly? Tina wondered. Or is she copying and pasting from a story she's already composed?

The white lady – her name was Rita – made small talk with my mother, trying to distract her – or comfort her? – until they got to Edmonton. "Is someone picking you up at the bus station?"

"I hope so," my mother answered.

You see, she'd never been there. My dad had just gotten a job in Edmonton a couple of weeks earlier. He'd gotten them a place to live, but my mother hadn't seen it yet, didn't even know what buses to take to get there.

Rita patted my mother's hand, which was kneading her knee.

I don't think it was the baby — me — that scared my mother. I think it was moving to Edmonton. That makes her sound like a hick, but she was a hick.

This scene Sandy was creating, through words rather than her usual images, was remarkably specific. Was any of it true? Surely her father, Russell, wouldn't have told her about her birth in such detail, not when Sandy couldn't have been more than five or six years old.

Maybe this was a family history that Sandy had constructed, woven together from anecdotes her father and grandparents told her. Or was it a story that she was writing on the spot, exhaling each burst of detail like someone who'd been holding her breath, holding in her narrative, for far too long?

Rita asked my mother what she was going to name the baby.

This was something they'd fiercely debated. If I'd been a boy, no problem — I would have been named Lawrence, after my dad's uncle. But they couldn't agree on a girl's name. My father wanted to call me Irene, but my mom had been in the residential school with a girl named Irene, and she was a snake, a slippery, spiteful girl.

Okay, this was clearly invented, or at least embellished. Even if Sandy's account was based on stories her family told her as a child, there's no way they'd gotten this precise. But all power to her, Tina thought. It was riveting.

Just then, she felt her panties get all wet. She hadn't needed to pee, but suddenly, she was soaking. She looked down. "I think my water broke."

Rita leapt up. "I'm just going to talk to the bus driver for a moment, dear. I'll be right back."

My mother nodded, unable to speak. This contraction was boring right through her like an oil drill.

The next thing she knew, the bus driver was announcing that they were going to take a little detour and stop at the hospital before going on to the bus station.

"But Russell," my mother whimpered. She felt her nose running now too. Jesus, she was wet everywhere, a sniveling mess. "How will he know where I am?"

"Well, when we get to the bus station, I'll just look for someone waiting for someone who doesn't show up."

The kindness of strangers, Tina thought. Rita probably told the story of the girl in labor on the bus for years after Sandy was born. But could she have imagined that stories would be told about her?

I imagine that my mother tried to focus on something outside herself as the bus progressed all too slowly. I've taken that ride from Drumheller to Edmonton. Through the window, scrubby fields of new corn streak past, each with its own square brick house up a dirt road from the highway, each with its own silo, bending the slanting late afternoon light, standing sentry over the whole enterprise. As you get closer to the city, the fields get smaller, the houses closer together. You pass an abandoned Fina gas station, its red-white-and-blue shield faded to gray, and right next to it, a brand-new, bright yellow Sunoco station with a store built right into it. Then a new car lot, then the skyline off to the right, made of tall cool buildings with glittering white and blue lights.

Suddenly Sandy was speaking in her own voice.

They loaded my mother up with drugs and she had no memory of giving birth to me. Later she told my father

The message ended there. Frantically, Tina scrolled down, but there was nothing more. Could the story—quilted together from passed-down recollections—end here? That seemed unlikely. She pressed Reply.

"Dear Sandy," she typed, "I'm so glad you wrote. Your message ended very abruptly, and I'm not sure if it was cut off. Perhaps it would be easier if we just talked. Would you like to give me your number or else just call me? My number is below."

But as she was hitting Send, a new message from Sandy arrived, again with no salutation, no real acknowledgment that she was sending this message to anyone.

She told my father that while she was under, she dreamt of riding the elevator down the coal shaft in Drumheller. Thin shards of light would slice through the car every now and then, and when they did, it would shake and rumble.

When she woke up, she saw the doctor who'd delivered her baby – Dr. Swanson, his name was. He was a skinny man in tortoise-shell glasses and a sour-smelling white coat. I know this; my father told me this man smelled like the onions in a day-old Teen Burger.

That detail – the oniony-smelling doctor – rang a bell. Hadn't she read something like that before, perhaps on Sandy's blog? This had to have been the product of her father's memory, burned into the mind of a young Sandy.

Kimi's mouth was dry as dirt, her temples were throbbing, she had a sharp, tight pain between her legs.

"Where's my baby?" my mother asked him.

He waved vaguely towards the door. "Oh, she's probably down the hall."

"Why isn't she with me?"

"Your baby might have been born in a tepee up until a decade ago instead of a modern hospital," he scolded. "Lucky for you – and for her – she's just in the nursery getting weighed and cleaned and swaddled." He paused, trying to be jovial, to act like he cared. "So how are you doing?"

"I've been better." She felt jittery and prickly, and her forehead was steaming like a tea kettle. "Hot and then cold, and a little sore down there."

"Of course you are," he boomed, now halfway to the door. "You've just had a baby. But you'll feel better in no time." Then he was gone.

No physical exam. No temperature-taking or blood-pressure monitoring. Here it comes, Tina thought, the beginning of the end.

Seconds after Swanson left, my dad darted in. He bent over my mother, took her cheeks in his rough hands, and kissed her forehead, her nose, and then gently, her mouth. "You did it," he said. "You are the champion mama." He'd just seen me in the nursery and told my mother about me, told her I was tiny and shriveled and adorable, like a prune with hair.

Before Peter and Grace took me away, my grandmother told me about my history. She said that Russell told her Kimi was sweating hard, panting and rubbing her belly as if trying to ease its pain. She said that he should have known that there was something wrong.

That was a terrible thing to tell a five-year old about her father. Besides, how could he have known? He'd never fathered a child before, never been with a woman who had just given birth.

Ah, so Sandy's anger wasn't reserved solely for Peter.

Peter, who was the reason Tina had reached out to her.

I imagine that by now, Kimi was seeing spots and diamonds and crystals of all different colors in front of her eyes, as if she was looking at my father through a kaleidoscope. She willed herself to stay with him, though.

This message ended there. Tina picked up her cellphone, went to The Traveler's last post, and typed in the Comment field, "Can we talk?" Then she erased it, afraid that Sandy would simply stop doling out her story, one installment at a time, and once again disappear. She updated her in-box. Nothing. Pulling on her bathrobe, Tina went to the kitchen and made herself a cup of Scottish Breakfast tea. When she returned to her room, now bifurcated by morning light, she refreshed her screen again. And there it was—Sandy's next message.

"We have to name her," my mother said.

"How about Irene? Irene LaFountain Desjardins."

"No offense to your Auntie Irene — but I want her to have a special name, a new kind of name."

"Like Pringles? Or Sergeant Pepper?"

"You're a nut. No, something that takes in the world, like she's going to do. Like Galaxy."

"Galaxy Desjardins?"

"Like the sun." Kimi felt another surge of pain and heat, like someone had taken a branding iron to her insides. "Hot like the sun," she muttered. "Wait, what day is this?"

"It's Sunday. It's" — he looked at his watch — "it's almost 6 a.m. on Sunday morning."

Kimi widened her eyes, and my father's handsome, worried face came into focus for just a moment. "Sunday!" she said. "Sunday Desjardins."

They took her name, Tina thought. They took her, and they took her name.

He nodded slowly. "Okay. Our daughter is Sunday Irene LaFountain Desjardins." Russell tucked the sheet and thin cotton blanket up under her chin. "Now sleep. Sunday will be here soon."

My mother must have been delirious by now. In her fevered mind, I think she was back on the res. Her little brother Oliver was digging, digging with his spade and then with his hands. The sun beat down on them. She was soaked in sweat — her hair, her breasts, between her legs. Each time Oliver stabbed into the earth, my mother felt a bolt in her belly. And each time, something in the earth cackled and wailed.

"Wake up, beautiful," my father was saying. "Sunday's here."

Kimi forced her eyes open, then shut them again, pained by the bright lights overhead.

"Open your eyes and take a look at your daughter," Russell urged.

She looked at the tiny baby in his arms. She reached out her own and enfolded me in them. Blindly rooting around my mother's chest with an open, toothless mouth, I looked to my mother like a baby mouse and sounded like a Siamese cat. "Hello, Sunday," she whispered. "Hello, little girl. I'm your mama."

Would this be the last message? Tina didn't know, but she couldn't keep reading in invisible silence. "I'm so very sorry," she hurriedly responded.

But another message arrived almost instantly. Sandy, or Sunday, approaching the climax of her story, either didn't notice or wasn't interested in Tina's sympathy.

My dad told me that she was getting sicker by the second as she held me. I imagine that she felt a buzzing noise and her skin prickled everywhere, like she'd been caught in a swarm of black flies. Perhaps I started to cry. The pain in her belly flared out in all directions like the rays of the sun.

"Jesus," she would have heard my father gasp. "Jesus, you're bleeding! Doctor?" Then his voice would have faded.

End of message. Tina refreshed her screen over and over, but no new emails arrived. She looked up from the screen. Outside her window, the rising sun had turned the water behind Refugee Island a luminous gold.

Rather than reply to the last message, Tina started fresh. "What a haunting loss," she wrote after numerous false starts. "And now another parent..."—no, that might inflame her. "And now Peter is dying. At least with him you have the chance to say goodbye."

She pressed Send. A long silence. She could hear a blue jay announce its presence with a barrage of irritated squawks. Then a small ding, and on her screen, *"I said goodbye a long time ago. I don't need to do it again."*

As Tina struggled with how to respond, one more message appeared, this one with nothing but a message in the Subject line: *"He doesn't either."*

May 2012

Once the hospice nurse came and started giving him the morphine and Ativan that would help keep him calm and free of pain, Peter's death had come shockingly fast. He'd retained moments of consciousness, enough to give Melissa a fleeting but tender smile when she showed up at his bedside, enough to mutter something unintelligible about the sea and to ask Tina, with sudden poignant clarity, if his wife had died. But within days, he stopped speaking and his eyes stopped opening, even when he moaned or more audibly labored for breath.

Tina, Jean-Pierre, and Melissa spelled each other at his bedside. They read and watched golf matches on television, finding a peculiar comfort in the quiet, intent voices of the broadcasters and the sudden, considerate silences of the crowd before each tee shot. Tina watched Peter closely, as she had her mother in her fast few days of life. But unlike then, Tina wasn't wracked now by astonishment and grief. Her sorrow was more contained, leaving room for curiosity. Was he afraid? Did he see or feel anything? She was absurdly reminded of being a spectator at the Toronto Marathon, holding out tiny paper cups of water to the passing runners, some hurtling past, swift and indifferent, others limping and lurching their way to the finish line. They were usually too exhausted to make eye contact, let alone to reach for the extended gifts. All seemed to see only the finish line.

Mostly, though, she was struck again by the singularity of this journey towards death. She and the others at his bedside could line the route, but he drifted alone towards the unknown. At least he has an audience, she thought. He would like that.

Though she loved walking in cemeteries, Tina had not stood at many fresh graves. Until now, just those of her father, her mother, and her friend Chris, felled by a drunk driver as she walked home from the appointment in which her oncologist had pronounced her cured.

The plump willows drooped with age; the copper beech above them had a broad embrace, expansive enough not only to canopy the headstones of the Brights but to shade those of many families. It was an old and stately oasis in northern Toronto, a beautiful, rolling landscape that dwarfed their party — party? — of six. Until Melissa told Tina of the gravesites Peter had bought for the whole family, she hadn't known that Strathcona Cemetery was admitting newcomers.

But there it was — Peter's cedar coffin gleaming in the ray of late-May sun that sliced through the trees. And there they were — Melissa and Michael, Jean-Pierre, Peter's nephew Ambrose and his wife Dawn, and herself. Melissa had briefly considered a memorial service in the chapel but decided against it. "That lifetime achievement award ceremony he had — jeez, less than a year ago? — that's where people got to pay tribute. Another service six months later would just be overkill, right?" Melissa had asked her a few hours after Peter's death.

She was clearly seeking Tina's agreement that a fast graveside service would be best, confirmation that Tina was more than willing to supply. "Absolutely. He would have described another ceremony so soon as wretched excess."

So, at Melissa's insistence, the obituary that Tina placed in the *Toronto Globe and Mail*, the *Thousand Islands Weekly Caller*, and the *National Post* had no information about a funeral service or even the burial.

Peter had written the obituary himself months earlier, back when he still hummed with energy and wit. Sitting before a cup of tea in the kitchen, he'd written it easily, his long sloping script filling multiple pages of a yellow legal pad, until he got to the last sentence.

"Bright is survived by ... by whom? By what?" he'd wondered aloud. "Bright is survived by his loving daughters — by his daughters, Melissa Bright Blumenthal and Sandy Bright — his handcrafted museum of a house and national debt-sized mortgage, and a collection of baseballs and photographs that may yet mean something to someone else ... even if only the holders of the aforementioned mortgage."

"What do you think?" he'd chirped, looking up at Tina.

"I think you should and will say whatever you want, so no comment."

"Clever girl," he'd answered approvingly.

Now, striding like an animated cartoon skeleton, tall, gaunt Melissa led them from the limo to the open grave where they huddled in a loose, contact-free scrum. A backhoe sat next to it at the ready, its driver sipping from a bright blue thermos bearing a Raptors logo.

Melissa turned to face them. "As you know, my father wasn't a religious man and he wouldn't have wanted a Minister present," she declared in a needlessly loud voice. "So it's just us chickens. Would anyone like to say anything before he's lowered?"

Ambrose—who Tina had never heard of before yesterday, let alone met, cleared his throat. "I know how much he meant to my father. Even after we moved to England, Dad and Uncle Peter would get together for a golf weekend in Scotland every year and Dad would come home from it pleased as punch. And of course he meant so much to all of Canada—Uncle Peter, I mean. He'll be missed." Ambrose paused, looking for something more to say, but found nothing.

Michael cautiously lifted his arm.

"You don't have to raise your hand, Michael," Melissa said.

"I just want to echo Arnold's fine words," he said. Seeing Melissa's puzzled face, he quickly added. "Ambrose's fine words. Peter Bright was a gentleman and a scholar, and a mercifully uninvolved father-in-law. He made me feel welcome and generally left me alone, which I appreciated. Still, I'll miss him. He was a good father to Melissa ... and, I'm convinced, to Sandy too, and a devoted husband, I believe." Then, in a spasmodic attempt to stand at attention, Michael brought his gleaming shoes together, threw back his shoulders, and touched the fingers of his right hand to his temple. "I salute you, sir."

An amused look flickered between Tina and Jean-Pierre, and Tina, dazed by the unseasonable heat and her cluelessness about what would happen next in her life, found herself suddenly struggling to hold back a grin.

But Jean-Pierre's sweaty face quickly turned somber. "He was a good man," he said quietly. "Kind to me, smart, a man with principles. He stood for something. Not enough people do." Then, turning his gaze from the others to the coffin, he quickly genuflected and murmured "Repose en paix, mon ami."

It was Tina's turn and she had nothing prepared. "I came to your father's house as a bit of a wanderer," she began slowly, addressing herself to Melissa. "I was hired as the help, but over time, Peter allowed me to become his partner." She paused. "My own father used to tell me that the hallmark of a strong relationship wasn't always agreeing with each other, but being able to fight. Peter was willing to argue with me. He taught me. He believed in himself, he believed in you—"she nodded at Melissa—"and he believed in me. He was a cantankerous, smart, brave, and generous man."

They stood in silence. "I can't top that," Melissa finally said. Then, turning to the grave, she said in a clogged voice, "I love you, Dad, and I know that in your way, you loved me." She touched the cool marble of her mother's headstone, shaded by a giant willow. "You too, Mom."

Then Melissa nodded to the grave digger. The backhoe's engine kicked into life, and the engine-powered shovel drove into the mound of dirt. Seeing the sheer volume of earth captured in a single jab, Tina realized that the grave would be filled in just a minute or two.

The mechanical speed of the burial felt wrong. Her family had observed Jewish ritual when both her parents were buried. At Bob's funeral, Joan—stunned but stunning as always—had bent, lifted the trowel stuck jauntily into the pile of dirt next to the grave, scooped out soil as if loading an ice cream cone, then tossed it into the grave. She handed the small shovel to Tina. Despite her youth and strength, her movements were weaker, more tentative than her mother's. She half-filled the trowel, then tilted it, letting the dirt and stones dribble down, gently pelting her father's casket. She hated that sound, and abandoned the trowel, reaching for a shovel instead. Charlie, Bob's brothers, her aunt Carol, and uncle Barry picked up shovels as well, and together, in urgent silence, they dug out the moist, rubbly dirt and tossed it into the grave until it was filled, until her father was fully buried, enclosed, and safe from the elements.

But Melissa had already started leading the small procession back to their cars when her phone beeped. She stopped abruptly, causing Michael to step on the back of her sensibly clad foot.

She stared down at it, then looked up. To nobody in particular she said, "It's a message from Sandy. She wants us to know that her heart is with us."

"Yeah, well her body isn't," Ambrose snapped.

"I'm sorry you missed him," Melissa said as she typed out those words. "He would have loved to see you." After pausing for another moment, she hit Send, and continued walking back to the car.

How could Sunday have forfeited the chance to say goodbye? Tina wondered. Her brain knew the answer—she already had, and once was enough—but Tina's heart ached nonetheless. For me, Tina realized as she sat down behind the steering wheel. I'm grieving for me, for the goodbye I never got to say.

* *

September, 1984, London

It was the first time that Tina had gone on vacation with Bob and Joan since childhood.

"Come on," Bob had cajoled over the phone. "Now that you don't have Richard tying you down, and no kids yet—it's the perfect time for a trip to London with the old folks!"

"Richard and I broke up ages ago."

"Not Richard. What's his name, the most recent guy?"

"Sean. It doesn't matter, but Sean."

"I knew it was something Irish … But you're free of him, no? A free woman?"

"Yes, Dad. I know I have no husband or children. But I do have a job, one I actually sort of like."

"No need to be touchy, Tina. I'm just trying to treat you to a vacation, not insult you." He paused and over the phone Tina could hear him take a deep, deliberate breath. He dramatically tried to keep his voice neutral as he asked, "I assume you're entitled to some time off?"

"I am."

"Listen, don't do me any favors. I just thought you might want a free trip to London, and maybe, God forbid, a bit of leisure time with your parents."

"I'm sorry, Dad. I don't mean to sound ungrateful. Of course I'd love to see you guys and go to London. I just need to ... I don't know how much time off I can get." But as the words were coming out of her mouth, she already knew that her answer would be yes.

And three months later, when she tapped on the door of their room at London's Dolphin House and heard her father call, "Just a minute," multiple times—he was probably looking for his pants—she was glad she had. It had been at least a year since she'd last seen her parents.

They looked different—smaller, as they blinked at the sight of her in the hallway light streaming in from behind her. They'd just awakened from a nap—"Just to cope with the jet lag," Joan had hastened to reassure her. Older maybe, and a bit less certain.

What to do with this new feeling of protectiveness? Resist it, Tina decided. They would hate to feel patronized.

"I'm sorry, Dad," she said gently the next morning over a wet breakfast of scrambled eggs, glistening sausages, and mushrooms that looked as though they'd been sautéed in a muddy puddle. "I promised my boss I'd check out this Sophie Calle exhibition at the Tate—he's thinking about showing her work—and I know you'll hate it." How strange it was to realize she could hurt her father's feelings. Weren't father-daughter relations supposed to get simpler with age? "But I'll meet up with you as soon as I'm done, okay?"

Her parents were almost submerged in the deep, overstuffed dining room chairs. Joan managed to look regal despite the embrace of the claret-colored seat back, though her hand faintly trembled as she sipped her tea. ("It's benign. An essential tremor, my doctor called it," she'd reassured Tina, "though I don't see anything essential about it.") But Bob, sweaty and gripping one floral-clad chair arm, had a vaguely panicked look as he tried to rise. And his hands, one pushing off the furniture, the other clutching a baggy pant leg, were defaced by splotchy liver spots that seem to have blossomed overnight. It took all of Tina's will not to offer him her bent forearm to use as a grab bar.

Joan pursed her lips, though Tina couldn't tell whether she was annoyed by her daughter's plans or her husband's grunt as he finally lurched to his feet.

Tina forgave her mother her unusual snit. She knew Joan would have preferred to go look at art rather than cool her heels for a few hours, but Tina wanted to view the exhibit at her own pace, without worrying about whether she was going too fast for her mother or too slow for her father. "Okay, so I'll see you at 1 pm," she said brightly, and stood to go.

On her way out the door, Tina heard her father's never-quiet voice behind her say, "She's always dancing to her own drummer."

She paused, waiting to hear her mother's response.

"Marching, dear. Dancing to her own tune," Joan corrected, "marching to her own drummer."

When Tina arrived at the Churchill War Rooms later that day, ten minutes ahead of the planned rendezvous, she found her father pacing outside the building, on the edge of St. James Lake, driving the geese to scurry out of his path with each heavy step. Her mother sat on the bench watching him, her eyes flitting between amusement and concern.

"I think he's just excited," Joan said as Tina sat down next to her, "with maybe a bit of dread thrown in as well."

"Why dread?" Tina asked, thrilled that her mother was confiding in her. Had this ever happened before?

"His time here still looms large. You know how it is when you revisit some place that was important to you when you were young? It may bring back a lot of happy memories, or it may just look small, or dingy, or just lacking in the power it's exerted over your imagination all that time."

Tina thought about her last visit to her parents' apartment on West End Avenue. Yes, she wanted to say, but wouldn't.

Bob turned and saw her. "Ready?" he asked briskly.

"Let's do this thing," Tina answered with joking valor.

They descended the stairs to Churchill's War Rooms, a warren of dimly lit spaces in a Whitehall basement. The bunker—top secret during the war—had served as a military intelligence center and emergency meeting facility for Winston Churchill and his cabinet.

They passed through a room honoring the women who'd worked in this basement, maintaining lists of supplies needed for every battalion in the European theater. Through the glass cases, Tina studied pages and pages of ledgers listing mundane but essential items (cases of soap, ration kits, socks ...), quantities, destinations, and dates.

"Logistics," Bob sighed. "This is how the good guys kept the trains running on time."

They moved on, past the glassed-in, soundproofed room that held the telephone Churchill would use when talking to Roosevelt, as secured as it could be. And when they got to the Map Room, Bob stopped dead in his tracks. He craned his head over the barrier to look in, his face as rapt as Tina had ever seen it.

"When I was transferred from Whitley Bay to London in May of 1944, I worked in a room like this," he told her.

On three walls hung enormous maps of every continent and ocean, each veined with delicate lines denoting supply convoys and battle fronts. Here, around the clock, representatives from the Army, Navy, and Air Force would continuously receive new information on the movements of troops and ships, and update the maps' jagged garlands. Next to each map, a large case held small wooden boxes filled with the yarn and push pins used to create the lines.

"I liked the night shift the best," Bob continued, his voice hushed and dreamy. "I mean, look at this." He gestured around the room, as if introducing each map to her, his daughter. "Each of these fragile lines represented tens of thousands of human beings connected by mud, bullet casings, and blood."

Tina took in the dim quiet and yarn sculptures veining the maps. Fraying, their cheerful colors muted by the windowless light, they were relics of a visual imagination linked by bits of yarn to an empathetic one. "It's like they were literally knitting people together, isn't it?" she said, placing a hand on her father's sweat-damped back. "Kind of like making a vest."

Her father cast her a grateful glance, nodding and seemingly too choked up to speak.

Such depth of feeling, she thought with wonder. What else don't I know about him?

Normally chatty and expansive, her father remained mostly silent as they passed through each room, reading every plaque, notecard, and exhibit. And his quiet lasted as they boarded the Tube to return to their hotel, the three of them standing silently in the din of the train's shuddering progress, gripping the pole that stood between them far more tightly than was necessary.

Tina studied the train car—its perky blue-and-orange benches, the crush of tourists and hatless men in blazers and open-necked shirts, the poufy-haired girls chewing gum and leaning into the logoed t-shirts on the chests of their boyfriends. "Does this look very different than it did in 1945?" she yelled into her father's ear.

"Unrecognizable," he shouted back. "No uniforms, no hats on anyone's head. Ads—sorry, adverts—for *Back to the Future* and Cadbury's Chocolate. Back then the posters were all warnings and propaganda."

Tina gave him a quizzical look.

"You know," her father bellowed, assuming a terrible English accent. "Chin up! *We Beat 'Em Before, We'll Beat 'Em Again*. Oh, and warnings. *Careless Talk Costs Lives*." He shook his head in amazement. "And the thing is, it all worked. The propaganda worked." Then turning to Joan, "Didn't it, love?"

•   •   •

"I realize how little I've asked you about your war experience," Tina said over dinner that night. They were in a huge, ornate Indian restaurant, more a theme park than a dining room, with a drink menu the size of the Ten Commandments. "I don't even know if you were in combat."

"Nope. I was in Logistics. An office job all the way."

Tina hesitated, then asked as delicately as she could, "Did you want to be in combat?"

"Hell, no," her father answered jovially. "I was completely unashamed at my lack of combat experience. I saw enough guys dazed and shattered to know that I didn't want to be one of them."

Joan nodded solemnly. "Amen to that."

"Besides, World War II was a logistician's war, a massive jigsaw puzzle where the pieces were trains, foundries, laboratories, syringes, chocolate bars, boots, rifles, and razor blades. Not that it was easy. I worked eighteen-hour days procuring, storing, and distributing everything from bullets to condoms to K-rations. Sometimes I arranged the transport of the troops themselves."

Tina heard an unfamiliar pride in her father's voice, and only now realized what a humble man he generally was.

"Still, weren't you scared? I mean there were bombing raids over the whole country, weren't there?"

Bob nodded as he dotted his naan with each of the four condiments the waiter had set down in front of them. "London got the worst of it, but it wasn't the only target." He took a bite of the quadrant containing a green chili sauce and nodded approvingly. "But I'll tell you," he continued after swallowing, "in the Planning Room—it was a hut, really, a goddamn damp hut on Whitley Bay—I felt ... serene."

Joan gave him a startled look. "Serene?" her mother challenged. "I can't even imagine that."

"Oh, probably not at first," her father answered cheerfully. "But after a while, the blare of air-raid sirens wasn't so much scary as just annoying. Incoming aircraft are a distraction when you're trying to locate 10,000 more operating tables or plan the distribution of a billion pounds of meat."

"Who did you supply?"

"The whole European theater," Bob answered. "You could find my grubby fingerprints on the purchase orders for over 69 million cotton khaki shirts and over 73 million flannel ones."

"Wow, that *is* a lot of apparel." Tina studied the prawns vindaloo that had just been set before her as if they were the crown jewels, then lifted one to her mouth. "What about equipment? Did you have to organize the movement of tanks and guns and soldiers?"

"Seven million rifles. Twenty-five billion rounds of .30-caliber bullets. Four and a half million miles of communication wire."

Tina studied her father, animated and almost grinning at the recollection of, what, transports? Bullets? Or maybe of feeling useful. "Do you miss those days?" she asked.

"What, you mean the war?"

"Well, not the war per se. I mean I assume nobody misses war …"

"You've got *that* right."

Tina waved her fork around and grains of rice cascaded gently to her plate. "No, I mean the effort, the coordinated effort."

"In a way, I guess."

"And your friends?" Tina persisted. "I imagine that when you're faced with so many life-or-death situations, you must form really close relationships, really quickly."

"Not really," he answered vaguely, then busied himself trying to get the waiter's attention. When the painfully thin young man came over—Jesus, his Adam's apple is the size of a baseball, Tina thought—her father jabbed his finger towards his nearly empty glass of beer. He looked inquiringly at Joan and Tina, who both shook their heads. Then, brightly—too brightly, Tina thought—he asked, "How about your day? How was the exhibit?"

"Oh, so we're done with the war?" She was surprised by this sudden pivot.

"Yup."

Tina looked inquiringly at her mother, as if Joan could explain it. But her mother just shrugged.

"The exhibit was … strange," Tina answered after a pause. "Very conceptual."

"What does that mean?" Bob asked.

"The artist, Sophie Calle, got a job as a chambermaid at a Venice hotel so that she could look at people's belongings and photograph them."

Bob's eyebrows shot up. "Really! That doesn't sound kosher."

Joan chuckled but held her tongue.

"No, it wasn't. But she only did it for three weeks, just long enough to shoot pictures of what was in the twelve rooms she cleaned each day. Then she created twenty-one diptychs, which made up the exhibit."

"What's a diptych? A dipstick, I know. Check your oil, buddy? But a diptych?"

"Two panels," Joan jumped in. "Just a pair of pictures, one on each panel."

Bob pulled an adjustable lead pencil out of his shirt pocket and started looking for something to draw on.

"Forget the diptych," Tina said. "That part doesn't matter. What matters is the pictures. Well, not just the pictures—which were actually pretty plain and unrevealing—but the commentary she wrote on the pictures."

"Are you allowed to do that?" Bob asked.

"To do what?"

"To write explanations of your pictures. Isn't that against the rules?" Tina and her mother exchanged a look. Bob raised his wagging index finger, and his voice along with it. "Now, don't patronize me, either of you. This is not a dumb question, especially when the art in question is a photograph, for Christ's sake! Why should a photograph—whose purpose is to capture things as they are—why should that need the photographer to explain it? Doesn't that defeat the whole point?"

"No, and no. Some people use cameras and film to create completely non-representational images. They're just interested in shape and shadow and light. And no, Sophie Calle didn't write explanations of the pictures. They're more ... speculations. She's like an archaeologist, documenting what she finds, and then interpreting these objects—the clothes and shoe brushes and toothbrushes and books and receipts—as if they're relics."

"I know I'm going to sound like some old crank, but seriously, is that art?" Bob turned to his wife. "Okay, now you can make fun of me."

Joan petted his hand and blew him a kiss.

"I don't know if it's art, but it's interesting," Tina answered. "She's drawing our attention to what we all do, which is make up stories about people based on what we see of them and their stuff." Bob spread his hands, mystified. Tina tried again. "The photographs aren't the art, they're the stimulus for the art. It's the stories … "

"She's saying that looking is an act of imagination," Joan said crisply. "It sounds like Calle is just using the photos to draw our attention to the process we unconsciously engage in all the time." She took a sip of her Martini, then dabbed the corners of her mouth with her napkin.

Though she wasn't about to admit it, Tina hadn't actually liked the exhibit. She understood Calle's voyeuristic impulse — hell, she shared it — but the deliberate artlessness of the images made them almost flamboyantly documentary, like Weegee crime-scene photos. A hairbrush streaming almost iridescent gray hairs; a wadded-up shirt stuffed into the corner of an open suitcase as if burrowing under the crisp, immaculately folded ones still unworn; two pairs of shoes on the shoe rack in the closet, one with its laces drooping downward behind the heels like seaweed; the back of a postcard not yet addressed; one slipper poking out from under the bed ruffle in a static game of peekaboo; a toilet with the seat up adjacent to a towel-filled bidet, the two of them looking like gaping, hungry porcelain mouths. Calle had managed to make the personal look tawdry. The images were just props, soulless and self-serving. And the fact that Calle breezily described scenting herself with one guest's perfume, adorning herself with another's cosmetics, eating the leftovers from someone's room-service breakfast left Tina more queasy than admiring. Calle had struck her as a Goldilocks driven less by simple curiosity than a disturbing sense of artistic entitlement.

And so, while Joan was, as usual, astute in her assessment of an exhibit she hadn't even seen, Tina found herself saying with conspiratorial pleasure, "You know, Dad, you're right. It's not art." Bob bowed in his chair, then cast Joan a triumphant grin. He was so easy to please — a realization that left Tina feeling both admiring and sad. "And it's certainly not world-changing. It's not history with a capital H like you were a part of during the war."

Bob chuckled. "Believe me, that's not how we thought of it then. Seeing the world, staying alive, meeting girls, learning new skills, sometimes being scared shitless — that's how it felt to us in those years. We were just kids, and you know how it is when you're that age. The eternal present."

"You didn't find yourself thinking, 'Someday we'll look back on this moment and —' well, I don't know and what. But didn't you realize you were part of something momentous?"

Her father cocked his head. After a long pause, he said, "Only in the abstract. I mean, sure, we knew this was a world war, that important things were happening — terrible things — on an unprecedented scale. But moment to moment, we were just living our lives. Capital-H history was something always behind us." He paused. Then, "It still is."

With her purposeless butter knife, Tina made geometric shapes out of the spilled rice on the white linen cloth. Across the table, she could feel her mother staring into her soul.

"You don't agree?" Joan asked.

"I'm not sure. Freud and those guys would say that we always carry our childhood into our present, right? So if that's true on an individual level, maybe it's true on a broader scale. I mean, not all of our formative experiences are personal, right?"

Joan set down her drink and leaned in, her chin now in her hand. "What were your formative experiences?"

Tina knew that question was coming the moment the words were out of her mouth. Her mother was a pro, speedily slipping through the door marked Private no matter how briefly or narrowly it had opened. "Well, you guys, of course," she answered with faux sweetness.

"Not people. Experiences."

"Pretty much what you'd expect, Mom. The Vietnam war — well really, the anti-war movement. The commune in Vermont. That Peter, Paul, and Mary concert you took me to when I was little. My first ride in an airplane."

"Peter, Paul, and Mary?" Bob asked. His bafflement sounded sincere.

Tina shrugged. "I know. They're kind of cheesy, right? But I liked that they were just a woman and two guys collaborating, making harmonies, without any apparent sexual games between them. They were just musicians, craftsmen, doing more with three voices than they could with one. I wanted to be like that—one of the guys, only with straight blond hair and loud, husky voice."

Her father nodded several times. "If you had a hammer ..." he sang, then stopped as the waiter proffered a small silver tray containing three wrapped mints and the bill. Bob reached into his pocket and pulled out his glasses, his wallet, his hanky, and a roll of Tums.

"A pocket like a clown car," Joan murmured.

"You're not the first person to call me a clown," Bob declared happily. "And you won't be the last."

"Ah, but you're a history-making clown, Dad—a veteran, a pioneer of the football replay and satellite communications."

Her father blushed, so visibly pleased that it shook her. Did her approval matter so much to him?

"History, shmistory," Bob said, letting his palms drop to the table in a conclusive thump. "Nobody agrees on what the past means anyhow. How you interpret 1939, how you assess its impact, is different in 1940 and 1950 and today. They call history a social science, but it's not science at all. It's subjective as hell." He pushed back his chair and stood. "Me, I look to the future."

Behind him, the waiter carrying a huge platter of steaming vindaloo dodged, barely avoiding a collision.

That's what happens when you never look back, Tina thought, not knowing what she meant, but nonetheless proud of the thought.

•　•　•

Now she was grateful for these opportunities to look back. That was the last time she'd ever seen her father; he died five months later. If I'd known, I would have said thank you, she thought, holding back tears. But everything else—I got to say everything else. He knew I loved him.

When they got back to Peter's house in Brockville, they were greeted by a small knot of helpers — nurses and housecleaners, Leo, the guy who plowed the grounds in winter and mowed them in summer, and his vivacious wife — and the handful of neighbors Peter had gotten to know when making an appearance at the occasional Fish Fry or Casino Night to raise money for the boys' and girls' hockey teams. As the community transitioned from retirees to young families, Peter's celebrity had faded, but there were many who had still been awestruck by their proximity to the man who spoke to the nation five nights a week. This afternoon gathering would be the extent of the formal mourning. It was an awkward gathering of people who didn't know one another and didn't have an especially intimate relationship with Peter's survivors, either. But this would be their first and only chance to set foot inside his house.

Inside the pleasantly cool kitchen, Ambrose sidled up to Melissa as she loaded a plate with the party sandwiches Peter's absent literary agent had thoughtfully ordered for them.

"Did Sandy respond to your message?"

Standing next to Melissa, Tina froze, awaiting the answer.

"Yes."

After waiting expectantly, Ambrose demanded, "Well, what did she say?"

Melissa hesitated. "She said she loved me. She said she was sorry not to be with me, but coming for Dad's death when she'd severed ties with him in life felt dishonest."

"How very principled," he ridiculed.

"She is principled," Melissa said with weariness but no judgment. "My mom and dad were well-intentioned, but let's face it. They kidnapped her, at least that's how she sees it. She couldn't — you don't just embrace your kidnapper, no matter how nicely he treats you."

"Oh come on!"

Melissa raised her hand. "I don't agree with her. I wish she'd found a way to forgive him. But she didn't hound him. She didn't publicly condemn him. She found her own path with her own band and made a life for herself. She could have done far worse."

Ambrose shook his head in disgust.

Melissa grabbed his shoulder. "You have no right to judge," she said harshly. Then, taking a deep breath, "Please, she's still my sister. Please just let it go, okay?"

Ambrose wandered off, and Tina looked at Melissa with new respect. Beneath her artless exterior was a core of both steel and heart. "Sandy's lucky to have you," she said.

Melissa's eyes welled up. "We haven't had much contact since she left home—mostly just the annual exchange of birthday letters—but she was a good kid. Is a good kid, despite everything."

"I envy you. I'm an only child." Well, almost an only child, she reminded herself, if you don't count the half-brother I've never met.

Melissa nodded in acknowledgement. "Yeah, it was good to have an ally in this house. Well, not *this* house, but in the house we grew up in."

Not "my parents' house," Tina noticed, let alone "my house." I might not have had sisters or brothers, she thought, but my childhood was a lot less lonely than hers.

That evening, after everyone but Melissa and Michael had left, Tina went into the kitchen to clean up. She stood at the sink, gazing out over the river. It was absolutely still in the humid dusk, the crystalline reflection of willows and maples slowly fading to black as the sun went down. She tried to evoke the vista in winter, but while she could remember its bleakness on cloudy days and the hard, glittering brilliance of the ice on sunny ones, what she recalled was a feeling, not an actual sight. But then, wasn't that happening more and more as she aged? Her emotional recall was as robust as ever, maybe even stronger, but the actual details of how things looked or sounded or smelled were obscured by how she felt about them.

"I'm going to miss this view," Jean-Pierre said behind her.

She jumped, then turned to see him holding two wineglasses. Under one long arm he pressed a bottle of Rioja and a bottle of brandy to his chest.

"When are you leaving?" Tina asked.

"Tomorrow." He set the bottles on the table and pulled out a chair for her.

"So soon?!" Tina slapped her hand to her chest, stricken.

"I'm not like you, with a project to finish," he said gently. "My work ended when Peter ended."

"Where will you go? What will you do?"

He pointed to the wine bottle and she nodded. As he poured some Rioja into Tina's glass, then his own, he said, "One question at a time, girl." He lifted his glass, and she did the same. "To Peter. To the future."

They each took a quiet sip. Then Jean-Pierre said, "I'm going back to Montreal, and I'll get another job like this one. There are not enough men in my line of work, so I never have a problem getting a placement." He paused and took another sip. "Of course, some people are scared to have a big black man in the house."

"But you wouldn't want to work for those people anyhow."

He grinned. "Exactly." He pushed back his chair, sighed heavily, and stretched his legs out in front of him. "You know, one thing I will not miss is this chair. This is a million-dollar home —"

"At least."

" —at least, and yet it has nothing comfortable for a big man to sit in."

"Or a medium-sized woman."

He nodded. "So you will not stay here forever either?"

"Heavens, no."

"Where will you go, mademoiselle? What will you do?"

She and Melissa had discussed that the previous day, during that odd waiting period between the removal of Peter's body and his upcoming burial. Once the funeral home had been notified and Melissa had sent out emails to the handful of relatives and surviving family members, the two of them sat restlessly in Peter's study.

"What's left to do?" Melissa asked as she blindly leafed through the binder of manuscript pages on her father's desk.

"The final chapter is only half-written, so there's that to finish. Maybe a foreword. And then there are footnotes to double-check and a bibliography to pull together. Then it'll need to be copy-edited and proofread, but presumably the publisher will do that."

"So how long will all that take?"

"Probably another two months of my time to make the manuscript ready for editing. Then hours or days here or there to make whatever edits the publisher requires ... but only if you want me to do it."

"Of course I want you to do it. Why wouldn't I?"

"Well, I'll need to make a living, so there would be money involved."

Melissa grimaced and waved her arm around the handsome room. "Does it look like that'll be a problem? I mean we're not billionaires, but honestly, paying your wages for a few more months isn't going to break the bank, if you know what I mean. Besides, I think Dad got an advance."

Tina spoke carefully. "And then there's the question of authorship."

"What question? It'll say 'Written by Peter Bright and Tina ...' " She looked skyward and blushed as she struggled to remember Tina's last name.

"Gabler," Tina supplied.

"Right. Sorry. I'm just a little ..." She circled a finger next to her temple.

"Of course you are," Tina reassured her. "You've just lost your father. Who wouldn't be at a time like this?"

Melissa shook herself and sat up straighter. "All right, then, do we have a deal? I'll pay your salary for two more months and the odd hour here and there needed to finish the book. You can stay here or go ... somewhere else ... while you're doing it. If you stay, though, you have to be willing to let realtors show the house."

"You don't want to keep it?"

"God, no." Melissa laughed mirthlessly. "This was my dad's castle, but it was never home for me. I mean, I like art and views of the river, but not enough to drive hours to see either, thank you very much. Not when my down time is so scarce."

Tina stuck out her hand. "We have a deal."

Melissa shook it, then scanned the room, her shoulders once again slumping. "God, I hope we can get someone to buy this place as is, with all the furnishings and art and ... stuff. I just don't know what I would do with it all."

It took everything in Tina's power not to offer to pack, consign, sell outright, and otherwise become the estate manager. *Stop being so goddamn helpful*, she told herself, then smiled. Her father would have been proud.

Now she poured a refill in Jean-Pierre's glass and said, "I'll leave— probably soon—and go stay with Carl at the observatory for a few months until his fellowship ends."

"And then?"

"And then I have no fucking clue." Tina burst out laughing. "I haven't changed a bit since I was seventeen!"

Jean-Pierre looked at her gravely. "Oh, I'm sure you have. Just a little, no?"

"I guess so. I sag. I have age spots on my hands. I occasionally wear glasses for reading." She paused, thinking, What else? "I'm a better cook than when I was young, and a marginally better artist ... Oh, and I don't moon over eighteen-year-old boys anymore, which is good." Then brightly, "What about you?"

"I don't lust after eighteen-year-old boys, either." They both laughed, then, as they drifted into silence, he added, "I am stronger now than I used to be. I am a father, and that turned me from a boy to a man overnight. I still chase the ladies more than I should, but I've learned to treat them better. I know now what I like"—he pointed to the bottle of wine on the table—"and don't like."

"What don't you like?"

"Liars. People—like politicians—people who don't mean what they say. What's the word?"

"Hypocrites?"

"Exactly. I don't like hypocrites. I don't like mess. I don't like feeling my body get old, but ...." He shrugged. "I am wiser than when I was young. At least I hope so."

Tina gazed at his practically unlined face, then at his arms and hands, supple despite their broadness. She realized with a start that she'd never drawn a Black person, and wondered what, if anything, she'd do differently. What else hadn't she done?

She looked away from him and back out the window. The sun, about to disappear below the horizon, was sending out one last shard of gold. It cut across the water, almost blinding her. Such brilliance, she thought, so much power in those final rays.

June 2012

Carl had picked her up at the Tenerife South Airport mid-morning, after she'd been flying or sitting in Heathrow for the past twelve hours. She was hungry and exhausted. And when she caught sight of Carl's pale, stubbly face beneath a jaunty straw hat, it looked strangely unfamiliar.

"Good morning," he'd said, smiling broadly, when she entered the gleaming, quiet Arrivals lobby. He folded her into his arms, inhaled the scent of her hair, and gave her a dry, emphatic kiss tasting of sunflower seeds.

She returned the kiss — which felt like a pleasantly firm handshake more than an intimate touch — and then stepped back to study him. He had developed a few brown age spots on his right cheek and temple. His frame, which used to strike her as lean, now seemed merely bony, despite the slight, soft belly that protruded over his woven, Canary Islands souvenir belt.

What must I look like, she grimly wondered? "Well, hello there," she said. "Fancy meeting you here."

"I hang out here most days looking for beautiful women to pick up." He was grinning helplessly.

"Any luck?"

"Not until today."

They gazed at each other in awkward silence. "Do you have a car," Tina finally asked.

Carl smacked himself on the side of his head. "Sorry, of course. I was just lost in reverie." His cheeks flushed, and Tina felt instantly remorseful for having even asked this rational question. "Well, not of course, actually. No, I don't have a car, since I so rarely leave the observatory. But don't worry—there's a big line of taxis out there waiting for us."

"Where are we going?"

"Wherever you want. I figured you'd want to just unwind and relax, but if you want to do some sightseeing, we—"

She touched his hand, which was reaching for one of her suitcases. "You figured right, sweetie. I just want to take a shower, lie down on a bed, gaze at the stars if you'll let me, and gaze at you, all right?"

"Oh, absolutely all right."

"But I do want to be a tourist tomorrow, or soon," she hastened to add. "Once we go up there, will I be able to come back down?"

"Oh, sure," he answered happily. Dragging the larger of her two bags behind him, Carl put his hand in the small of Tina's back and steered her towards the exit. "There's a shuttle bus that runs regularly up and down Mount Teide, and we can always rent a car in town for the day ... or the weekend, if you want to go exploring."

They stepped out of the air-conditioned terminal and into blistering sunlight. Carl kept up a steady patter of small talk about Tenerife as he hailed a cab, helped the driver load it, and issued a few brief instructions in slow, flat Spanish. The travelogue continued as they got onto the highway that hugged the coastline. Dazed from sun and fatigue, Tina tuned in and out, periodically asking questions about the active volcano in the middle of the island, the national park, the distance from the other Canary Islands, and the color of the boulders and cliffs on either side of them as they began their ascent to the Observatory.

"How high up are we going?" she asked.

"About 2,400 meters ..."

"Which I've never comprehended ..."

"Or 8,000 feet. High enough that you'll feel a little breathless until you adapt."

"I feel breathless at sea level."

Carl creased his brow. "Seriously?"

"No, not literally," she reassured him. "I meant metaphorically. I was making a joke."

"Because, you know, we're not young anymore."

Tina studied his anxious face, trying to channel a sudden surge of affection and annoyance. "Trust me, honey, I know." She'd thought more about her own mortality in the past year than she had in all the years preceding it. Even during the SARS epidemic nine years earlier, she'd felt invulnerable, conscious of statistics but almost hermetically sealed from any real suffering beyond having to ration her beans, canned goods, and toilet paper and wear a mask on the subway.

"In fact, I'm the oldest guy on the mountain … by a lot."

Tina was startled. Carl had always been so lacking in vanity, in self-awareness in general, that now it was her turn to be suddenly concerned. "Is that weird?" she asked.

"No, it's fine. We get along fine. It's just strange to not know anything about the music they listen to, or the games they play, or the equipment they buy for their kids …"

"But you've been working with younger people since … well, since you became an older person. What makes this so different?"

"The isolation," he answered promptly. Behind his backlit head, Tina saw that they were ascending. The stands of palm trees, already sparse even down below, thinned out still more, then disappeared. The landscape was ochre and green, volcanic rock and scrub, punctuated by cacti and succulents that jutted up like stalagmites from the arid earth.

"I see what you mean," she murmured. "Canary Islands. I'd pictured this place as tropical."

"Well technically, it is in the tropics…" Carl began.

Tina felt a stab of annoyance. She'd forgotten just how nerdy he could be. "I mean jungle. Humid."

"No, not humid. Especially at this elevation. And the soil, well, it's barely soil. The ground here is pumice and clay and, in fact just around this bend …" He leaned towards Tina and peered out her window "… lava fields. Not very conducive to flora and fauna."

The mountainside was laden with a tumble of rock, a chaotic heap of arid black, brown, and grey boulders and stone and dust. "It's looks

226

like an explosion at a fertilizer factory," she marveled. "Like all the desiccated cow shit in the world was scooped up and just dumped here."

He pointed to a pointy-peaked mountain in the distance. "It was blown here, by that."

"Is that a volcano?"

"Yup," he answered happily.

"When was the last time it erupted?"

"There was a fairly small eruption in 1909, and before that, a much bigger one in the mid-1700s."

"So every hundred and fifty years or so?" Tina asked.

Carl shrugged grandly. "There's not enough data to make any kind of prediction. Of course, there are earthquakes all the time, but—"

"Here? Earthquakes all the time here?" Next to tornados and poisonous snakes, earthquakes were what Tina most feared in the natural world.

Carl laughed and put his arm around her. "Relax. Just shallow, mini-quakes. The earth is moving under our feet all the time, by degrees so slight that most of the time we don't even sense it."

He was right, of course, figuratively as well as literally. Being here now, at the age of 60, driving up to an astronomical observatory in the Canary Islands, certain of where she would be for the next few weeks and knowing nothing about what would happen after that—all of this felt familiar, just another transition in her unplanned life. And the past year, living in someone else's palatial home on a river, helping a dying old man cement the legacy he'd chosen for himself—that had felt equally natural. The trajectory from that crowded childhood apartment on West End Avenue to this slope, littered with ancient rock that had once been magma, was both inconceivable and inevitable, a product of minute shifts in the earth under her that had silently informed her steps.

"Oh, just mini-quakes." She smiled at this man who felt such comfort in the chaos of the physical world. "Okay, then. I'll sleep well tonight."

She didn't, of course. They'd reached the observatory, and Carl led her straight to his dorm room. It was small for one person, tiny for two, with a single bed and a nubby orange-and-white couch that he'd pushed up against the mattress in a sweetly hopeful attempt to turn it into a double.

She put some of her clothes and toiletries into the dresser drawer he'd emptied out for her, then slid her still half-full suitcase under the desk. Then they stripped and cautiously maneuvered themselves onto the hybrid bed.

They made love with neither ferocious passion nor quiet languor, but with the practiced grace of carpenters planing wood to reveal its color and grain. Carl fell instantly asleep afterwards, having been up all of the previous night. ("Doing the usual," he'd sighed as they passed by the Telescopio Carlos Sanchez. "Mapping stellar oscillations in the Orionis Sigma cluster. Nothing to write home about.") Tina dozed fitfully, exhausted but unable to stay asleep with such bleached and starchy light slicing in between the slats of the Venetian blinds. Finally, she got up, put on a sundress, and went outside.

Paved paths wove between the buildings, a collection of medieval, Moorish-looking turrets and domes bleached white from the relentless sun. Knots of tourists stood in front of one, and Tina eavesdropped as the guide recited facts about solar, optical, infrared, and radio telescopes—a litany equally unintelligible to her in Spanish, English, and French. This young woman, while skilled in languages, lacked Carl's ability to explain the arcane in a way that she could grasp.

"Tell me again what you've been doing here," she asked as she climbed back into bed at dusk, suddenly overwhelmed by jet lag.

"Finding brown dwarves," he answered, caressing her shoulder.

"And they are ..."

"Old stars that have grown small and dense and dark but haven't caved in on themselves."

Resisting collapse, Tina mused. Was that any way to live? She drifted off into a dreamless sleep.

Four hours later, she slid back into consciousness, roused by Carl's hand on her cheek.

"I brought you some dinner," he said softly. He was perched on the side of the bed, his grizzled face bathed in the light of a desk lamp.

Outside the window behind him, there was nothing but inky black. "Paella. It's not bad."

She sat up, rubbed her eyes, and gratefully took the ceramic bowl from him.

"I thought you might want to do a little stargazing," he continued. "Just for a few hours. Then you can go back to bed until you figure out what kind of schedule you want to be on—my crazy up-all-night one, or something more conventional."

"Conventional! God forbid," she answered. "Let's split the difference. I'll stay up late and sleep late. It'll be like I'm a teenager all over again." She gobbled down the first few forkfuls of paella, then forced herself to slow down and savor its smoky tomato scent, the flaky chunks of fish, and the small, pearly clams. The night was as cold as the day was hot, and wrapped in a blanket, enclosed in a halo of light, she felt the food's spicy warmth in her belly as an animating force. "Let's take a walk."

Outside, the temperature had dropped about thirty degrees, and Tina hugged Carl's winter jacket around her. The avenue of domes and towers that had seemed so bright and solid during the day now looked ghostly, with only faint outlines of light emanating from their entrances. They stopped when they reached the fence at the edge of what Carl told her was a steep cliff and looked upward.

"See," Carl said, pointing at a spot about forty degrees above the horizon. Tina could discern only the faint outline of his arm. "Canis Major, one of Orion's hunting dogs."

Tina laughed. "I see a bowlful of stars. Hundreds of them. I don't know how you make out any constellations in a sky like this."

"Millions of them, actually," Carl gently corrected her. "But Canis Major—that should look familiar to you. It's pretty easily seen in the Northern sky year-round."

"Sorry, but the only constellations I've ever been able to make out are the Big Dipper, the Little Dipper, and Orion's Belt. I've never understood how the ancients found these shapes in the night sky, let alone how the moderns like you do."

"Necessity. They found them because they had to. Their navigation, even their agricultural practices, depended on recognizing their changing position relative to the night sky. Those ancient sailors and astronomers were looking for something to set their course by, so they found patterns that illustrated the stories they already knew. Orion, the hunter. Cassiopeia, the queen."

Tina started to laugh. "Years ago I heard a podcast about an art theft in Boston. Two guys dressed as cops were buzzed into the museum, where they proceeded to steal thirteen paintings, including Rembrandt's only seascape, and a Vermeer. For decades the FBI and amateur detectives and journalists tried to find the paintings. The museum offered a huge reward."

"And? ..." Carl's puzzled voice sounded disembodied in the dark.

"And the podcasters — a couple of journalists — finally got a tip that some mobster had them buried under his patio in Florida. So they went down there, hired a guy with ground-penetrating radar equipment, and asked him to survey the now-abandoned house of the now-dead mobster. So as not to bias him, they didn't tell him what they were looking for."

"Did he find anything?"

"He did." Tina was so delighted to have remembered this story that she wanted to draw it out. "He found a large, rectangular shape about four feet below the concrete, big enough to house all the artwork. So with some ambivalence — because they were afraid of being iced out of the story — they took their discovery to the head of security at the museum, and he in turn informed the FBI."

"So, did they find the pictures?"

"I'm getting there." Tina petted his arm as if he were an impatient child, then resumed her story. "Sure enough, both the security guy and the FBI refused to tell them what, if anything, they were going to do with the information. But somehow, our intrepid reporters found out that they were going to dig up the box, and when. They flew back to Florida, reintroduced themselves to the guy who lived across the street from the abandoned house, and he let them stake out the gangster's house from his front porch."

"This is getting good," Carl said raptly.

"It gets better. The FBI came with a backhoe and started breaking through the concrete. The din was awful. Then suddenly it stopped.

As the reporters craned to see from their perch, the FBI guys picked up shovels and started digging by hand. Finally, the reporters heard one of them abruptly tell the others to stop. They gave up all pretext of hiding and dashed across the street to get closer to the action. They saw the guys huddled around the hole in the ground. They heard the clanging of metal shovel against metal box. After two years of chasing this story—for one of them, twenty years—the suspense was almost unbearable." She paused.

"Yeah, so ..."

"Suddenly they all stepped away from the hole, and a couple of them pulled their shirt collars up to cover their noses and mouths."

"Was there a dead body?"

"No. The long, rectangular metal object large enough to hold stolen art was a septic tank."

Carl snorted, then chuckled. "Well, duh."

"Exactly! Duh! Had anyone just shown the reporters or the FBI a picture of the shape beneath the patio and asked, 'What's this thing buried in the backyard?' nine out of ten of them would have said, 'It looks like a septic tank,' then gotten back to work."

"And the tenth?"

"I don't know what the tenth person would have said, but probably not, 'It's a hiding place for a stolen Rembrandt.' "

Carl chuckled, then fell silent. They turned and headed back towards the telescope Carl would be looking through that night. "And what does this have to do with Cassiopeia?"

"We start with the story, then we see what we're looking for."

•   •   •

The next morning, while Carl slept, Tina brought her laptop to the plain but welcoming dining room. She had to start writing the foreword to the book.

"Peter Bright and I argued frequently as his life wound down," she began.

Though long gone from the airwaves and no longer a national icon, he had lost little of the fire and none of the integrity that had made him such a trusted, even revered, journalist.

She deleted "even revered." Peter would have repudiated such hyperbolic language even as he thrilled to think it was true.

"Aging gives you focus," he'd told me early in our relationship. "It helps you pare down your wandering attentions and home in on what matters."

What mattered to him was unbiased truth, an attribute that he believed photographs were uniquely equipped to capture.

I disagreed. In our generally convivial but sometimes quite heated debates, I argued that bias – cognitive, political, and aesthetic – was present in every shot. Truth, I maintained, was fact infused with narrative, and thus inherently subjective.

We were both wrong, and both right.

Not for the first time, Tina felt torn between pride and foolishness as she saw her words on the screen. She was certainly no philosopher. Who the hell was she to pontificate about truth? And yet she believed what she was saying. But then, wasn't that precisely the danger? *Don't believe everything you think*, warned the bumper sticker on a car she'd often parked behind in Toronto. Words to live by.

Peter wrote this book in an era, our era, when everyone believes that every image can be invented, altered, and falsified. And indeed it can. But that's nothing new; the practice of doctoring pictures developed alongside the practice of taking them. Early technicians mastered the art of composite images. In the 1860s, some enterprising photographer who was hired to shoot a portrait of Abraham Lincoln perched that distinctive head atop the body of southern politician John Calhoun. A hundred and fifty years later, some TV Guide art director similarly united Oprah Winfrey's head with Ann-Margret's body. In Matthew Brady's photo of General Grant with his generals, taken around the same time, Francis P. Blair was added to the picture even though he wasn't present. Fast forward another century and a half, and in photos circulating among the Alt-Right, Barak Obama appears posing with Osama Bin Laden.

And in the same way that absent people were added, present people were erased. Stalin, Mao Zedong, and Adolf Hitler all had aides removed from photos when they fell out of favor with the boss. In a famous photo of Mussolini straddling a horse, his sword-wielding arm held triumphantly over his head, the horse trainer holding the animal's reins present in the negative is magically absent from the published print.

She paused, uncertain where to go next and distracted by a small troop of selfie-stick-wielding tourists traipsing into the dining hall. She looked around at the terra cotta floors, blond wooden walls, and elaborately paned windows that cast geometric shadows on the opposite wall. Why were they visiting the rectangular room where the scientists ate? Because, she realized, these tourists had come to see something, and since the astronomers were sleeping, and access to the telescopes was restricted, this cafeteria at the top of a volcanic mountain had to be a destination in its own right, imbued with, what, mystery? Coolness? What sort of significance could an empty dining hall have?

But while the practice of doctoring pictures was long established, it took a while for conspiracy-theory-driven skepticism to flourish. I first heard of it in 1969, when a fringe of disbelievers declared that the video of the moon landing was actually shot in a Los Angeles soundstage. But if that was simply wacky, subsequent claims were downright sickening. Photos of mass shootings? Bogus propaganda, some assert, doctored images designed to rob gun owners of their weapons.

When the act of perception becomes simply an act of finding the reality we want to believe — regardless of our political affinities — we are all in danger. That was the alarm that Peter Bright sought to sound.

"Sought to sound"? Ugh. Lose the BBC documentary voice, Tina scolded herself.

That was the alarm that Peter Bright raised. And what I learned from him is that while we can never coalesce around a single truth, we must at least acknowledge and agree upon a single set of facts.

Dear God, how could she get off this train of pedantry? Who, other than a political candidate, says "We must"?! Tina flashed back to — what was it? A movie? Or the girls in her class when she was about twelve, yanking back their shoulders and their bent arms over and over again, chanting "We must, we must, we must build up our bust!" And how did her mind veer from epistemology to weird puberty rituals in a microsecond?

Tina reread the paragraph she'd just written, then tentatively resumed.

But I learned something more from Peter about the merits of collaboration. Or rather, re-learned it. I'd long suspected that my preference for group productions over solo pursuits was a sign of weakness, an evasion, a fear of putting myself to the test. But as an aging woman supporting a very old man, I rediscovered what I'd known as an idealistic kid, that ....

That what? She looked up from the screen, then longingly out at the blue, blue sky flecked with starched wisps of cloud. She saved the file and pushed back her chair, wanting nothing more than to walk to the lookout at the end of the paved path and bask in the sun, immobile as a lizard.

But as she stood, her laptop began to gently shudder. Her chair and the one next to it slid slowly to the right. The drinking glasses next to the water dispenser clattered on their tray. The two men walking into the dining room paused, and one reached out to seemingly caress the doorframe. Tina froze, clutching the tabletop, torn between terror and disbelief.

Within a few seconds, the trembling stopped.

"Was that an earthquake?" Tina asked the guys in the doorway.

"Just a tremor," the red-headed one answered. "Nothing to worry about."

"At least not this time," the other guy intoned ominously from behind a thick black beard.

"Come on, give her a break," his friend protested. "She's not used to this."

The bearded guy flashed a wide smile, as fake as his warning tone had been a second earlier. "This isn't the one where the island cleaves and half of it falls into the Atlantic, raising sea levels still more and killing coastal property values once and for all. So cheer up."

The redhead pointed to his friend. "Ignore him," he advised Tina. "He's an idiot."

Slapping her hand over her still frantically pulsing heart, Tina said, "So am I." She smiled sheepishly and, on rubbery legs, made her way out of the building.

The landscape looked unchanged. If the rock piles had shifted or grown, it wasn't evident to her. If the chatting pairs of tour guides and astronomers traversing the path were unnerved, they didn't let on.

But of course, if they looked at me, she thought, they'd have no idea that for one screaming microsecond, I was afraid I was about to die.

As always, she realized, the gap between what we feel and what we show yawns wide.

July 2012

A few days later, Tina took a shuttle bus down the mountain, shedding layers of clothing as the bus descended. They entered the town, driving past brightly colored homes and whitewashed condominiums and restaurants and hordes of sunburned tourists wandering from one canopied patio to the next. Finally, the bus stopped in front of a hotel and the driver announced that it was time to disembark.

He stepped off the bus, then turned to help his passengers down its stairs.

"Donde es La Caleta?" Tina asked in what she hoped was Spanish.

The driver pointed to his left, down the drive that hugged the coastline. "Ahi," he answered. "Dos kilometres."

One of Carl's friends had told her that La Caleta was one of the quieter, less-developed beaches. But as she walked, it became clear that "beach" was a misnomer. There was little sand to be found, just porous sandstone and black volcanic rock posing a barrier between the sidewalk and the sparkling turquoise water.

Eventually she came to a small peninsula where the rocks were long and flat, easily traversable. As she got closer, she saw tents, chairs, sunbathers—a mix of children, bearded elderly men, and sinewy young women, many of them topless—and heard languorous laughter. Behind the slabs of rock, which served almost as docks, she saw caves carved into the base of the mountain. Many of them had curtains over their entrances, cookstoves in front of them, and a large tarpaulin covering a communal table had been set up in front of some of them.

As she picked her way over the rocks to get closer to the settlement, she was joined by an older man and his wife.

"Not quite the seaside homes we've been looking for," the man said cheerfully. He appeared to be in his mid-to-late 70s, and he reminded her of her paternal grandfather—tanned and pie-shaped, with the jowly cheeks that both her father and grandfather had had, broad shoulders, and a torso that tapered down into hairless, delicate legs. Even his pale blue seersucker shorts looked just like the kind that her father had favored fifty years ago.

"Certainly not," his wife agreed firmly. With her bleached eyebrows and boiled skin, she looked like the classic British tourist in a warm climate.

"Have you been looking for a vacation home?" Tina asked.

"Indeed we have," the man answered. "But the choices seem to be shoddily constructed condos—which we have at home, thank you very much—or the odd hippie commune like this one." He pointed to the cave-dwellers to their right, then extended his hand to Tina. "I'm Tom, by the way. Tom Collier, and this is my wife, Sally."

"Pleased to meet you. I'm Tina Gabler." She shook both Tom and Sally's hands, both of which were damp and limp.

"Shall we explore a little more?" Tina asked after a brief silence.

"Let's," Tom answered, and set off with surprisingly long strides across the hot rock. Clammy handshake aside, he seemed to do everything heartily. Her father had also been this way at the beach, eager and resolute.

An older man with bleached dreadlocks, a bird tattoo soaring up his arm, and a mangled beard, waved to them as they approached. "Welcome to La Caleta," he said in a startling Brooklyn accent.

"Lovely to be here," Tom answered. "What is this?" He gestured vaguely at the settlement surrounding them.

"Paradise," the man answered. "We're about twenty people who have opted for a simpler, more authentic way of life."

"How do you live?" Sally asked. She sounded both curious and appalled.

"Same as you do. Eat. Sleep. Breathe in. Breathe out."

"No, I mean—"

"I know what you mean. You mean how do we make a living? We fish. We have a boat that we take tourists out on. Some of us do day jobs in town, waiting tables and the like. A couple of us sell drugs—not the heavy stuff—just good old fashioned Moroccan hash."

"And you share your wealth?" Tina asked.

He snickered. "I don't know about wealth. But yeah, we share our food and drink. We help Brigitte—" he pointed to a topless blond woman at the next tent—"We help her home-school her kids. Shit like that."

Tina was fascinated by the contrast between his naked skin—so darkened and dried by the sun that he looked almost mummified—and his nasal New York City voice. He ought to have been wearing a Yankees t-shirt and selling boiled Hebrew National hot dogs from a cart. "How long have you been here?" she asked.

"Well, me, I've been here about twenty years. Fernando"—he pointed to a beefy young man who seemed to be digging for clams in one of the brackish tidal pools nearby—"he's an IT guy from Madrid who just got here last month. But Papito"—he stood from his deck chair and looked around, then plopped back down—"he's been here over thirty-five years."

"Wow, so this commune goes way back."

"Back to when we thought we were going to save the world this way."

"Right," Tom said. "We all thought we were going to save the world, didn't we?"

Sally snorted. "I didn't."

"But many of us did, didn't we, love. We thought whatever daft or mind-numbing jobs we did by day, never mind. We'd still find companionship and live peaceably and look out for each other, beyond just borrowing each other's spades and mowers. And what happened? We were seduced by the telly. Watching and watching, that's how we spent our evenings, each in our own little cave."

"Maybe we weren't a little Soviet, but we *did* look out for each other," Sally protested. Tina felt that she was watching yet another skirmish in a long-running battle.

"Sure we did," Tom cajoled. "Just not so differently than my mum and dad did in our flat on Wapping Lane."

"Well, now you're just spouting the Gertie and Martin party line, aren't you," Sally retorted. "His mum and dad," she explained to Tina and their new companion. "Solidarity and common courtesy, luv," she said with an affected Cockney accent, "that's what it's all about, ain't it?"

Gertie and Martin. What was it about those names that was so familiar?

Tom didn't rise to his wife's bait. "I'm with them. Mum and Dad got a few things right," he said.

Tina froze. Gertie and Martin, mother and adoptive father to her brother Tom. What other morsels had she'd gleaned from that letter in her father's nightstand? She couldn't just come out and ask if Martin had lost a leg in the war. "Do you have any siblings, Tom?" she asked, sounding, she knew, unconvincingly casual.

"A younger brother, Hugh," he answered after a pause.

"Baby Hughie, I like to call him," Sally offered. "Even now, at 70 years old, he's a big baby."

"Especially now," Tom corrected.

"Seventy? He's your *younger* brother?"

Tom looked at her, puzzled. "He is. Why, how old do you think I am?"

Tina frantically did the math in her head. Tom—*her* Tom—was born in 1946. So that would make him ... "Sixty-six?"

Tom laughed. "I'm flattered. You've just shaved seven years off my age."

"So you're actually ..."

"I'm actually seventy-three."

"Years young," Sally dutifully added.

"And where did you grow up?" Tina asked, though she already knew that he wasn't the one, that he couldn't be.

"East London born and raised," he answered with faux pride. "Home of Jack the Ripper and the West Ham Football hooligans."

"Rah, rah, Hammers," Sally cheered faintly.

Not Glasgow. Not her brother. That surge of excitement retreated as quickly as it had come, leaving Tina feeling foolish. Maybe it was time to stop looking for him. What was to be gained from finding someone who shared some of her genes and none of her life? A life, she was slowly realizing, that she had lived mostly with pleasure. And if there were times when it felt incomplete — no, when she felt incomplete — they were not caused by an absent sibling, but just by the understanding that she had not yet done all that she wanted to do.

Their host, Jay, invited the three of them to have lunch with him. Tina and Tom readily assented, and Sally didn't bother to answer. Over a meal of sardines and tomatoes and some sort of anemic boxed white wine, the four of them compared notes about their upbringings, homes, and the state of the world. It had been so long since Tina had been on vacation. She'd forgotten that this was what happened when you were suspended in the amber of freedom, with nothing you had to do.

Sated on food and talk, they drifted into silence and listened to the waves pour in between the rocks, then trickle out. A week ago, dripping in the humid Toronto heat, she'd lugged her belongings back into her old, sublet apartment. Today, baking under the dry Spanish sun, she sat inert, still as the lizards on the gravelly sand below her feet. Yesterday she'd submitted her final invoice for her work on *Framing the Shot, Shaping the Story* and today she was unemployed. Her purpose-driven "family" of the past year had dissolved, but in reuniting with Carl in this lunar landscape, she felt that she had come home.

Sally glanced at Tom and tapped her watch.

"Right," he said, rousing himself. "Time to move on. But let's get a memento of this lovely afternoon!" He stood, then patted the pockets of his shorts. He pulled out his phone and squinted at it. "Dead. Damn. Sally, do you have yours?"

She shook her head. "It's back in our room charging."

"Jay, I assume ..."

Jay shook his head. "No phone, man." Then, pointing to his own naked body, "And no pockets."

"Tina, if I give you my number, can you take a picture and send it to me?" Tom asked. "I'm one of those blokes, as my wife will tell you. I've got to document everything. It helps to slow the passage of time."

"I'm pretty terrible at selfies," she said. "My arms are too short."

"No matter," Tom cheerfully insisted. "Being distorted and out of focus is part of their charm, isn't it?"

And so, because she was nothing if not obliging, Tina pulled out her phone. As the officially designated photographer, she wanted to honor their time together by capturing an image that was in focus. As a subject, who hated posing for the camera, she wanted nothing more than to get it over with.

She knew that she'd remember this day with this ephemeral band of strangers sharing conversation, memories, and some temporary common ground. She also knew that if, years from now, she came across this picture independent of any others from this trip, she'd have no idea who these people were or where the photo had been taken.

They huddled together, arms cast gingerly over each other's' shoulders, squinting into the blinding sea. Tina stretched out her arm and adjusted the camera until they were all in the frame, four faces in various shades.

"Ready?" she asked. "Smile."

• • •

She showed the picture to Carl over dinner that night. "Doesn't he look like my Dad?"

"I never met your father," he reminded her.

"Yeah, but you've seen photos of him. Can you see why I thought for a second that this Tom might have been my Tom?"

Carl squinted at the image on her phone. "Nope." He ruffled her hair. "Sorry."

Tina studied it again, straining and failing to see the resemblance that had seemed so evident earlier in the day. She turned her phone off. "Can we look through your telescope?"

Outside, they ambled along the dimly lit path to one of domes closest to the road down the mountain.

"This is my observatory," Carl said.

The metal door groaned as he opened it, and suddenly Tina had to blink against the room's bright, sterile light. A young man with a scruffy beard peering intently at one of a dozen computer screens in the round, gear-filled room turned to face them.

"Alfonse, meet Tina, love of my life."

Alfonse looked up and waved at them. "Bonjour, Tina," he said in a thick French accent. "This is a good man you have here."

Tina waved back, smiling. He was a good man. "I know. Pleased to meet you too, Alfonse."

Carl wheeled a second chair over to his seat at a keyboard and gestured to Tina to sit.

As he clattered away, Tina looked up at the domed ceiling of the observatory, a latticework of connected steel tubes and rods. "It's like the world's largest jungle gym," she said. "Or like being inside a 3D model of the earth's biggest molecule. Sorry, the universe's biggest molecule."

Carl chuckled. "Yeah, the ceiling's cool, but what I'm about to show you is much cooler."

On his large computer screen, an elliptical pinwheel—a galaxy—was connected to a much smaller, rounder one above it by a swirling, S-shaped plume of dusty light. Together, they formed a gorgeous, diaphanous swan. "This is one galaxy eating up another one. And see all these things that look like stars and gassy discs?" he asked, pointing with his finger to the hundreds of clear shining dots and small, blurred circles surrounding the two galaxies. "They're all galaxies too, just much, much farther away."

"Oh, Carl, it's beautiful!"

"Yeah, isn't it?" Despite the room's horrid fluorescent light, Tina could see the joy in Carl's eyes.

"So, you took this picture?" she asked incredulously. "Like I would just hold up my phone to take a picture of a sunset or a stupid church sign or a misspelled slogan on the side of a truck? Just snap and—look at that—one galaxy a million light-years away slurping up another?"

"More like a hundred and fifty light-years away, and no, not quite that simple, but almost. I did press the digital shutter, probably about a thousand times over the course of an hour or so. Then this image-cleansing software we have here compared each image to the next one in the series, deleting the pixels that were just noise and keeping the ones that were consistent from one picture to the next."

"Noise?"

"Visual distortion, graininess, like a really bad cell-phone photo shot in low light. It eliminates the noise, the artifacts of the photographer's conditions, and then aggregates and amplifies what's left."

"So this isn't really one photo?"

"Right. It's the product of about a hundred photos of the same thing."

"And how does the software know that what it's eliminating is noise and not just some really faint star or unusual heavenly object that nobody's seen before?"

"We give it rules to follow, like, 'Ignore this if it is visible in one picture but not the ones taken a second before or after, or if it's flashing *Nude Dancers* in pink letters.' "

"So it's an aggregate image, based in part on what you expect to see," she said slowly.

"Well, yeah." Carl sounded hurt. "But that doesn't mean it's false. In fact, all that reinforcement means it's actually more likely to be true."

"Oh, I understand, sweetie," Tina rushed to reassure him. I wish I could tell Peter, she thought, that my boyfriend—a man of science, an evangelist for fact—is manipulating images to reveal a truth

"Now let me show you M15," Carl said.

"Wait, isn't M15 some British spy agency?"

"No, that's MI5, Miss Moneypenny. M15 is a globular cluster, about twelve billion years old. Want to see it?"

Tina nodded. Carl pecked at the keyboard, and the roof opened to reveal a sphere of sky. Tina heard a deep, metallic purr as the large, squat telescope above the viewfinder moved into position.

"Look through the viewfinder," Carl instructed. She did, and saw dots, hundreds of dots, some larger and blurrier than others, and one with a luminous white core. "You see the one with the really bright center?" Carl asked.

"You mean that thing that looks like a bright, fuzzy star?"

"That's Messier 15, and it's about 33,600 light-years from Earth, and 175 light-years in diameter."

"How does that compare to the sun?"

"Well, it's home to about 100,000 stars, many of which are comparable to our sun. And the cluster as a whole is about 360,000 times as luminous than the sun ... which is pretty impressive, considering that there's probably a big black hole in the middle of it trying to suck all that light into itself."

"You're saying that this one star is actually a group of 100,000 stars?"

"Yup. And it's one of at least three globular clusters just in our galaxy. And as you know, the universe is filled with clusters of galaxies."

He turned back to the keyboard and after one more flurry of key tapping, she heard the faint sound of a shutter opening and closing. Carl waved her over to look at his computer screen.

"Here's what that fuzzy star looks like after we've done some lucky imaging." It was gorgeous, a sphere of glowing confetti in shades of gold and brilliant blue and a white as diaphanous and seductive as a lone cloud on a sunny day. "Probably each one of those stars has planets, and many of those planets have moons, and on who knows how many of them, there's some sort of organic life."

"And to those life forms we look like—"

"Like a fuzzy dot."

None of this was new to her; Tina had heard most of it before. But here, on this barren, dark mountaintop, with cold, glittering infinity above her and blazing hot magma below her, she felt the authority of imagination as surely as she felt Carl's warm breath tickling the back of her neck. The data points assembled to create this astonishing image—they were facts, but borne of intangible vision. If asked *What do you see?* how would she have answered? The past. The future. The power of our collective inventiveness to connect us.

-The End-

Acknowledgments

This book would not have been possible without other books, time,
and the clear-eyed feedback and generosity of others.

Its inspiration was one simple, gorgeous paragraph in Suzanne
Berne's *Missing Lucile*. Five years after reading it, when I finally began
writing this book, I was particularly educated and influenced by Errol
Morris's *Believing is Seeing,* Sarah Sentilles' *Draw your Weapons,* Susan
Sontag's *On Photography,* and *Roman Vishniac Rediscovered,* edited by
Maya Benton.

Jessica Goodrider Loewen, a student at the University of
Lethbridge and member of the Blackfoot Confederation not only fact-
checked and gently corrected the chapters involving Sunday and
Kimi, but generously shared some of her own family history in
Residential Schools.

My long-time friends and writing group colleagues read and
kindly critiqued almost every iteration of almost every chapter. For
that I thank you, Carol Aucoin, Cindy Dockrell, Kevin O'Kelly, and
Anne Rutland. And of course, I thank Reagan Rothe and the staff at
Black Rose Writing for seeing some promise in this book.

Michelle Seaton, Janet Pocorobba, Lynn Peterfreund, Craig Matis,
George Eltman, Carla Wittes, Melanie Wittes, Mark Schlack, and
Emily Schilling all plowed through the entire manuscript in various
incarnations, providing invaluable feedback that helped shape the
final version.

My late parents, Glorianne and Si, and the love between them, infuse much of this book. Not only did they give me the gift of a happy childhood, but showed me the rewards of deep looking and active listening.

As always, my family has provided fuel and encouragement throughout this process. It is blessedly large, and I'll spare the reader from a long litany of names of cousins, nieces, and nephews, all of whom inspire and delight. But I can't end without offering particular appreciation for Bobby, Paul, Carla, Shelli, Chloe, Melanie, Layla, Katie, Talia and Safia. You are the essential cord running through my past, present, and future. And I am profoundly grateful to and for Mark – insightful reader, ruthless editor, champion spooner, sometimes guide, and my always precious companion.

About the Author

Julie Wittes Schlack's memoir in essays, *This All-at-Onceness*, was named one of *Kirkus Reviews*' Best Independent Nonfiction Books of 2019. She reviewed books for *The Boston Globe* and writes for NPR station WBUR's journal of ideas and opinions, Cognoscenti. Her fiction and essays have appeared in numerous journals such as *Shenandoah, The Writer's Chronicle, Ninth Letter,* and *Tampa Review.* Julie lives with her husband in a co-housing community in Northampton, Massachusetts.

Note from the Author

Word-of-mouth is crucial for any author to succeed. If you enjoyed *Burning and Dodging,* please leave a review online—anywhere you are able. Even if it's just a sentence or two. It would make all the difference and would be very much appreciated.

Thanks!
Julie Wittes Schlack

We hope you enjoyed reading this title from:

BLACK ROSE
writing™

www.blackrosewriting.com

Subscribe to our mailing list – *The Rosevine* – and receive **FREE** books, daily deals, and stay current with news about upcoming releases and our hottest authors.
Scan the QR code below to sign up.

Already a subscriber? Please accept a sincere thank you for being a fan of Black Rose Writing authors.

View other Black Rose Writing titles at
www.blackrosewriting.com/books and use promo code
PRINT to receive a **20% discount** when purchasing.

CPSIA information can be obtained
at www.ICGtesting.com
Printed in the USA
LVHW101536221221
706954LV00014B/631

9 781684 338429